Double Down Desperate

D1710547

Enjoy

Jannet Hoffman

Double Down Desperate

By Jannifer Hoffman

Resplendence Publishing, LLC
http://www.resplendencepublishing.com

Published by Resplendence Publishing, LLC
2665 N Atlantic Avenue, #349
Daytona Beach, FL 32118

Double Down Desperate
Edited by Jessica Bimberg and Venus Cahill
Cover art by Adrian Nicholas

Print format ISBN: 978-1-60735-564-9

Print Release: November 2012

Lovingly dedicated to a very special family who share my North Dakota roots:

Leona Nies
LaVina and Vic Kaul
Ervin Hoffman
Marion Hoffman
Diana and Clinton Martell
Gary Hoffman
Ronnie and Sandy Hoffman
And in memory of
Mary and Christ Hoffman
Clarence Hoffman

Acknowledgments:

Heartfelt appreciation to all my fans in Ashley, North Dakota

Many thanks to:
My sister, Patsy, who in no way resembles the Patsy in this book
My son, Tony, for supplying a male's point of view
My dear friend, Marie Kirk, who always has an answer to my questions
And special thanks to my editor Jessica Bimberg

Chapter One

November first

Patsy Bartlett glanced at her watch. "So what in the world does he want with us this time? I'm going to miss my aerobics class."

"Well, I'm already late for a hockey game," her brother, Conner, complained. "I have no idea what's on his mind. I just received a summons to meet him here in his office at two o'clock. By text yet. I didn't even know he knew how to text."

"That's how he notified me, too. It's very annoying to have to take time out of the middle of my day. I had plans." Patsy shifted in her seat to pull her tight skirt down. "After aerobics, I had an appointment to get my hair frosted and styled. I'd hoped to get my nails done, too. Good heavens, we just saw him last week at dinner; he could have talked to us them."

"He's been acting weird lately," Conner said. "Like insisting we have dinner at home with him one night a week. We haven't had to do that since…well, since Mom died."

"He probably got teed off when you left before dessert."

"Yeah, well, the only reason you stayed was because he complained about you charging twenty grand on your credit card so you and your friends could fly to Paris for the weekend."

She grimaced. "Maybe that was a bit extravagant. But why should he care anyway? It's not like it was a million bucks."

"My thoughts exactly. And, to top it all off, he's late," Conner groused. "I just may give him a piece of my mind."

"Yeah, like that's going to happen. Wouldn't that be like biting the hand that feeds you? If you feel that way, why did you show up?"

Conner made a rude sound. "For the same reason you did."

Patsy drew a deep breath and sighed. "I just hope he's not on the get-a-job kick again."

"Really," Conner muttered. "Like the time he asked us to work in the family business. Heck, I actually thought that might be kind of fun until he said I had to start at the bottom and work my way up. That would have been downright embarrassing. Give me one reason why we should work anyway when our father is a multi-millionaire. That doesn't even make sense."

"Shh," Patsy whispered. "Here comes Daddy Megabucks now."

Charles Bartlett sat at his desk and perused the fruit of his loins waiting impatiently in chairs before him.

Patricia, or Patsy as she insisted on being called, had turned twenty-eight five days ago. As usual, she was shrink-wrapped in spandex, with a skirt too high and cleavage too low, one short step above centerfold. Didn't leave much for the imagination.

It was a crying shame as far as he was concerned. She was a beautiful woman, with a perfect, well-endowed figure. Why did she insist on dressing like a tramp and wearing enough makeup to frost a three-layer cake?

All he could say was he liked her hair. It was wild and kinky with tight ringlets, and as far as he knew, the copper color was natural—the same as her mother's had been. She had the same sea green eyes, too, and right now, they were narrowed on him with distain.

Sitting next to her, twenty-nine-year-old Conner was attired in an expensive golf shirt and immaculately pressed wool slacks. Everything about him screamed neatness, from his manicured fingernails to his perfectly groomed golden-brown hair. His dark eyes and sun-touched hair matched Charles' own at that age. Similar to his sister, Conner's eyes gleamed with irritation for being summoned in the middle of his *very busy* day.

Charles loved his two children dearly, and that was the reason he'd called them in. That and the fact he'd spent two hours that morning with his heart doctor. Patsy and Conner were not going to be happy with his announcement.

"Could we move this along?" Conner said impatiently. "I have tickets to a game at the Excel Center starting in half an hour."

"Yeah, and I'm missing my aerobics class." This from Patsy.

"I'm afraid this is one time you might have to miss those important events. I've made some arrangements with my lawyer, Morty Chambers, and they're going to impact your lives." Scowling, he looked at each of them in turn. "Just so you understand why I made the decision I did, let me explain. The two of you are spoiled, greedy, and lazy. I take full responsibility for the spoiled part. The greediness—I just don't know where that comes from. It's the laziness, the refusal to work, which was the catalyst for this plan."

"I offered to work in the company," Conner griped defensively.

"So did I," Patsy chimed in.

Charles sighed. "So you did. Conner, you requested a position that paid two hundred grand a year to do a job you didn't have a clue how to do—"

"I have four years of college."

"Yes, and you squeaked by with C-minuses. And your skills are in computer technology, which is a good field, but you wanted into the business end.

"Now, Patsy, you weren't quite as greedy. You only asked for a hundred thousand, but you didn't want to work more than three days a week.

"I have other interests," Patsy protested.

"I'm sure you do. What it all boils down to is I'm looking at two healthy young adults who still live at home and receive an allowance—a substantial one, I might add. That is about to change."

The two healthy young adults in question exchanged a curious glance between them.

"I've instructed Morty to write you each a check for twenty-five thousand dollars." Charles saw then both visibly relax. "I figure that should hold you over until you can establish yourselves. I expect you to move out of the house by tomorrow. Take your clothes and electronics and anything that belongs to you, including your expensive cars, but you'll have to pay your own insurance. I'll pay off your credit cards before I cancel them. If you want another, you can apply for it on your own without my backing. Just make sure you aren't carrying a balance on October thirty-first next year. You need to learn to pay off your debts as you make them—live within your means. If you don't understand that concept, I'll be happy to explain it."

"Where will we go?" Patsy asked incredulously.

"Wherever you choose," Charles told her. "It's time you both found places of your own. The stipulations are as follows—you have one year to make it on your own. If either of you calls and asks for more money within that time or borrows money against your inheritance, my name, or this company, it will not bode well for you. Other than a twenty-five-thousand-dollar–per-year stipend, you will be stricken from my will. In addition, do not use my name or this company for a reference when applying for a job. In fact, it would please me if you don't mention my name at all to anyone who doesn't already know you.

"I'd appreciate it if you called periodically to ask me how I am, if you care, or to talk about anything going on in your lives as long as it has nothing to do with finances. For that, I'll continue to pay for your cell phones so you can keep in touch with me and each other in the event you leave the Minneapolis area. Consider it an early Christmas gift because it's the only one you'll get." He paused and sighed. "The only exceptions to these stipulations are if you are hurt, sick, or dying."

Conner shifted in his seat frowning heavily. "I can't live for a year on twenty-five thousand dollars."

"I'm sure you can't. That's why you will have to find a job."

"Why should I get a job when you're a millionaire?"

"That's exactly right. *I'm* a millionaire. You are not. I earned the right to say that. You have not. And just so you know, this wasn't my idea."

Conner's head shot up from a pout. "Let me guess," he snarled. "It was Morty Chambers, your know-it-all lawyer?"

"He's never liked us," Patsy put in.

"I wasn't Morty; it was your mother."

They both gave him disbelieving frowns.

"Three nights ago, she came to me in a dream. She accused me of spoiling your chances to become decent, self-sufficient human beings."

"Mom would never have done this to us!" Patsy said angrily. "She loved us. I wish she was here."

"So do I, Patsy. So do I. I wouldn't be in this predicament if she were."

Conner made a rude snorting sound. "How do you figure that?"

"Tell me, Conner, what were you doing the summer when you were fifteen before your mother died?"

Conner shrugged. "Hanging out with my friends. What else?"

"And what did you do for spending money."

He gave a little laugh. "Mom made me get a…paper route," he finished slowly.

"Exactly," Charles said turning to his daughter. "And you were thirteen. What did you do?"

Patsy chewed on her lower lip. "I had to take care of the Johnson's three dogs while they were in Europe for a month."

"And whose idea was that?" Charles asked.

Patsy made a scrunched face. "Mother's."

Patsy leaned against Conner's bedroom door as he packed. "So…where are you going?" she asked.

He threw his college football trophy into a box. "Damned if I know. I might try and bunk in with Casey until I can find an apartment or something."

"Casey's a meth-head loser. He lives in a rundown dump, for Pete's sake. Why on earth would you go there?"

"He's my best friend."

Patsy snorted. "The only thing he ever wanted from you was a free ticket. I never did understand why you hung out with him at all."

"So you think your friends are any better? How often did you pick up the tab when you went out with them? What are your plans?" he asked without waiting for a reply to his previous question.

"I'm going to the Radisson until I decide."

"That's high buck, Patsy."

She walked over, plopped down on his bed and sighed. "I know, but it won't be for long."

"Do you believe that crap about Mom visiting him in his dreams?" Conner asked.

Patsy shrugged. "Who knows? It's not the first time he's claimed to have heard from her. Remember four years ago, when he didn't want you going deep sea diving off the coast of Australia? He talked you out of it, and then the ship sank."

"Pure coincidence," Conner scoffed. "The only reason he didn't want me to go was because he insisted I had to be home for his big birthday bash." He began stuffing multiple pairs of shoes in a canvas bag. "I think it's just a smoke screen. If you ask me, I'd bet Morty's behind it. He's always carping about my spending habits. Like it was his money I was using. Big damn jerk."

"At least you have your Escalade. I'm stuck with my little Maserati. I can't even get half my things in there. I'm going to have to rent a locker or something."

He gave a harsh laugh. "You wanted that pissant of a car. I told you to get a Honda CR-V."

"Yeah, yeah, yeah," Patsy grumbled. "You were right. But I never expected to be thrown out of the house—and just before the holidays. Happy Thanksgiving, Merry Christmas, and Happy New Year."

"Who knows, maybe it'll turn out for the best," Conner said. "I'll see you back here for Thanksgiving dinner."

* * * *

"How can you be down to twenty-five hundred dollars?" Conner asked. "It's barely July. What are you going to live on for the next four months?"

Patsy was almost sorry she'd called him. "I don't know. How are you doing? Still living with Casey?"

"Hell no. Like you said, he's a junk-head. I rented a one-room efficiency. But I need to get a job or I'm going to be in the same boat you are."

"Have you looked for work?" Patsy asked.

"Yeah, but it's impossible in the Minneapolis metro area. Every place I go, they recognize my name, and they want to know why I'm not working at Bartlett Shipping for my father. What about you?"

"Well…" Patsy hesitated. No sense trying to lie to Conner. He could see right through her. "I haven't exactly been looking."

"Geez, sis. I suppose you're still living at the Radisson, too. You're going to end up on skid row."

"Gordy asked me to move in with him."

"Aw shit, Patsy. You aren't going to do it, are you? I know you've been dating him but the a-hole is a worthless misfit, and a womanizer to boot. As soon as he knows you're broke, he'll dump you like last week's garbage. I'll bet you haven't even told him about dad's ultimatum."

Of course he was right. "I don't have many choices available. I'll run into the same problem you have if I try to find work."

"But you haven't even tried. You're in denial about this whole thing, aren't you?"

Patsy gulped back a sob. She wasn't going to let him hear her cry. She hadn't cried since her mother's funeral, and she'd be damned if she was going to start now. "I'll find something."

Conner sighed. "I'm not going to harp on you. I'm not in a whole lot better shape. I can't make it another four months either unless I get some income. I think I'm going to head to western Minnesota. There's a small town near the South Dakota border that's looking for someone to teach computer know-how to seventh graders."

Patsy laughed. "You want to teach preteens? You don't even like kids."

"I don't have to like them to teach them how to boot up a computer."

"They can be very obnoxious, but you know your stuff, and it's only a few months."

"That's what I figure. I can stomach the little urchins for a while if I have to. What are you going to do? You better get on the ball and find something."

Conner's plan gave her an idea. "Hey, maybe I'll drive out to North Dakota and visit Grandma Summers. I could stay with her a while then head to California, try modeling." *And maybe she got a bunch of money when she sold the farm.* Grams was always very generous.

"Now you *are* dreaming. Besides you haven't seen or talked to Grams since Mom died. So now you think she'll lay a few bucks on her long lost granddaughter?"

"It could happen. She sent us birthday gifts every year until two years ago."

"And did you ever send her a thank-you note?"

Patsy swallowed a lump in her throat. Conner had an uncanny insight that was extremely annoying.

"Did you?" he persisted.

"No. Just like you, I never appreciated it. We had plenty of money. Getting a hundred-dollar gift was so insignificant. Do you suppose Dad was right about us being greedy and spoiled?"

Conner let out a hearty laugh. "Ya think?"

* * * *

Morty Chambers stood, electronic notebook in hand, facing Charles Bartlett. "What's on your mind?" Morty asked.

"We need to talk. I have some plans to implement," Charles said, motioning to a side chair. He was going to have to do something he'd hoped to avoid but… "It's been almost eight months, and I can't see any evidence that either Conner or Patsy is taking my threat to disinherit them seriously."

Morty's heavy brows arched. "Are you really going to go through with it?"

"Yes. It's necessary—for their own wellbeing."

Morty booted up his notebook. "Okay, tell me what you have in mind."

Charles took a deep, laborious breath. He wasn't happy about it, nor was he proud of what he was going to do. Especially since he knew it was mostly his fault his offspring had turned out the way they did. For years, he'd ignored the feeling that Mary Beth was frowning down at him. His greatest wish was that they'd see the light before it was too late. If he wanted to accomplish that goal, he needed to show his hand.

The fact he'd sensed Mary Beth's approval in the last eight months convinced him he was moving in the right direction, but it didn't seem to be making a difference.

"I'd like you to set up a trust fund for Patsy and Conner." He noted Morty's frown and went on. "Each of them will receive twenty-five thousand dollars a year for as long as they live."

Morty typed for a moment, and when Charles didn't continue, Morty looked up expectantly. "That's it?" he asked incredulously.

"Stipulate that the money will continue to go to their legal heirs if they have any."

"So," Morty said, "this means you're changing your will. I don't need to remind you that you are worth millions. What are you going to do with your company, and the balance of our wealth?"

"Everything else in the will concerning people, other than my children, will stay as it is. With the remainder, I'd like you to set up a trust that will give scholarships to young people who can't afford to go to college. Maybe it will benefit some ambitious youngsters more willing to make something of themselves than my two.

"Of course, there's a remote chance they'll make it the year, and at that point, we'll formulate another plan. If fact, we'll need to write something up to take care of that, in case something happens to me before the year is out. I'm starting the ball rolling now so they know I intend to make good on my promises. They need to be aware I'm setting this plan in action. Of course I won't sign anything until the year is up. If something happens to me before that time, write up a document expressing my wishes. I'll sign, a 'just in case' kind of waiver. I'm guessing you know how to do that."

"Certainly. I can take care of it." Morty stood to leave then hesitated. "Charles, I'm concerned about this huge step you're taking…and the references to 'just in case'. Are you having some health issues I don't know about?"

Charles waited a lengthy moment before answering. "No," he lied. "Nothing to concern you."

After Morty left, Charles turned to stare out the window of his elegant high-rise office overlooking the Mississippi River. He wasn't ready to share his problem with Morty, or anyone else, for that matter. He'd debated heavily whether to tell Patsy and Conner about his diagnosis.

It was called atherosclerosis. Charles had never even heard of it before. His doctor had explained it to him in straightforward terms. In his case, three arteries in his heart were plugged, one at one hundred percent and two others fifty percent. It was serious, and without surgery and lifestyle changes, he'd likely die from it. How soon was undetermined at this point.

It wasn't that he was afraid of dying. He wasn't, but leaving the two kids he loved more than life did scare him. And he shouldered the guilt because it was his fault they were the way they were. His wife had had a firm and loving hand. She'd had an insight he couldn't begin to fathom when it came to raising children.

How was it he had no trouble running a multimillion-dollar shipping business, but he seemed to have no aptitude when it came to his own children?

He'd hoped to see some change in them by now, but they clearly weren't taking any steps to becoming self-sufficient. He'd asked Morty to keep tabs on their progress, but to this point, he'd had nothing favorable to report. Patsy hadn't changed her style of living one whit, and Charles was surprised she wasn't already broke. Conner was at least watching what he spent and looking for work, albeit unsuccessfully.

The only thing they had going for them was they were both stubborn as hell. Charles was hoping some ingrained Bartlett pride would set in before it was too late.

Morty experienced a surge of elation. No doubt in his mind Bartlett was lying about his health. He'd had a doctor's appointment one week before he'd called those two spoiled brats in to give them the ultimatum—grow up or the fairytale life ends.

Charles trusted Morty explicitly. It would be easy setting up his own personal trust fund, making it appear to be for unfortunate kids. He was a good money manager. Under his hand, Bartlett's wealth had increased ten-fold—now when push came to shove, he wanted to give it all away to more worthless brats who hadn't done a thing to earn it. The paltry sum he'd left Morty wouldn't be enough to buy a decent car. Sure, he'd managed to siphon some off over the years, but he wanted it all.

Patsy and Conner would cut their own throats, Morty was sure of that. No way would those two be able to last another four months without whining to Daddy for more money. But, if either one exhibited any chance they might make it, Morty had ways of taking care of that.

Chapter Two

Patsy stared at the endless landscape that was North Dakota. Sweeping fields of ripening grain—she remembered her grandfather identifying at one time—stretched out like tall, waving carpets. She wasn't sure but she thought since it was the second of August they would be harvested before long.

Neatly planted rows of trees skirted the farms that were spread out every five or ten miles. Some were farther apart, and even more dotted the rolling hills in the distance, as far as the eye could see. She didn't understand why anyone would want to live in such isolation so far from a major city. Even gas stations were few and far between, forcing Patsy to keep a constant eye on her gas gauge. She hadn't seen a shopping mall or even a McDonalds since leaving the freeway a hundred miles back.

The only surprising thing was the amount of water. It seemed they'd had an abundance of rain because there were a lot of small lakes she was sure hadn't been there before. In a couple of spots, water even covered the roads. Other places, small dams banked the road on either side. It was an eerie feeling to drive with water beside you sometimes as high as eye level. Of course, if she'd had a bigger car, like Conner's Escalade, she might have felt safer.

Except for the excessive water, she remembered most of this trip from driving with her mother when she came up to visit Grams once a year. Conner rarely came along after he became a teenager.

It hadn't been so much that she didn't want to see Grams as that it was boring, especially without Conner. While Grandpa Hank was alive, they lived on a farm with a big old house and lots of animals, which had been kind of fun when Patsy was little, but after he died, Grams moved to a little house in Ashville. A town that was so pathetically small there was nothing to do, and Patsy had missed her friends. The only good part about visiting Grams was her cooking. She knew how to make raisin strudels and dumplings and wonderful chocolate chip cookies.

According to her map, Patsy was only about twenty miles from Ashville. Patsy hoped she'd remember which house Grams lived in. Located somewhere in the southwest corner, it had bright yellow siding and brown shutters. Of course, Patsy hadn't been there for fifteen years. The house could have been repainted by now or Grams may even have moved. Knowing it would be dark in a couple of hours didn't help Patsy's anxiety level any. She should have timed it better so she'd arrive in full daylight, but she couldn't afford to spend any more nights in a hotel than she had to.

Passing a thick row of trees, Patsy contemplated on how she'd approach the older woman she'd ignored for so many years when something flashed out of the corner of her eye. The next thing she knew a large object leaped in front of her car, hit the grille then the windshield. Too late, she slammed on the brakes and swerved. Screams tore from her throat as her car careened toward the steep ditch. The vehicle came to a sliding stop at a precarious tilt but fortunately stayed upright.

Heart hammering and breathing heavily, Patsy stared out through the shattered glass wondering what had hit her. Steam spewed over her pretty red car, and smoke billowed from the wrinkled hood.

Still in shock, she was vaguely aware a car had stopped on the road. She tried unsuccessfully to open her door against the high tilt of the car when a strong arm pulled the door open for her. A man leaned in to look at her, concern etching his handsome features.

"Miss, are you okay?"

She nodded shakily. "I—I think so. What hit me?"

"A deer. You hit a deer." He reached in for her arm. "Here, let me help you out."

When she turned to get out, she was aware her head hurt at the temple. She touched the spot with shaky fingers. Her heart rate jumped when she saw the tips were bloody.

"Oh, my gosh, I'm bleeding."

"Your head must have bumped the steering wheel," the man said as he half-helped, half-lifted her out of the car. "Didn't you have your seatbelt on?"

Of course not. It wrinkles my clothes. "I—I guess I must have taken it off and forgot to put it back on," she mumbled, sensing he wouldn't understand her reason for not wearing it.

His dark gaze flicked over her from leopard print chinos to cropped-off designer tank top. She could tell by his raised brows he appreciated what he saw in a naughty male sort of way.

"Maybe I should take you in to see the doctor," he said.

And rack up a huge bill? "No, no. I'm okay. Just a little bump I'm sure." That was when she got a look at her crumpled Maserati. A hand flew to her mouth. "Oh, my gosh, my car! Look at my beautiful car."

He frowned down at her, and she realized then how tall he was—tall and gorgeous with a body-builder physique. If she'd been in a better state of mind, she might have thought about flirting with him.

"The car can be fixed," he was saying. "Just be glad you didn't roll it. I was right behind you. The last thing you want to do is try to swerve away from a running deer. That's how people get killed. You're lucky this isn't a steep ditch."

It certainly looked like a steep ditch to her. "What am I going to do?" she said, trying to choke down the panic building in her chest.

The tall man shrugged. "Get it towed in to Ashville, I imagine. I can give you a ride to town, and I know the guys at the station who do towing, if that will help. Where were you headed in such a hurry?"

Good grief, she must have been so deep in thought she was speeding. "Ashville, I was going to Ashville to visit my grandmother."

"No kidding? You have a grandmother in Ashville? What's her name?"

"Wilma Summers. Do you know her?"

"Huh. Not sure. I live on a farm northwest of here. I don't know everyone who lives in town. I can give you a lift, then you can see about towing."

Patsy glanced at her mangled car and sucked up her misery. "Yeah, I guess. I'll need to get my things, though."

"Sure, I can do that for ya." He reached in the car and pulled out her keys and her purse. Handing the purse to her, he went to the trunk, opened it, and grimaced. "You need all this in here?"

She flushed. She'd filled every corner to get as much in the tiny trunk as she could. Sighing, she gave him a look of resignation. "I guess I can get by with the suitcase in the back seat—but I don't want everything else to get stolen out here."

He pulled in a deep breath of air then blew it out in an exasperated huff. "If you have a cell phone, I could call the tow truck right now. I don't carry one. My wife has it since she usually has the kids with her when she drives. Martin has probably gone home by now, but I'm sure he'll come out anyway."

Patsy pulled the cell out of her purse and handed it to him. While he made the call, she used a tissue to dab at the blood on her temple. Thankfully, there wasn't much there but she'd probably end up with a nasty looking bruise. She heard him tell the man on the other end of the phone what kind of car she had and where they were. Two miles east of the Schott's farm, he'd said.

"Martin Bower will be here in twenty minutes. If I wait with you, I'll need to call the wife and tell her I'll be late."

"I'd appreciate that," Patsy said numbly, wondering what she was going to do for transportation until her car was getting fixed. Maybe Grams had a car she could borrow.

"My name is Darren, by the way," the tall, studly, married-man-with-kids said, holding out his hand.

Patsy gave him a firm shake. "Glad to meet you, Darren, really glad, actually. I'm Patsy Bartlett. You better call your wife so she doesn't worry."

He laughed. "She won't worry—unless I mention I'm with a dazzling redhead driving a Maserati."

Patsy felt her face heat up even though he seemed to be joking. He turned his back while he made his call, and she heard him laughing again. She could just imagine he was telling his wife about the rich bimbo who slammed into a deer. Little did he know she was traveling on her last seventeen hundred dollars.

How was she going to survive another three months, carless and homeless? Even if she could survive being homeless, she had to get her credit card paid off. She wasn't sure how much she owed, but it was at least five hundred dollars, and that was without interest.

She stared sullenly at her car. Now this little debacle dropped in her lap. The worst of it was she'd changed the insurance on her car to a thousand-dollar deductible to save money.

When Darren hung up, he turned back to her. "Peg said she thinks your grandmother is in the assisted living side of the nursing home. Seems she broke a hip a while back and hasn't fully recovered. Nobody was aware she had any family."

The tow truck showed up, sparing Patsy from having to tell Darren about Wilma's poor excuse for relatives. Maybe Grams wouldn't even acknowledge her. Sadly, Patsy knew that was exactly what she deserved. Grams was in North Dakota growing old alone, and Patsy hadn't even bothered to send thank-you notes for all the gifts she'd received over the years.

The towing guy, Martin, drove straight into the ditch and backed up to her car. He got out and stared in awe at the damaged vehicle. He squinted and sucked in a low, whistling breath. Either he'd never seen a car that hit a deer before or he'd never laid eyes on a Red Gran Turismo Maserati. Patsy would bet on the latter.

"Wow, we might be able to fix the hood, but you're going to need a new radiator, a grille, and a windshield. They could take a while to get. I don't know if they have parts for this little contraption even in Bismarck."

Patsy's heart sank to her toes. Not only was her beautiful car mangled, but the cost and time it would take to fix it, along with paying off her credit card, would deplete her remaining cash. She was heartsick and soon to be desperate.

Following the tow truck in Darren's old club cab pickup, Patsy decided she had to fess up to her situation and see if Darren could help. She had to find some work at least until her car was ready.

"I need to find a job while my car's getting fixed. Do you know of any place in town that's looking for help-wanted?" she asked, trying to sound casual about it.

Darren gave her a look that implied, *are you joking?* "Ashville's a pretty small town. I doubt if there's anything available."

"What about a low-rent motel?" she asked, swallowing her pride.

He gave her a curious look, and she could almost read his mind. She drove a hundred-thousand-dollar car and was looking for a job and a cheap place to stay?

"There's only one motel in town, probably cost you forty or fifty bucks a night. Is that expensive?" he asked.

Darren would be horrified if he knew her lavish background, but she was going to keep that information to herself for the time being. She shrugged. "Depends on how long it takes to fix the car."

"Could be a while. Sounds like they'll have to order parts." His eyes suddenly light up. "Hey, come to think of it, my neighbor is advertising for an older woman to hire on as a cook and housekeeper." When she turned a shocked look on him he quickly held up his hand. "I do realize you're not an older woman, but he hasn't exactly been swamped with applications. You could probably just help him out until your car gets fixed and he finds somebody else. Plus, he lives in a big house—he might even be willing to put you up."

Patsy could have sworn he had a mischievous glint in his eye. "I don't know a lot about cooking," she admitted glumly. She didn't add that she'd never even made coffee and knew nothing about housekeeping other than what she'd seen maids do.

"Hey, no problem," Darren chirped, a little too enthusiastically. "We live less than a mile away. My wife, Peg, is a great cook. I'm sure she'll be glad to give you some pointers."

Pointers? Patsy almost laughed. Like how to turn on the stove? She had a bad feeling about this.

* * * *

On May twenty-first, after fifty-nine days behind bars, Luke McAlister had walked out of the Bismarck courthouse a free man. He was free, but Kelsey, Lola and Betsy were still dead.

An empty farmhouse awaited his return, but the memories of the last night he'd spent there, along with the final argument he'd had with Kelsey, would be etched in his brain for eternity. He was only thirty-four years old and would forever be a haunted man.

He hadn't wanted to go back to his farm, but he had nowhere else to go, and his land had been neglected long enough.

Almost three months had passed since that day, and Luke still hadn't mastered the art of feeding himself. He set his plate of burnt chicken and soggy baked potato on the table, glaring at it in revulsion. After two weeks he hadn't received a single call on his ad for a housekeeper/cook. Certainly, there were women in town who needed a little extra income, but those old biddies were all afraid of him. Either he was going to have to learn how to do it himself or go hungry. Already, he'd been gulping down Tums after each meal, trying to stay an unsettled stomach. You'd think he'd have picked up a few things by now. Hell, he couldn't even microwave a potato without it shriveling to an unrecognizable lump.

He poured a large glass of fresh milk and sat at the counter to eat his paltry meal. The one thing he'd perfected was instant pudding—pour milk in a bowl, add the dry pudding mix and whisk it until it got thick—too bad everything wasn't that simple.

He knew he could go in to the local Asheville Café and eat, but he still wasn't comfortable doing that. Too many people looked at him like he was a monster who'd gotten off murdering his family. These were the same people he'd grown up around, gone to school with, who were friends of his parents. He'd left for two years to do a stint in the Army but had returned to run the family farm when his mother and stepfather were killed in a car accident. At that point, he'd been accepted right back in to the fold until the night that had forever changed his life. Now, except for a small handful, they'd turned on him like he'd grown two horns and a red, pointed tail.

He refused to even drive in to the grocery store, choosing instead to make the forty-mile trek into Jamestown where nobody recognized him. Which reminded him, he needed to start making a shopping list. Maybe find some boxed stuff that was as easy to make as the pudding with simple directions on the carton. Hell, he didn't have time to learn how to cook. He had a farm to run.

He'd gone straight from his mother's cooking, to the service, to marrying Kelsey and letting her take over. She'd been a whiz in the kitchen, even with taking care of Lola and Betsy.

A stab of pain shot through him at the thought of those two little girls. They weren't his by birth, but he couldn't have loved them more if they had been. They'd been only two and four when he'd married Kelsey. The two cutest little blue-eyed buttons you ever did see.

God, he missed them and their playful voices filling the house that now stood in silence. After nearly five months, the ache was still fresh whenever he came in the house. Outside doing farm work and operating machinery, he could allow himself to be distracted, but here in the house… He often thought he should take his brother Glen's advice and sell the place or turn it over to him. But how could Luke do that when it was what Kelsey had wanted— she'd hated the farm, and it had been the reason she was leaving him. Sometimes, he missed her, but then, the night of their last argument would come back to him, putting a damper on his memory of her.

The ringing phone pulled him from his reminiscing and his plate of unappetizing food. It was Glen, who was almost seven years younger than Luke and had still been in college when their parents had died. He'd used the cash he received in compensation for Luke getting the home place to purchase another slightly smaller farm ten miles away. Glen had never married but at least he had the good sense to date local girls—women who understood about farming and the cold North Dakota winters. Luke, on the other hand, had brought in an outsider he'd met in a bar. Kelsey had been beautiful and classy, a big city girl who'd hated everything about farming.

"So, how you doing, Luke?" Glen asked, interrupting Luke's musings.

"I manage. I got the last of the hay put up today. Just need to get the combine ready to go and I'll be set for harvest—"

"I wasn't asking about the farm," Glen cut in. "I was asking about you."

Luke sighed deeply. "If I don't find a cook pretty soon, I'll be lucky if I don't starve to death or poison myself."

Glen laughed. "Maybe you should take some cooking lessons. Either that or find yourself a woman."

"A woman is the last thing I need," Luke grumbled. "They're nothing but trouble."

The line was silent for a moment, then Glen said, "I still think you should sell that place and get away from all the memories there."

Glen had been offering to take the farm off Luke's hands since long before Kelsey and the girls had died. Luke suspected Glen resented the fact he hadn't gotten the farm, especially since it had been Glen who spent the summers and weekends working there while Luke was in the service. Yet he never mentioned it or scorned Luke because of it.

Luke's father had owned the farm and willed it to him when he died. Luke was seven when his mother had remarried and had Glen, but the will had remained ironclad. Besides, it'd been Luke who saved his paychecks and was able to pay off the liens when he took over.

Luke would be forever grateful to Glen for stepping in and helping Darren, Luke's neighbor, finish the planting and taking care of the cattle while Luke had sat in the county jail awaiting his trial.

Luke ended the call from his brother and went back to his sorry meal. After loading his dishes in the dishwasher, he grabbed a beer and his guitar and went out to sit on the porch to enjoy the cool August evening. The hour before dusk was his favorite time of day. He'd barely taken two swallows when he saw Darren's pickup coming up the drive.

Patsy's felt a sudden chill when Darren turned into the farmyard he said belonged to Luke McAlister. Several buildings of various sizes made up the farm, including a modern split-level house and big red barn with an attached short silver silo. She also recognized a chicken coop and what appeared to be a large gray granary. Various pieces of farm equipment she couldn't identify were lined up in a row beside the granary, including a huge green John Deere tractor. Her grandfather had owned one of them, and she remembered riding on it.

Typical of North Dakota farms, trees bordered the outskirts of the buildings on the north and west sides. Grandpa Hank's farm had the same type of trees growing in rows. He'd called it a shelterbelt. The bright sun hovered over the trees.

The truck came to a halt, and Darren told her to say put while he broke the news to Luke. She saw him on the porch in the wicker rocker, his upper body and face hidden in the early evening shadows, which danced back and forth as he rocked. A large Irish setter lay at his feet. It stood and came forward, tail wagging, to greet Darren.

Darren reached down and vigorously rubbed the dog behind the ears. "Hey, Reggie, how ya doing, buddy? Keeping your master out of trouble, I hope."

Her first thought was maybe McAlister was a doddering old man especially since he'd requested an older housekeeper. Maybe he wouldn't even notice if she couldn't cook, and with any luck, his eyesight might be bad enough to not notice her lack of housekeeping skills. Rolling her window down a notch, she tried to listen to their conversation.

Darren did most of the talking, and though she couldn't hear his words, she guessed by the gestures he continued to make toward his truck he was trying to explain her situation to the rocking Mr. McAlister and that she needed work and a place to say.

When Darren stopped talking, Luke McAlister still hadn't said a word, at least not that she could tell. Suddenly, Darren looked toward the truck and, with a wave of his arm, gestured for her to come forward.

The tempo of Patsy's heart kicked into high gear. She tugged on the lower edge of her spandex top, hoping to pull it down far enough to cover her mid-section, but it slinked right back in place when she moved. There was also little she could do about her form-hugging, leopard print chinos. If Mr. McAlister was as old as her father, he'd be horrified by her clothes, just as she knew her father was. Too bad she hadn't taken time to pull a pair of jeans and T-shirt out of her suitcase. She'd used the restroom at the service station where they'd taken her car and could have changed there. A day late and a dollar short, her father would have said.

Having already decided this man would never hire her, she shrugged, stepped out of the truck, and made a feeble attempt to appear confident and dignified.

She slowly tottered toward the porch, her strappy sandals with the pointy heels digging into the gravel drive.

Luke stared at the housekeeper, pseudo-hooker, walking awkwardly forward. He set his guitar aside and gave his neighbor a glare that could have melted the polar ice cap.

"Are you fricking nuts?" he growled.

"She's a nice girl," Darren said quickly. "Give her a chance. The poor kid is in a bind."

"What kind of bind can a female who looks like that and owns a Maserati be in?"

"Did I mention she was on the way to visit her grandmother in Asheville?"

"Good, take her to her grandmother's. I don't need help that bad." He did need help but not the kind this carrot-topped floozy could give him.

"Can't. She's in the assisted living home."

"Well, take her home to your place."

"Are you kidding? Peg would kill me—or worse. How about you just keep her overnight and drive her in to her grandmother in the morning."

Luke gave a rude snort. "You're talking like she's a lost dog."

Darren grinned. "Well, she is sort of, although you could hardly call her a dog. Look at that cute—ah—face. Those big green innocent eyes. Besides, you know perfectly well nobody around here is going to answer your ad."

Luke ignored that truthful statement and watched as the woman finally made it to the first step.

"I don't need her," Luke snarled, shoving to his feet, intending to go in the house.

Patsy almost backed up when Luke McAlister unfolded his six-foot-plus frame and came to his feet. When his facial features came into the light, she stared up at him in shock. Holy crap, talk about tall, dark and ruthlessly handsome. With his flannel shirt and worn jeans, this farmer dude could have come straight from a woodsman catalog. He had an unruly shock of black hair, desperately in need of a combing, and haunting gray eyes that were zeroed in on her like laser beams. His gaze slid from her face to her feet and back to her face, pausing a mere microsecond on her breasts.

He looked about as approachable as a coiled cobra, but she was never one to back down from a snake, two-legged or otherwise. She had to say her piece before he could open his mouth to tell her to hit the road. "I need a job real bad, Mr. McAlister, I'm willing to work."

McAlister glanced at Darren. "I requested an older woman. She doesn't look more than seventeen."

Patsy wasn't sure if that was a compliment or not. "Actually, I'm twenty-eight. And I'm willing to do whatever needs doing. I also need a place to stay until my car is fixed. In the meantime, if you find someone else, I'll…I'll leave."

"*Whatever* needs doing?" he said allowing his gaze to rest on her form-fitting top, specifically her breasts.

All right, now, he was pissing her off. Conner would have thrown his head back and laughed at the insinuation, and had Patsy been in a better mood, she may have laughed herself. But her car was wrecked, she was bordering on poverty, and this *farmer* had plucked her last straw. Job or no job, she marched up the last two steps, stood in front of the hunk of a Neanderthal—the really *tall* hunk of a Neanderthal, she realized—and placed her hands on her hips.

"*Whatever* means whatever you were expecting from your *older* lady. If you have anything else in mind, you can stick your job where the sun doesn't shine."

A muscle twitched in the corner of his eye, and his gray gaze hardened as it locked with hers. "Where did you get this mouthy twit?" he asked Darren without looking away from her face.

"I may be a lot of things," she snipped, "but a twit is not one of them. I desperately need a job, I'm willing to beg for it, but that's as far as I go."

He unlocked his gaze from hers and turned to his smirking neighbor. "She can stay the night; that's all I'm agreeing to for now." His piercing glare swiveled back on her. "You can take it or leave it—and you better be a damn good cook."

Patsy swallowed the constricting lump in her throat. "I'll take it."

Chapter Three

Conner stared woefully at his first class, wondering why he ever though he'd want to teach adolescent miscreant to run computers. He watched his students file in, a sick feeling building in his stomach. Little did they know he had a low tolerance for dealing with kids. Especially these kids. They were the misfits. The ones that needed a boost to start the coming school year. And if he wanted to be offered a job in the fall, he needed to succeed at this one. The committee that hired him was willing to overlook the fact he had no teaching experience if he could bring these kids up to speed.

They'd really have a good laugh if they knew the sole reason he was here was to save his inheritance. What would he do when the fall term started and he'd have three classes a day? How would he survive an entire school year caged up in a room with nothing but juveniles? Truthfully, he only had to survive three more months, but he wouldn't make any points with his father if he quit his job just because the time was up. It surprised him he really did want his old man to be proud of him. Something he hadn't considered before taking this job.

Well, he didn't have to make a decision until November first—if he lasted that long.

He'd noticed when he came in there were only five computers. How the hell was he supposed to teach without equipment? What kind of a school, he wondered, couldn't afford to supply students with sufficient tools?

Groaning, he picked up a marker to write his name on the white board then hesitated. What did he want to be called? Mr. Bartlett? Hell, why not? All through twelve years of school, he's had to address his teachers as Mr., Mrs., Ms., whatever.

He wrote the name then turned to look at the students all gawking back at him like zombies. Four girls, three of them looking at him with adoring doe eyes and the fourth with a try-to-make-me learn-something scowl. All four boys clearly would rather be any place else than in a classroom on a sunny summer day. Well hell, so would Conner.

But, wait, there should be six boys. Two were missing, late. Skipping class on the first day? Conner had a sudden flashback to his own school days. The last thing he wanted was kids who behaved like he had.

He glanced at the clock; they still had two minutes. Scuffling and screeching came from the hallway, then two boys more or less tumbled in. One large, overweight boy had his hand on the back of the neck of a smaller, slimmer kid. The smaller boy was all but in tears as he was shoved aside. Laughing, the big kid took a seat at the back of the room while the other one picked himself up off the floor and slinked into the first seat he came to.

Conner gritted his teeth. Very few things bugged him more than a bully picking on a kid who was half his size. The cruel action evoked unwelcome memories of his own unhappy elementary years. He hadn't started his growth spurt until he turned twelve. Before that, he was an inch shorter than Patsy even though she was almost two years younger.

"What's your name?" Conner asked the smirking kid in the back.

"Raymond Calder," he answered.

"And you?" he asked the slinker.

"Willard—Willy—Jenson," he said sniffling.

Conner regarded them both a moment then looked at Raymond and pointed to the chair beside Willy. "You sit up here."

Raymond shrugged, got up, and shuffled forward. As he sat, he gave Willy a none–too-gentle tap on the back of the head. "Why do I have to sit beside him?"

"Because," Conner said, "you're going to need his help."

Raymond's eyes widened angrily. "Why would I need his help?"

"Because Willy is smarter then you are."

"How do you know that," Raymond groused.

Conner smiled. "You told me when you walked in. The only reason a big kid picks on somebody smaller is because he's envious of the other one being smarter. Otherwise, why would he bother since it wouldn't be much of a challenge?"

* * * *

Luke stood like an unfriendly statue while Darren unloaded Patsy's suitcase from the back of his pickup. Patsy had a feeling of approaching doom as Darren hefted it on the porch beside her.

"Can you manage it from here?" he asked.

"No problem," she lied, not because she couldn't handle the suitcase but being left alone with the sinister farmer was more than a little frightening. And the snarky look on Darren's face didn't help. If she didn't know better, she'd think he'd run that deer out in front of her so he could set her up. That, of course, was ridiculous but there was something the two men were hiding. Darren was enjoying the uncomfortable situation far too much, and he had the feeling he couldn't wait to get home and tell his wife about it.

And why was he so sure nobody would answer McAlister's ad? That statement alone was enough to dub him Mr. Rochester. Well, certainly Darren wouldn't leave her here if McAlister was an ax murderer, so what did she have to be afraid of?

As Darren pulled out of the yard, Patsy released the handle on her suitcase and looked up expectantly at the brooding farmer. "Where will I be staying?" she asked, hoping he wouldn't say the barn.

Without a word, he turned and walked into the house. The screen door would have slammed in her face if she hadn't caught it.

Stepping into the foyer behind him, Patsy was amazed at how large and nicely decorated the modern, split-level house was. She saw no resemblance to the old, boxy farmhouse her grandparents had lived in.

The sitting room was set up like a den with plush blue and white brocade furniture, big screen television and lots of glass-top oak end tables. In front of the sofa sat the most interesting coffee table she'd ever seen. It looked like three giant books with dark leather binding sitting on top of each other. A stone fireplace covered the far wall, while several informal, but nicely framed photos of kids graced the elegant mahogany mantel.

The pastel blue curtains and crisp white doilies along with flowered paintings told her a woman had decorated this room, and for the first time, Patsy wondered if he had a wife. Darren hadn't mentioned it. Maybe McAlister was recently divorced. Did he have children? She wanted to ask but wasn't in the mood to start up a conversation with him.

The only masculine thing she saw was through an open door into what looked like an office. From her vantage point, she could see a desk with a high back brown leather chair and some bookshelves.

She glanced around at the somewhat cluttered room. A menagerie of magazines, newspapers, and discarded mail adorned most of the surfaces including the sofa.

He must have noticed her frowning disapproval because his irritated voice cut into her thoughts. "If I were neat and tidy, I wouldn't need a housekeeper; besides I have a farm to run that's been neglected for two months."

She wondered where he'd been for two months but didn't care enough to ask about it. Shrugging, she gave him a thin, satisfied smile. "Well then, I guess you do need me, after all." She didn't feel it was necessary to mention the only cleaning she'd ever done was in the confines of her own room; everything else, the maid had taken care of.

He grunted, making a noncommittal sound and pointed toward a short flight of steps descending to the lower level. "You can stay down there. First room on the left. Bathroom's connected to the bedroom as well as having a door to the hallway. No one's been in there for some time so what you see is what you get. If it needs cleaning, I suspect you can take care of it. Whatever else you need— hunt for it."

He nodded, indicating behind her. "Kitchen's back there. You can familiarize yourself with where everything is. We'll talk about salary tomorrow—if things work out."

Thanking him, she nodded and pulled her suitcase toward the stairs. She wouldn't bother unpacking since it was doubtful he'd be keeping her around.

His voice stopped her. "If you have any intentions of staying, you better have some different clothes to wear."

She turned to glare at him. "I'm not wearing any cutsie little maid's uniform if that's what you have in mind."

She thought she saw his lips twitch but it could have been an angry tick. "I was thinking more of jeans and a shirt that covered your bellybutton. I don't get many visitors here, but in case anyone sees you, I don't want them getting confused as to the reason you're here. If you don't own anything respectable, I can drive you to Jamestown and give you money to go shopping—if you'll be staying."

Geez, her father would love this alpha male. Her first reaction was anger, but she stifled that quickly. She needed this job, and even more important, she needed a place to stay until her car was fixed. Mumbling a hasty, "Okay," she headed for her room, calling over her shoulder. "But I am not addressing you as Mr. McAlister."

She carried her bag down the stairs and located the room. It was small but adequate, a fraction of the size of her room at her father's house where she had her own sitting area with a large television she rarely watched.

But this room was comfortable looking in spite of the sparse furnishings—a queen size bed, a long dresser with mirror, and matching bureau. The walls were painted a lemony yellow and a big, old-fashioned rocking chair filled an otherwise empty corner. Again, the feminine touch was present with white lace curtains, floral paintings that complemented the spread and pastel afghan draped over the arm of the rocker.

Everything seemed clean until she noticed the dust on the surface of the dresser. It was so thick she wrote her name in it. Patsy didn't have a clue how much time had to pass to accumulate so much dust. Mrs. Mimi Dinkler, their fussy housekeeper at home, would be horrified. That thought made Patsy want to laugh and cry at the same time.

She set her things down and went to inspect the bathroom. No dust. Obviously this room had been used. She checked the door leading to the hallway, locked it, then wound a wad of toilet paper off the roll. After dampening the wad, she returned to the bedroom to do her first job as servant to Luke McAlister, dusting her own room. That done, she sat on the bed and flopped to her back, feet dangling, wondering how she'd gotten herself into this mess.

Her growling stomach reminded her she hadn't eaten since breakfast. Glancing at her Rolex, a Christmas gift from her father two years ago, she realized it was after seven o'clock. Small wonder she was hungry.

Deciding to check out the kitchen, she slipped off her strappy heels that had been a bitch to drive in and dug into her suitcase for a pair of flat sandals. Surely she'd find something to eat that didn't require cooking, even if she had to chance running into *him*. Lord have mercy, how was she going to fake her way through meals? Maybe she could find a cookbook.

Darren, whom she'd dubbed as a total smart-ass, had laughed when she'd mentioned she couldn't cook. He'd told her he had confidence in her, and if she ran into trouble, his wife, Peg, would be happy to help her out. Patsy got the feeling she was the butt of a joke Darren was playing on his neighbor.

As she made her way up the stairs, she hoped something would go her way on this awful day, and the crabby Mr. McAlister would have gone to bed early. She knew she was out of luck when she heard the television playing on low volume—so as not to disturb her? She snorted. Yeah right. More likely he'd been hoping she'd stay down in her room.

She was surprised to discover he was watching Jeopardy instead of some mindless sports channel. Fortunately, the recliner where he was sitting was positioned so she didn't have to walk in front of him to get to the kitchen. He didn't say anything but his gaze slipped to her flat shoes. If he was pleased about the change, he didn't say anything.

"I'm going to check out the kitchen," she said, waiting to speak until she was behind him.

His reaction was a wave of his hand as though he didn't care what she did. Something about him was strange. She wondered if that had anything to do with him not being able to find a housekeeper.

His dog, Reggie, who'd been lying at his feet, got up and followed Patsy into the kitchen where he sat on his haunches staring at her as though wondering what she was doing there.

When Luke spoke suddenly, breaking the silence, she realized he was blurting out the answer on the game show. Good, let him be preoccupied with the program so he wouldn't pay any attention to what she was doing. Amazingly, the kitchen was fairly clean. No dirty dishes, thank goodness, and her feet didn't stick to the floor when she walked—the official Conner Bartlett test. As kitchens went, this one was pretty nice, and the strawberry curtains were definitely a woman's touch. She wished she'd asked Darren about McAlister's wife. Maybe getting friendly with Peg might yield some answers.

First thing she did was check the refrigerator. Along with the usual condiments she found milk, cheese, and eggs. She snuck a quick glance back at Luke then broke off a hunk of cheddar cheese with her fingers and stuffed a large bite in her mouth. In the freezer she found chocolate ice cream that had frost crystals growing in it, and several packages of meat, including ground beef, steaks, and pork chops. None of which she had an inkling of how to prepare. Lord, she was going to be so busted.

Groaning, she opened all the cupboard doors in quick succession but found nothing readily edible. Then, she saw a narrow door off to the side. She pulled it open, happy to discover a fairly well-stocked walk-in pantry—the mother lode. Unfortunately, she didn't have a clue what to do with any of it—until she found a box of microwave popcorn bags. Hey, *that* she knew how to make. Still chewing on her cheese, she snatched a bag out of the box, intending to head straight for the microwave, when a stack of cookbooks caught her attention. She grabbed the one that said *Pillsbury*, tucked it under her arm, and carried it with her.

Another glance over her shoulder confirmed Luke hadn't moved. The weirdo was still calling out answers. She wondered if he did that when he was home alone. All she could say was, for a hick farmer, he was pretty damn smart.

Waves of buttery popcorn smells assailed Luke's senses. Damn, if there was one thing he couldn't resist, that was it. That and the fact that *she* was out there making it about did him in. He'd never been one to lust after a loose woman, but it had been a long time since he'd had a sexual encounter of any kind. He'd hoped the next time he saw her she'd be dressed a little less provocatively. At least she'd ditched those ridiculous Hollywood heels.

By the time the popping stopped, he'd missed three Jeopardy answers including a bonus question. He always got those.

He snapped the recliner down, got up, and walked to the kitchen. She was seated at the counter, cheese in one hand, a mouthful of popcorn in the other, studying one of his mother's old cookbooks.

Her cheeks flushed a bright shade of pink when she looked up and saw him staring at her.

"You sharing that?" he asked.

She gave him a weak smile. "I guess I better, since you own it. Sorry, I haven't eaten since this morning. I suppose I should have asked."

"Not a problem," he said, taking a stool at the counter across from her. Since she'd obviously been eating from the bag, she now jumped up and took two bowls down from the cupboard and divided the remaining popcorn between them. She must have been hungry because there wasn't a lot left.

Shrugging guiltily, she smiled. "I'll get another bag."

She had a captivating smile, he thought as he took a peek at what she was reading while she disappeared into the pantry. The page was open to *pancakes*. The page had food smudges on it. He'd heard once that was the indication it was a good recipe. Apparently, she knew that. There might be hope for her yet.

He watched as she came back to pop the corn and had to admit she had a figure that was easy on the eyes. For his own personal comfort, if she stayed, she needed to stop dressing like a tramp, and wear something less—revealing.

He'd emptied his bowl when she came back to the counter with the newly popped bag. She was in the process of dividing it when a sharp tat-a-tat-tat knock sounded at the door. Recognizing the signature knock, Luke mouthed a string of silent curses.

Patsy stared at him, curious why he wasn't answering the door. Then, she wondered if that was supposed to be her job.

Before she could decide, she heard the front door open followed by a male voice. "Hey, Luke, you home?"

"In the kitchen," Luke called, giving Patsy a strangely withering look. It occurred to her that he might be embarrassed to have her in his house dressed as she was.

With his dark hair and gray eyes, the man who walked in had a distinct resemblance to Luke. But that's where the likeness ended. This man was at least two inches shorter and slightly overweight. He also didn't have the muscle mass Luke did.

His curious eyes lit up with mischief when he spotted Patsy. "Wowee. What do we have here? Am I interrupting something?"

"No!" Patsy and Luke snapped at the same time.

"This is my brother Glen," Luke muttered unenthusiastically.

"And this is—?" Glen asked, waiting.

"Patsy. Patsy—what is your last name anyway?" Luke asked her.

Patsy didn't appreciate the way Luke's brother was ogling her. Granted, her looks and style of dress brought that on a lot, but something in Glen's eyes made her uncomfortable.

"Bartlett," she said. "Patsy Bartlett."

"Patsy answered my ad for a housekeeper/cook," Luke supplied.

Brows risen, Glen perused her with interest. "You hired someone, and you don't even know her last name. Now, that's interesting." He reached around Luke and snagged a handful of popcorn.

"She just got here tonight."

Glen chuckled. "Looks like that, and can cook too? Man, Luke you hit the jackpot with this one." He turned to Patsy. "I don't recall ever seeing you around these parts. Where'd you come from anyway?"

None of your business, asshole. Patsy bit her tongue. Glen was Luke's family. If she wanted this job, it would not serve her purpose to get on the bad side of him.

"East of here. I came to visit my grandmother," she explained, keeping a check on her temper. "I hit a deer outside of town, and Darren helped me get my car towed then brought me here. Luke offered me a place to stay while my car's getting fixed, and in return, I'll help out around the house."

That was stretching the truth since Darren had, more or less, forced Luke to take her in, and he hadn't actually agreed to hire her yet…but she'd let Luke clarify that if he wanted to.

Luke did not look amused with her explanation, especially when Glen took a seat at the table making no attempt to stifle the grin on his face.

"What brought you out here tonight, Glen?" Luke asked. "Other than to harass my help."

"I was in the neighborhood and you sounded a little down when I called so I thought I'd stop and visit. I haven't seen you in town lately."

"I don't go to Ashville, you know that."

"I don't see why—"

"Drop it, will you?" Luke snapped.

Glen held up his hands in surrender. "Okay, pal. That's your field to plow anyway. Did you get your haymow pulley fixed?"

Luke's face clearly relaxed at the change of subject. "No. Tomorrow morning, I'm going to go up and take a look at it. If I needed more hay up there, I'd get a conveyor track but as it is…."

Patsy had no idea what they were talking about. But she was curious as to why Luke didn't go in to Ashville when it was the nearest town. She'd seen a grocery store, a drug store, and several machine shops. He had mentioned going to Jamestown, which was at least forty miles farther?

Glen suddenly stood. "Well, I've got to get going." He held a hand out to her. "Nice to meet you, Miss Bartlett. I hope to see you again."

"Good to meet you too, Mr. McAlister," she lied, accepting his proffered hand.

He frowned at her. "It's not McAlister; it's Johnson. Luke and I had different fathers."

* * * *

Patsy woke up early—before eight, which was early for her. She'd heard music playing softly upstairs long into the night. It must have been a CD because it was all the same singer. Judging by some of the songs it sounded like Vince Gill.

Now she heard Luke's footsteps above her and knew he'd probably be ready to eat soon. Nervous as she was she actually looked forward to making pancakes; she'd studied the recipe over and over until she had it memorized.

Slipping into her two hundred dollar designer jeans and the Reba McIntyre T-shirt she'd bought at a concert last winter, Patsy hoped her somewhat modest outfit would make her potential boss happy.

He was already in the kitchen. Not the way she'd intended to make her first meal—with him watching over her. She pasted a smile on her face and gave him a cheery, "Good Morning."

"Same to you." He gave her an overall appraisal without scowling so she hoped that meant he approved of her attire. "I thought I'd start the coffee since it's the one thing I can do, he said. "Then I have a few chores to do, and I'll be back in for breakfast."

Patsy gave a gigantic sigh of relief and sidled up next to him to watch how he made the coffee. "Will pancakes be okay?" she asked, willing him to say yes.

"Sure, and there's some bacon in a drawer in the fridge. Make four strips for me and whatever you want for yourself. Coffee should be ready in a few minutes. I'll go take care of my chores. That'll give you about half an hour."

Patsy stared after Luke as he walked out the door, trying to swallow the lump of panic in her throat. Bacon! He wanted bacon. She charged down to her room and got her cookbook. The index had nothing about bacon. Then she remembered their cook had made bacon in the microwave for BLT's. How hard could that be?

She found the bacon, took a plate out of the cupboard, and cringed. The bacon was greasy and slimy and the most disgusting thing she'd ever touched. Choking back nausea, she pulled the pieces apart with her fingertips and laid them on the plate. Four slices. She liked bacon but that was before she'd touched it uncooked. Next, she located the ingredients she needed for the pancakes and quickly started mixing them together, flour flying everywhere. If Conner could see her now, he'd be rolling on the floor laughing. *Let him laugh*. She was determined to learn how to cook if it was the last thing she did.

With the batter ready to go, she dug a frying pan out of the cupboard, set it on the stove, added a little oil, and checked the clock. Ten minutes to go. Two minutes later, she had the first pancake sizzling in the pan, and the bacon looking less disgusting. Hoping to impress her potential boss wither her efficiency, she hurriedly started to clean up the mess she'd made. As she was about to put the cover back on the flour container, she noticed some little specks in it. On closer examination, her heart gave a jolt.

Bugs! Tiny, little, wormy-looking bugs—in the flour.

Unable to breathe, she grabbed a spatula and turned the pancake that was getting brown on one side. She glanced at the bacon—it had a while to go yet. Then she went back to the flour container, hoping if she had another look she'd find she was mistaken about the bugs.

Oh yeah, they were there all right, but they weren't moving. They were dead. Out the kitchen window, she saw Luke walking toward the house, carrying a small plastic bucket.

The first pancake was done. It looked brown and beautiful. She flipped it onto a plate and examined it very closely. She couldn't see a thing out of the ordinary, specifically a bug. Moving quickly, she poured more batter in the pan to make a second one then dumped the flour that was left in the canister into the trash container.

Luke walked in and set his pail of eggs on the counter. "Chickens were busy this morning," he said. "Sure smells good in here. I'll just go wash up and be right back."

His dog, Reggie, had come in the house with him. He sat there staring at her, and she could have sworn he was frowning like he knew exactly what she was doing.

Patsy gave herself a mental shake and flipped the second perfectly round pancake. What choice did she have? The bugs were, after all, dead. What harm could it do? The heat would kill any germs. The guard dog made a deep sound in his throat like he could read her thoughts. Great, a mind-reading dog. Just what she needed.

Quickly rescuing the bacon from the microwave, she set it out on a paper towel like she'd seem Mimi do, stunned to see how nice and crispy it looked. When Reggie's big tongue came out and slurped his chops, she informed him he wasn't getting any bacon, but if he wanted pancakes, there was enough batter left for at least two or three more.

She quickly set the table and poured two cups of coffee, wondering how she was going to explain not eating any pancakes. The third one was done when he got back and took a seat. She heaped it on top of the others on his plate and set out the syrup she'd found in the pantry.

He started chewing on his bacon and drenched the pancakes with syrup. She sat frozen while he took his first bite. Her stomach roiled, and she raced for the bathroom.

Chapter Four

Luke frowned at her hasty departure until a thought hit him. Her face had turned a sickly shade of green for a moment, and that's exactly how Darren's wife, Peg, had looked in the morning when she was pregnant. He swore and continued eating, intending to have it out with Patsy when she got back.

He had to admit he was surprised. The bacon was done perfectly, and the pancakes were some of the best he'd ever eaten. Even Kelsey, as experienced as she was, had never made them from scratch.

When she returned from the bathroom, she sat and took a sip of her coffee, keeping her gaze anywhere but on him

"Not hungry?" he asked.

She shook her head. "I must have eaten too much popcorn last night. I don't seem to have an appetite this morning."

"Darren's wife had that some problem when she was pregnant."

Her head shot up. "I'm not pregnant if that's what you're suggesting."

"Are you sure?"

She snorted. "Positive. I haven't had— never mind. Just trust me on that."

"Okay. By the way, both the pancakes and bacon were excellent. You did a great job. Thank you. If you're still inclined to stay, we can work something out regarding salary later. In the meantime, if you take inventory and make a list of the things you need, and we can make a trip to Jamestown to pick it up. Right now, I have to go out and check that pulley, Chances are I'll need a part or two, and we can drive in this afternoon."

Patsy was starting to breathe easier until he said, "I may as well take the trash out. I noticed yesterday it was getting a little full."

He went to the sink and pulled out the trashcan, but as he was removing the bag, his brows drew together. "What's this? Why did you throw the flour out?"

Patsy's throat seized tight, her tongue stiffened, as panic edged its way into her soul. She couldn't have uttered a sound if her life depended on it. Of course, he automatically examined the flour, and she could tell the moment it dawned on him what she'd done.

His face was a mask of ill-concealed fury. "Did you feed me bugs?"

She gaped at him, suddenly stricken with fear. He was going to kill her.

"Answer me dammit. Did you make those pancakes with this flour? I want to hear you say it."

At this point, she didn't think it prudent to mention they were dead bugs. And she was beyond coming up with any feasible lie or even an excuse, especially when she felt the heated truth flaming in her face. Swallowing thickly, she whispered, "Yes."

He stared at her for a long moment then spoke in a deadly controlled voice. "You have two options, Miss Bartlett. And the only reason I'm giving you choices is to see just how badly you want this job. I'm going out to look at my pulley, because right now, I need to get away from the sight of you, but when I come back in, you can either have your bags packed or sit down and eat one of those pancakes in front of me. Not a bite, not half, but the whole damn thing. And don't even think about barfing it up." He grabbed the trash bag and stomped out of the house.

Patsy stared after him in shock. Then, she realized Reggie hadn't followed him out. He was sitting back on his haunches watching her intently, smiling? Was he guarding her to make sure she wasn't going to try to mix up another batter?

"There's no more flour, you idiot," she yelled as much to the dog as to herself. He stared back at her with big brown eyes and long wet tongue hanging out. Was he laughing?

This, she didn't have to put up with. She marched to the door opened it and ordered the dog to follow his master. Reggie hesitated a moment then strutted though the door like a pleased peacock.

She took a large gulp of cold coffee to get control of her stomach then sidled cautiously over to the counter to peak in the bowl. There was enough batter for at least two more pancakes. She stirred it slowly, examining it. When she actually saw a tiny dark spec she jumped back with a sickening squeal.

Her heart hammered, and her stomach did crazy little flip-flops at the thought of eating insects. She wished she could call Conner, but she'd tried that last night. Her cell phone wouldn't work out in this Godforsaken country. Probably just as well. She couldn't call the guy who could swallow a live minnow. He'd most likely enjoy bragging about eating flour bugs.

Patsy shuddered and walked down the five steps to her room to do a backup plan, replacing the few things she'd taken out of her suitcase so it would be ready. She'd already decided she would eat the pancakes. Really what other choice did she have? However, she wasn't sure she could do it without vomiting, and Luke had warned her upchucking wasn't in the deal.

When she'd woken up that morning, she'd been hungry and looked forward to eating a breakfast she'd prepared herself. Now, she'd completely lost her appetite.

By the time she got back to the kitchen, a half hour had passed. She poured a fresh cup of coffee and collapsed into a chair to wait for her doom. When an hour had gone by, she cursed him. Obviously he was making her sit there and think about what she had to look forward to. The man had a cruel streak in him.

The worst of it was she had hunger pangs, something she wasn't accustomed to in her pampered life. She supposed poor people in third world countries would eat the pancakes, lick their plates clean and ask for more. No doubt that depressing thought came straight from her mother—maybe Dad *had* spoken to her mother from the grave, after all.

Rubbing her hands over her face in frustration, Patsy tried to stop thinking about buggy pancakes and world hunger. Reggie barking at the door brought her out of her thoughts. Heart pounding and feeling sick, she waited for Luke to follow. When the door didn't open, she went to investigate what Reggie was barking about.

The sun was a brilliant ball in the sky. The yard was empty. No sign of Luke McAlister. The dog looked at her in an odd way, making a low sound akin to a whine —he certainly wasn't smiling.

Walking out on the porch, she looked down at the barn and saw a long ladder lying on the ground, beneath it was Luke. She leaped down the steps and raced toward the barn, a sunken feeling twisting her unsettled gut.

He was awake but grimacing in pain, holding one arm. When she flung the long telescopic ladder off of him, she noticed one leg of the ladder was twisted and bent. It must have collapsed while he was on top of it. The heavy pulley he'd been working on lay very near his head.

Patsy saw no sign of blood. "How bad are you hurt" she asked, remembering something about not moving an injured person for fear of doing further damage.

"It's my left arm and the ribs on that side. I don't know what the hell happened. I was working one minute, and the next, I was lying on the ground, and that damn pulley came slamming down an inch from my head."

"Should I call an ambulance?"

"No, just help me get up."

She put her hands on his wide shoulders where he didn't seem to be hurting and pulled. A pained hissing sound came through his clenched teeth as he rolled with her help to a sitting position.

He took a moment to catch his breath. "Can you drive the pickup over here?" he asked.

She'd never driven a pickup before. "I—I guess. Where are the keys?"

"In the ignition. Wait, help me get to my feet first."

"Are you sure? Do you want me to call Darren?"

"Not yet. Let's see if we can do this first. Go behind me and lift under my arms just be careful of the ribs on the left side. I think my legs are okay."

He leaned forward, gritting his teeth and groaning in agony, but managed to get to his knees then stand. He wasn't standing straight but he was on his feet, breathing heavily.

"Okay, now, get the pickup," he said hoarsely.

She hesitated, not sure if it was safe to leave him. "You're not going to fall?" she asked.

"Not unless you plan to stand there chatting a while first."

She whirled around and ran for the vehicle then paused a second, wondering if she should get her purse. Looking back at him, she realized he had hobbled over to look at the ladder, so she ran in the house and down to her room, taking the steps two at a time. She snatched her purse off the dresser then yanked a pillow off the bed and raced back outside. Jumping in the club-cab truck, she flung her purse in the back and placed the pillow on the seat beside her. Sure enough, the keys were in the ignition.

She didn't have time to dwell on the practice of leaving keys handy for thieves. People likely didn't even lock their doors around here. Thankfully, the engine roared to life on the first turn, and Patsy backed up and drove the forty or so feet to the barn.

Luke was walking around, examining the ladder. The man must have grit of iron. So why were her hands shaking? Leaving the engine running, she hopped out of the truck and scurried over to him, wondering why he didn't seem to be in much of a hurry.

"We should get going," she said.

"Take a look at that," Luke said, pointing to the twisted leg of the ladder about six inches from the bottom.

"Can't you worry about that later?" she said.

He gave her a hard look. "Somebody sawed the leg almost clear through and filled in the saw marks with putty."

Patsy shrugged. "So?"

He gave her an incredulous look. "So somebody tried to kill me. That's…so…" The exertion of anger caused him to double over, clutch his side and wince. He swore profusely and wiped sweat from his brow with his sleeve. Clearly, this man was not used to vulnerability.

"We better get you to a doctor. Your concern over the ladder can wait until then." She grabbed his good arm and steered him toward the truck.

He mumbled a curt, "Yeah," and went along with her.

She opened the truck door, grabbed the pillow from the seat and waited to see if he could manage to get in by himself. With the help of a few choice words, he finally managed to squirm his body into the seat.

"Are you comfortable?" she asked.

"Hell no! Do I look comfortable?"

Patsy caught herself to keep from laughing. Certainly his pain wasn't funny but for a big manly man he sure was acting like a baby. "Lean forward and I'll put the pillow behind your lower back so you can get the pressure off your ribs."

"What? You're a doctor now?"

"Do you want to take my advice or sit there and grumble until you puncture a lung?"

He gave her a skeptical glare but did as instructed. She stuck the pillow as low behind him as she could then eased him back. He was pale and gasping by the time she had him settled.

She raced around to the driver's side, jumped in the truck then hesitated when she saw Reggie staring at them, his big brown eyes etched with concern. "What about the dog?" she asked. "Does he need to go in the house?"

Luke let out and exasperated huff. "He's a farm dog not a mollycoddled pet."

Patsy felt a rush of annoyance sweep over her. Stifling it, she jerked the truck in gear and took off up the driveway not caring if she hit bumps in the potted gravel road. Each time she did he sucked in another breath.

"Do you have to hit every hole in the road?"

"Yeah," she muttered, "I want to make sure I don't mollycoddle you." She made a right turn at the end of the drive then, going past Darren's farm, she came to the main road and signaled to make another right turn.

"Where are you going?" he asked, scowling.

"To Ashville. This is the way we came yesterday."

"We're not going to Ashville; we're going to Jamestown."

"Ashville has a hospital; why would we go forty miles farther to Jamestown?"

"Because," he replied, enunciating every word through gritted teeth. "I don't go to Ashville."

"Well, that's just plain silly. Unless you can give me a reasonable explanation, like they have a lousy doctor or something, we're going to Ashville. I don't want you passing out on me because we have to drive all the way to Jamestown. So what's it going to be?" She hesitated, waiting for his answer.

"Has anyone ever told you you're a pain in the ass."

"Regularly," she said, turning right toward Ashville.

She smiled to herself while he muttered under his breath something derogatory about females in general. Let him grumble, she thought. If he'd have said they had better doctors in Jamestown, she might have gone that direction. Somebody in Asheville must have pissed him off or some such menial thing. Too bad. It was time he got over it. She wanted to see her grandmother, and she also needed to check on her car.

Luke laid his head back and closed his eyes. He'd known her less than twenty-four hours, and he was so annoyed he wanted to strangle her. Starting from when she'd wiggled her little ass up the steps, looking like a high-class hooker. He could have popped Darren for bringing her. What really upset Luke, though, was the way his body responded to her. Granted, it had been six months since he'd been with a woman but he'd gone longer than that in his life. And she wasn't even close to the kind of woman he was normally attracted to.

Then, she'd fed him those disgusting pancakes. Which reminded him—the wench had gotten out of eating them. Truthfully, he didn't believe she would have. She'd have had her bags packed instead. He'd half expected her to offer him sex when he came in the house in exchange for not eating the buggy cakes. He was so damn distracted on that ladder, trying to decide if he'd take her up on it, he hadn't even realized he was falling until he hit the ground.

That brought up another question. Who sabotaged his ladder? The list of people who believed he belonged in prison for committing a triple murder was endless. A good share of the residents of Ashville were on that list. The remaining few either believed him or were undecided. He didn't feel like explaining to his chauffeur about the incident that had made him an outcast in his hometown. Fortunately, Doc Flanders was on his side. Luke could get his injuries treated by someone who'd rather see him alive then dead and get on home.

He leaned back and heaved a huge painful sigh. Maybe Glen was right. Maybe he should sell out and make a new start someplace else—someplace they'd never heard of Luke McAlister. That could mean leaving the state of North Dakota entirely.

The other option was finding out what really happened that night. Somebody had set him up, killing Kelsey and doing whatever they did to her beautiful little girls. A familiar ache shot through Luke's chest that had nothing to do with physical pain, as it did every time he thought about them. He brushed the moisture from his eyes with his sleeve. God how he missed their giggles, their energy, their presence around the house. They were so young, had so much life to live. If it was the last thing he did, he'd hunt down whoever was responsible.

He'd been so distraught he'd second-guessed himself at the time, yet he knew damn well he couldn't have harmed one hair on their heads, but somebody had. He suspected it was that same somebody who tinkered with the ladder and drugged his drink that night. Whoever it was didn't want him remembering or nosing around in an unsolved crime.

His companion kept passing him furtive glances as though she expected him to pass out at any moment. Let her think the tears pooling in his eyes were from his throbbing ribs. They sure as hell hurt enough to bring a man to his knees.

Patsy pulled up to the emergency door at the Ashville Hospital. She remembered the big sprawling brick building from when she'd been there before. Her mother and grandmother used to walk with her to the playground just below the hill. On rainy days, there was even a little stream running through it. She noticed a spacious new wing had been added to the hospital since then and guessed that's where the nursing home was.

She shoved the truck in park and jumped out to come around and assist Luke, but when she opened the door for him, he waved her away. "I'm fine. I can make it on my own."

"You are one stubborn macho man," Patsy said, standing back and letting him get out by himself. He was pale as a ghost and gasping for breath.

"It has nothing to do with stubborn," he hissed. "If you grabbed me in the wrong place, I might pass out, after all."

"Well, I wasn't going to grab you *there*."

He gave her a bleary-eyed look. "If you're trying to make me laugh, it's not working."

A young man in a blue medic uniform sprang from the swinging doors, pushing a wheelchair. "Luke, what the hell happened to you?" He gave Patsy an interested appraisal.

"Hi, I'm Richard. What happened to him," he repeated, addressing her when Luke didn't or couldn't answer. He positioned the chair behind Luke and set the brakes. "Okay, buddy, ease back slowly."

"He fell off a ladder. I think he broke some ribs," Patsy said, breathing a sigh of relief when Luke, after a few grimaces and groans, was finally seated.

Chapter Five

"Mr. Bartlett, have you lost your mind?"

Conner looked up from the papers he was studying to see a shapely young brunette standing over him with her hands on her hips and a decidedly angry scowl on her cute perky face. He liked what he saw—except for the pursed lips and glaring violet eyes. With that unusual color, she had to be Willy's mother.

"Ah, not that I'm aware of," he said. "Why? Have you found it?"

"This isn't funny," she snapped. "You have a lot of nerve putting ideas of karate lessons in my son's head. He has a hard enough time as it is being the smallest child in his class, now you're suggesting he learn how to fight."

"No, not fight," Conner said evenly. "Defend himself. Not the same thing."

"How can an undersized kid defend himself against bigger boys without getting the hell beat out of him?"

"Are you aware that he's being bullied?" Conner sensed by the shock on her face that she didn't have a clue.

"Willard hasn't said a word about being bullied," she admitted, her voice having come down an octave. "There are laws against that."

Conner shrugged. "Yeah, well, laws don't always keep kids from being kids."

"And how in the world do you figure karate lessons will change that? By getting him into fights?"

"No, by being smarter than his opponents. Karate lessons would give him the confidence to stand up for himself. Being a bully isn't any fun if you can't intimidate your victim."

She gave him a bodily once over and snorted. "By the looks of you, you're experience comes from being one of the bullies."

Conner leaned back in his chair, taking a moment to decide how much he wanted to tell her. He gave a heavy sigh. "If that'd be your guess, Mrs. Jensen you'd be wrong. I didn't develop until I was fourteen. My sister was taller than I was. Talk about wounded pride," he added. "She came to my rescue more than once when somebody tried to pick on the runt of the class."

Her eyes widened. "I find that hard to believe. I mean, look at you." She made a sweeping gesture toward him. "You're...well...not exactly undersized."

Conner chuckled. "If that's a compliment, thank you, but as I said, I wasn't always built like this."

"And that changed when you took karate lessons?"

"No," Conner said, laughing. "It changed when my sister took karate lessons. She started when she was ten, and believe me, nobody messed with her. She never even had to fight. What does Willy's father think about the idea?"

She averted her eyes. "His father is gone."

"Oh, sorry. Willy's records didn't indicate you were divorced."

"I'm not. I'm a widow. Sam was killed in Iraq eighteen months ago. You'd think that would be enough for kids in a small town not to pick on Willard, but as you said, kids don't always abide by adult standards."

"Yeah, sad to say, but true," Conner said with a shake of his head. "Look, I'm finished up here. Would you like to go for a cup of coffee? We could talk more about this."

Her back visibly straightened. "I don't date."

"Going for coffee isn't exactly a date."

"In a small town it is. You think there's one person who wouldn't know that the Widow Jenson went to the diner with the new computer teacher?"

Conner gave himself a mental shake. "Is that so horrible? I'm not exactly Jack the Ripper."

"I— All right, I guess it would be okay. As long as we talked about Willard."

Stifling an idiotic grin, Conner stood and shoved his papers in his briefcase. "Deal, then let's go. By the way, Mrs. Jensen, it's none of my business, but your son told me he prefers to be called Willy."

Her cheeks turned a pretty shade of pink. "Thanks, I guess I should have known that. He loved it when his father called him Willy. And, please, I'd rather be called Debra."

"Hmm. Debra having coffee with Conner. That ought to give those gossip mongers something to chew on. I wonder what they'd say if we actually had something to eat along with the coffee. I'm kind of hungry."

* * * *

After leaving Luke in the hands of the doctor, Patsy walked down the long hallway leading to the nursing home. She was told they had four rooms slated for assisted living. Wilma Summers lived in unit one-one- three.

Patsy wasn't sure why her heart was pounding at the thought of seeing her grandmother after all these years. Could it be that guilt pressed on Patsy for never responding to all the gifts she'd sent and never making any attempt to communicate with her for—how many years since she'd seen Grams? Patsy was thirteen the last time she'd been to North Dakota with her mom. Fourteen years ago. Would Wilma Summers even recognize her inattentive granddaughter, her only granddaughter?

How old would Grams be now? Grandpa had died when Patsy was eleven and Grams was sixty-seven. Patsy did the math in her head and came up with eighty-three. Not so very old, she thought.

Patsy recalled all the wonderful times she'd had on the farm with her grandparents. A spark of pleasure washed over her, followed immediately by shame. She wouldn't blame Grams one iota if she snubbed Patsy.

The door to Grams' room was ajar. Patsy stuck her head in, snapped the knocker and called out. "Hello, anybody home?"

"Is that you, Shirley? I left the door open for you. Have a seat. I just got out of the shower. I'll be out in a minute."

Patsy wasn't Shirley, but she went in and had a seat anyway. Leaving the door open while Grams took a shower seemed like a foolhardy thing to do, but then, this was Ashville. As Patsy remembered they had virtually no crime worse than a kid stealing a candy bar from the general store or picking apples from somebody's tree.

While she waited, Patsy studied the compact apartment. A tiny kitchenette with the little table she was at took up one end of the apartment and a sitting room with a sofa and matching recliner filled the other end. A good-sized television stood between them mounted on a pedestal that swung to be viewed from either direction. A door to her left opened to what she assumed was the bedroom. The closed door on the right was clearly the bathroom. That door opened, and Grams appeared in a bathrobe and damp hair, walking with the aid of a cane, talking as she went.

"Shirley, I—" Grams halted her steps and stared at Patsy with wide eyes. "You're not Shirley."

Patsy gave her a little smile. "No, sorry. I'm not Shirley. I'm Patsy."

It only took Grams a split second to put it together. Her face lit up like a shining star. "Oh my goodness, my sweet little Patricia." She spread her free arm wide and limped forward.

Patsy was on her feet instantly, rushing into the hug, tears stinging her eyes. "Grams, it's so wonderful to see you." The older woman felt frail in Patsy's arms, yet her one-armed hug had amazing strength.

When the hug ended Grams pulled back to look at her. "Goodness gracious, child, you're all grown up."

"It's been a long time," Patsy said, leading her to a chair at the table.

Grams took the seat, her smile remaining intact. "Far too long. Tell me what you've been doing with your life?"

* * * *

"Patsy smashed her Maserati."

Morty Chambers nearly choked on his coffee. "She did what?" he asked Ben Fontaine, the guy he had tailing Patsy. Charles had asked Morty to keep tabs on his two worthless offspring, which fell right into Morty's plan.

"She hit a deer just outside of Ashville, North Dakota," Fontaine said. "They towed it into town, but it'll be three or four weeks before they can get parts."

Morty knew exactly what she was after in Ashville. Her maternal grandmother lived there, and most likely, the little brat was going to try to get money out of her. That gave him a good chuckle. The old bag was living off of her meager Social Security. In fact, Charles sent her a check every month to cover the rent on her apartment.

"So what's she doing while the car's getting fixed," Morty asked.

"Oh, you'll get a laugh out of this," Fontaine snickered. "She's staying with this farmer supposedly as his housekeeper and cook."

"Patsy cook? That stupid broad couldn't boil an egg if her life depended on it. Unless she's performing other duties under the guise of being a cook—wouldn't surprise me at all. But it certainly would interest her father. Stay in town there and keep an eye on her. She doesn't know you but keep a low profile anyway."

* * * *

Patsy's visit with her grandmother was cut short when Shirley came to take her to a dental appointment. Patsy left the cozy little apartment with a smile on her face, a notebook full of Grams' favorite recipes, and a promise that she'd return again soon. Grams had even helped her make out a list of items she'd need for at least three meals. She had intended to go to the local grocer anyway with the fifty-dollar bill Luke gave her when she left the hospital, but now she could go with specific things in mind to buy. Smiling to herself, Patsy had taken *that* to mean she still had a job—without eating her fiasco pancakes, particularly when he made a point of telling her to buy flour.

Thinking of Luke, she decided to stop and see how he was faring before she took the pickup downtown.

At the clinic, she was told—only after the intern confirmed she'd brought Luke in—that he'd be with Doctor Flanders at least another hour. Armed with that information, she drove to Rudy's Dry Goods Store to search for the items on her list. She'd been in this same store many times with her grandmother, but it was the first time she'd personally ever gone grocery shopping. It surprised her she enjoyed it and, even more so, that she was actually looking forward to learning how to cook.

Looking at all the food reminded her it was almost noon and she hadn't eaten yet today. She threw a couple of deli sandwiches in her cart, wishing she didn't have to wait until she got into the truck to eat one.

Shopping took longer than she thought. Twice she'd had to ask were to find something, but after half an hour, she finally pushed her load up to the checkout counter. A short woman who looked to be at least eighty with a roadmap of wrinkles on her craggy face pushed a cart up behind her. Patsy remembered the woman, who'd been giving her strange looks and seemed to be following her around the store. It didn't appear to be a coincidence that she came right up behind her at the checkout.

"So," the woman said in a raspy voice. "You must be that young thing staying out at McAlister's place?"

Patsy looked back and saw the carton of Marlboros in her cart. She wanted to tell her those things would give her wrinkles but that seemed a bit after the fact. Sighing, she thought she might as well take this opportunity to set people straight on what she was doing at the McAlister farm. She smiled as she loaded her groceries on the checkout belt and said. "Yes, I'm the new housekeeper and cook he hired."

"Oh, yeah," she said. "He had an ad in the paper. As I remember, he was asking for an older woman."

Biting back what she wanted to say to the nosy old biddy, Patsy kept her smile in place. "Yes, well, I was the only one who applied."

The woman actually cackled. "I'll bet. Guess he had to get someone from out of town who didn't know him."

The pleasant-looking man about her age—Rudy, his name tag said—who'd been sliding Patsy's groceries over the scanner while giving her furtive glances, gave the woman a stern look. "Now, Gertie, stop gossiping."

"It's not gossip," Gertie insisted. "It's fact. That man killed his wife and butchered those two darling little girls then buried them in his backyard. Anyone who goes there should be warned."

"He was acquitted," Rudy said. "Leave him alone, or don't you know what the word *acquitted* means."

Gertie gave Rudy an antagonistic glare. "I know what acquitted means, but I don't think you do. My cousin is a lawyer. He said you can't be *acquitted* unless you go to trial, and there weren't no trial, 'cause they didn't have enough evidence."

Rudy rolled his eyes. "Well, there you go."

Gertie snorted. "That don't mean he ain't guilty, and if they find new evidence, he'll go right back in the slammer where he belongs."

Patsy just stared at the two of them as they argued back and forth while Rudy rang her groceries up. Her heart was hammering so hard she couldn't think.

"Your total comes to fifty-three dollars and ninety-eight cents, Ms. Bartlett," Rudy said, bringing her back to reality.

How did he know her name? Moving in shock, she dug in her purse, handed him the fifty from Luke along with a five-dollar bill of her own. He gave her change back and started bagging her groceries.

"How did you know my name?" she asked as she snatched up the M&M's she'd bought and dropped them in her purse.

Rudy smiled and shrugged. "My brother–in–law, Martin Bower, owns the Ashville repair shop where you took your car. Nice set of wheels, by the way. Bummer getting it banged up like that." He laughed. "Martin's thinking of selling tickets to the parade of people stopping in to look at it."

Patsy swallowed, wondering if she'd entered a time warp.

Gertie made a harrumphing sound behind her. "Nobody in their right mind would drive a car like that around here. Sticks out like spoiled cabbage if you ask me."

"I didn't hear anybody asking you, Gertie," Rudy said as he loaded the last of Patsy's things back in her cart. "You need some help carrying this out?" he asked.

Another rude sound came from Gertie at that offer.

"No, I can manage, thanks." Patsy sent a scowl in Gertie's direction and pushed her cart out to the pickup, walking in somewhat of a daze.

As she loaded her bags in the back seat the conversation inside came back to her.

That man killed his wife and butchered those two darling little girls then buried them in his backyard. Anyone who goes there should be warned.

Patsy thought about the deli sandwich in the bag behind her but somewhere during that conversation she'd lost her appetite. Instead of hunger, nausea boiled up in her stomach.

She pushed the cart back and left it outside the store. When she got in the pickup, her hands shaking so hard she had a difficult getting the key in the ignition.

Had Luke McAlister murdered his wife and children? No, Rudy said he'd been acquitted, but Gertie said there was no trial due to lack of evidence. Patsy laid her head on the steering wheel and tried to think, to rationalize this out.

It explained why Luke didn't want to come to Ashville. Apparently, some of the people still believed he was guilty. He'd also suggested the number of people who might want to do him harm was a long list.

At least now she knew why he didn't refer to her as his ex-wife, Patsy thought as she pulled up to the Ashville repair shop. Maybe she'd get lucky, and they found some used parts for her car and were able to repair it. Fat chance. Her luck didn't seem to be running in that direction lately.

Martin, the man who'd towed her car, greeted her by name as she entered the garage. He smiled as his gaze swept her from head to foot.

"So," she asked, mentally crossing her fingers. "What's the story on my car?"

Marten repositioned his Minnesota Twins cap and shook his head. "No parts anywhere near here. We'll need to order them from Minneapolis, and they need to have them shipped from a warehouse out east. The soonest I can see gettin'em is two to three weeks. Won't take us but a couple of days after that."

Patsy's heart sank even lower than it had been.

"We tried to call your cell earlier this morning," Martin went on to say, "but it was out of range or something. So I called Darren and he said you were staying at the McAlister place. I didn't get an answer there at all."

Now, at least Patsy knew how the whole town was able to keep tabs on her. She thanked him and, with a heavy sigh, turned to leave but Martin kept talking.

"I'm surprised you didn't already know the scoop on your car. I gave your man all the information this morning when I wasn't able to get ahold of you."

She whirled around to stare at him. "My man? What man?"

Marten shrugged. "Some tall, skinny dude, scraggly beard. Looked to be about fifty-five, resembled Ichabod Crane." He gave her a searching look. "You mean you didn't send him in to check on your car?"

"No. And I don't know anybody who looks like that."

Marten scratched his chin. "Huh, I wonder who it was then? He seemed awfully interested in where you were. Of course, he's not the only one by far. He might just be a stranger passing through and heard the hype on your car."

"The hype?"

Martin chuckled. "Oh yeah, every male under the age of thirty has been in to see it and a few of the old farts, too. You're quite a celebrity—or at least your Maserati is."

Patsy stifled a groan. So by now there wasn't a person within fifty miles who didn't know about her being out at McAlister's.

"I need to get my things out of the trunk. Do you have a couple of large boxes I might use?"

"Sure, there's a bunch back by the dumpster. You can drive right around to the back. It's parked in the fenced lot behind the shop."

She was relieved to hear it was in a protected area.

"I'll get one of the gawkers to help you," he said as she walked out the door.

She wasn't sure what he meant but she nodded glumly, got into Luke's truck and drove around the station. Realization hit her like a slap to the head. At least fifteen people were back there, milling around her car.

So much for security.

Geez, didn't they have anything better to do here? All eyes swiveled to her as she parked as close to her car as she could without mowing down a few bodies. When she got out of the truck, she was met with a barrage of questions. She felt like she'd stepped into a press conference.

"Wow, are you the lady who owns this car?"

"You must really be rich, huh?"

"Is it true they can do one eighty-five?"

"Yeah, I heard that Joe Walsh song."

"Are you a movie star?" This from a youngster who couldn't have been more than ten years old.

"Can it, guys!" Martin came out the back door of the shop. "Leon, Mitch, go over to the dumpster and get Miss Bartlett a couple of boxes. The rest of you back off and give her some room."

The two youngest boys quickly did as they were instructed. The rest moved like the parting of the Red Sea as Patsy walked up to her car using the remote to open the trunk.

"Is it true you're staying at that killer's place?" a lanky teenager asked as the two boys arrived with the boxes. He was the same person who'd given her a wolf whistle when she'd stepped out of the truck.

Patsy decided to ignore him and started unloading the trunk, setting the suitcases aside and putting the loose things in the boxes.

"He's not a killer," another teen snapped.

"My pa says he is."

"You're such and asshole, Gabe. Just because you old man is the turd-head sheriff and has more money than anyone else in town doesn't make him smarter than the judge."

Gabe ignored the jibe and called to Patsy. "Are you McAlister's new whore?" His statement and ensuing laughter silenced the rest of the crowd as they waited for Patsy's response.

Patsy was in no frame of mind to put up with a smart-mouthed kid. "That question doesn't bear answering," she said. "But it does prove that the local sheriff is raising the village idiot."

Laughter exploded along with a wave of clapping.

Someone else from the small crowd yelled out. "Hey, Gabe, is it true most of the kids in the next county are your half brothers and sisters?"

A wrestling match followed until Martin showed up and pulled them apart. "Okay, that's enough. Everybody clear out. And I don't want to see any of you back here again."

"Or, he'll call the sheriff," somebody quipped loud enough for all to hear.

Amidst grumbling protests, they turned one by one to leave, all except for the kid who had defended Luke. "Can I stay and help Miss Bartlett load her stuff?" he asked Martin.

"Yeah, sure, David—if she needs your help. I have to get out to the pumps."

David grinned as Martin left. "You want me to put the suitcases in the back of the truck, Miss Bartlett?"

Patsy smiled at him. "Yes, thanks, David, I'd appreciate it."

When he came back for the second load, he said, "Luke's not a killer, Miss Bartlett. I've been out to his place working. He's honest and fair. He loved those little girls. I know he'd never hurt them or anyone else. His wife, Kelsey, now she was a—" his young face reddened, "—not a nice person."

He quickly picked up one of the boxes she'd filled and carried it to the truck.

Patsy closed the empty trunk and lifted the last box. David came up and reached for it. "Here, let me do that."

She gratefully handed the box over then walked around to the front of the car to examine the damage. It looked brutal. She gave a heavy sigh and swallowed a lump in her throat. When she looked up, she saw a man standing on the other side of the fence watching her—a tall thin man. She looked away quickly and approached David.

"Who's that man behind the fence, over there to the right?"

David looked, frowned, and shrugged. "Heck if I know. He's not from around here that I know of. I did see him back here looking at your car earlier."

"David, is there any way you could find out who he is and maybe where he's from?"

He snickered. "You bet. I love to do espionage work, Miss Bartlett."

"You can call me Patsy."

He gave her a wide grin. "Gee, thanks, Patsy. I'll give you a ring at Luke's place if I find anything out. My Aunt Milly owns the only motel in town. If he's staying there, she'll know where he comes from."

Chapter Six

Obviously her father was having her tailed. Driving back to the hospital, the more she thought about it the angrier she became. It shouldn't bother her, she reasoned. She hadn't broken any of his cardinal rules—yet. But he could at least trust her. She wondered if he was having Conner followed too.

She checked her cell phone for service and discovered it was working. Pulling up in front of the hospital, she switched off the truck and punched in Conner's speed dial number. After seven rings, a voice mail announced he was unavailable to take the call.

Patsy left a hasty message, explaining about Ichabod Crane and that she had no service out at the farm. She couldn't give him the number there because she didn't know it, so she briefly explained about her car and why she was stuck on a farm in the middle of nowhere.

What she didn't mention was that her employer was a possible murderer. Not only did she find Gertie's claim to be ludicrous, but even if it were true, Luke was pretty much incapacitated for the time being. She couldn't have planned her stay there any better if she'd fixed that ladder herself.

And to think about it, Luke seemed to be convinced somebody had monkeyed with it. If that was true, it could have been any of the people in the area who believed he was guilty of murder. Sheesh, of all the situations she could have gotten herself into this one had to take the cake.

Eighty-nine days. She had to survive eighty–nine more days with a total of sixteen hundred and eighty-five dollars in her pocket. A thousand of which she'd have to shell out for the deductible on her car and most of the rest to her Visa bill. Cripes.

Feeling depressed, she walked into the hospital and scanned the reception area, looking for Luke. Since he was nowhere in sight, she figured he was still in with the doctor. As she approached the front desk to ask about him, she was aware of a frosty glare coming from the blonde, blue-eyed, thirty-something woman seated behind the counter.

Patsy recognized that look, and the green tint around the edges. The woman was jealous. Of her? Because of Luke McAlister? Patsy marched up to her, prepared to set her straight about her relationship with *Mr. McAlister.*

Before Patsy could say a word, Wanda—according to her name badge—said, "So…you're the new housekeeper and cook Luke hired. It's hard to believe someone who drives a Maserati would know how to cook. How long are you planning to stay?"

The woman's snippy attitude seriously rubbed Patsy the wrong way. All thoughts of reassuring her vanished. Patsy gave Wanda her brightest smile. "As long as he needs me. And my talents aren't limited to pots and pans," she gave Wanda a wink, "if you know what I mean."

Wanda's mouth was still hanging open when Patsy asked where she could find Luke.

Wanda pointed to a hallway on the right. "Doctor Flanders' office at the end of the hall."

If Patsy thought Wanda's first look was frosty, it was now glacial. It reminded Patsy of a comic villain who could freeze people with a pointed stare.

"Thank you," Patsy said, smiling. She then turned and did her best exiting wiggle walk until she was far enough into the hallway to be out of sight. Muttering under her breath, she headed for the door marked DR. JAMES FLANDERS.

The door was slightly ajar. She raised her hand to knock when voices drifted through the opening.

Luke was talking. "...I didn't imagine that putty smeared on my ladder, Jim."

"Then you should report it to Sherriff Wilson." Patsy assumed that soft spoken, definitely not North Dakotan, drawl came from Dr. Flanders.

Luke snorted. "I hope you're joking. You want me to go to the sheriff, the same man who arrested me in the first place."

"That was before you were found innocent."

"Do I need to remind you I wasn't found innocent, Jim. I was released for lack of evidence."

"In the eyes of the law—"

Luke cut him off. "The same law that had eyes for my wife. Do you think I was blind to the little sexual innuendos they exchanged?"

Patsy heard Dr. Flanders heavy sigh. "You told me yourself nothing happened between them."

"That's not exactly how I put it. And until I find out what happened to Kelsey and the girls, everyone is suspect."

"Okay, suit yourself, Luke. Just be careful. Stop at the drugstore and pick up your pain medication. I called it in for you."

"I don't need it," Luke grumbled.

Flanders laughed. "Quit being a macho idiot and take the medicine. I have another appointment so I need to run. Let's see if your driver is here."

Patsy's heart rate slammed into overdrive. She backed away quickly then started walking slowly toward the door. When it opened and a tall, blond, unbelievably handsome man stepped out. His smile radiated confidence.

"Ah, there you are. You must be Patsy," he said holding out his hand. "I asked Wanda to send you in. I'm Doctor Jim Flanders, and I'm very pleased to meet you."

Patsy took his hand, returning the smile and wondering exactly what Luke had told him about her. "How's the patient?" she asked.

Flanders laughed. "Ornery as hell. He has two cracked ribs and a sprained shoulder. He's going to need help even if he won't admit it. I'm glad you'll be there to give him a hand. I put in a prescription for pain medication at the drugstore downtown. Pick it up before you leave. He's stubborn as an old mule so make him take it if he becomes too cranky."

He gave her a little wave but paused as he started walking away. "Oh, by the way, he has my home phone number. Don't hesitate to call if he has any problems. This is one case where I'd be glad to make a house call."

Wow. Patsy thought that was a rarity in this day and age. She was about to tell him how much she admired a doctor who made house calls when he said, "Or if you need any cooking advice, you can talk to my wife at that same number."

Hearty laughter filled the hallway in his wake. He didn't wait around to watch her face turn red.

Damn Luke, he'd told Dr. Flanders about the pancakes. Who else had he shared that little tidbit with? Wanda? That would explain the snide remark about Patsy not being able to cook because she drove a fancy car.

Her mind was working on revenge when she saw the target in question walk out of Flanders' office, pale as a ghost and trussed up like a Thanksgiving turkey, his shirt draped over his wide shoulders leaving his upper chest bare. She'd have to be blind not to notice all that skin.

When Luke saw Patsy standing outside Flanders' office, he had the feeling his emotions were in a blender along with the rest of his battered body. On one hand, he was relieved to see her since a small part of him had believed her capable of heading out of town with his truck never to be heard from again; on the other hand, he wished she'd just gone away, disappeared in a flash the same way she'd arrived.

The woman was trouble. He could sense it like a bad storm building on the western horizon.

He wondered how far she'd push him now that he appeared to need her more than she needed him. Little did she know that Wanda had offered to come out and assist him. Of course, Wanda was a total twit. She'd been pursuing him since high school. If he accepted help from her, he'd never get rid of her. But Patsy didn't need to know that.

She gave him a quick once over, pausing at the wide bandage around his ribcage with the attached wristband that held his left arm against his body. He hated being vulnerable and attempted to keep the pain from showing. She didn't buy it.

"Looks like it hurts," she said frowning. "We better get you home so you can rest."

"Yeah, let's get out of here. I hate the smell of hospitals."

She nodded and led the way through the lobby.

"Hey Luke," Wanda called from her station. "Let me know if you need anything. I have the next two days off. I'm a really good cook," she added with a toothy grin.

"Thanks, Wanda," Luke said. "I'll keep it in mind."

"Okay. You have my number; just give me a call."

Luke got a look at Patsy's face when she stepped back to hold the door open for him. She raised her eyebrows and seemed to be pressing her lips together to suppress a smirk.

What had he expected, jealousy? Wasn't happening?

Outside she followed him to the truck then reached around and opened the door for him to get in.

For some insane reason, it pissed him off. "I'm not an invalid."

She gave him a cheeky grin. "Good, I'll remember that when you ask me to wipe your butt cause you can't reach it."

He blew out a sound of disgust. "Not going to happen in this life." It was the last thing he could say since the rest of his energy was used up getting in the truck. He held his breath, hissing. Every damn inch of his upper body hurting like Hades on fire. She stood by patiently, waiting until he was settled then reached across his lap and buckled his seatbelt. Her warm breasts pressing against his thigh gave him an unexpected jolt. He couldn't be sure but the snide look on her face suggested she'd done that deliberately.

Closing the door, she rounded the hood then hopped in behind the wheel.

"Where are you going?" he asked when she took off for Main Street instead of going toward the farm.

"Doc said you have to pick up medicine at the drugstore."

"Dammit, I told him I don't need it."

Patsy shook her head. "Well, tough guy, he said I should get it and force it down your throat if you get too ornery. I think he also said something about you being more stubborn than old man Becker's mule."

Luke snorted. "That ancient mule died over ten years ago, before Jim Flanders came here. How the heck do you even know about it?"

She gave a little laugh that was close to a giggle. "It was something my Grandpa used to say."

Luke laid his head back and stretched out his legs, trying to find a comfortable position. It was no use. "Who was your grandfather?" he asked, hoping conversation would help get his mind off the pain.

"Hank Summers, I think Becker was his neighbor." Patsy pulled up in front of the drug store. "Are you going to pay for this medicine or do I have to?"

Luke gave an exasperated sigh. He reached for the wallet in his left hip pocket and drew in a sharp breath of air. "How about you pay for it and I'll reimburse you when we get home?"

She nodded and got out of the truck. Before she closed the door, she looked back at him and said, "Hurts to reach back there, does it?"

Watching her disappear into the drugstore, he would have laughed but it hurt too much. Sobering, he wondered if she'd be so flippant after she learned he'd been accused of killing two kids and his wife. It was hard to believe no one had told her yet.

When a few minutes had passed and she still hadn't come out, he glanced in the back where he'd noticed the grocery bags. Just the sight of them reminded him he was hungry as a bear coming out of hibernation. Any other time

he'd have reached back and fished through them but...
Damn, he hated being incapacitated.

Too bad this dot-on-the-map town didn't have a drive-in fast food service. He wasn't a big fan, but right now, he'd eat just about anything—except pancakes.

Chapter Seven

The first thing Patsy noticed when she got back in the truck was the grim expression on Luke's face. He was obviously in pain. "Sorry, I had to wait for it," she said.

"I told Flanders I didn't need pills."

Patsy stuck the water bottle she'd purchased in the console holder then reached in the Thrifty White bag and pulled out the small bottle of pills. He gave her an odd look when she opened the container and shook two little white tablets out in her hand.

"What are you doing?" he asked.

"Following doctor's orders. He said if you get crabby you take a pill."

"I'm not crabby. I'm hungry. I hope with all those bags you bought you have something in mind to eat when we get home. I haven't eaten since this morning."

"Well, consider yourself lucky. At least you had breakfast."

She ignored his pointed glare and held the pills out to him. When he made no move to take them, she sighed. "You may as well give in on this because I'm not moving the truck until you do."

He gritted his teeth and snatched the tablets out of her hand. "You could give lessons to Becker's mule. Open the damn water."

She twisted the cap off the water bottle and handed it to him. He tossed the pills in his mouth and chugged down half the water in a couple of gulps then handed it back to her.

"Satisfied?" he mumbled curtly.

"Yes…for now," she said, starting the truck and backing out.

"Do you have anything I can munch on?"

"We'll be home in twenty minutes."

"I'm hungry now."

So was she but she didn't think it was in her best interest to mentioning that he was behaving like belligerent a two-year-old. All right, she decided, allow him some slack. After all, he'd had a rough morning. She reached in her purse lying on the center column and dug out the bag of M&Ms.

"Here," she said, handing them to him. "This is all I have without stopping the truck and going in the back seat. You need me to open it for you?"

"No. I can manage." He snatched the bag out of her hand and tore it open with his teeth. He was angry with himself for being so snippy with her. She hadn't caused his handicapped predicament, but she sure as hell was causing his other issue. In spite of the pain in his ribs, he had a woody the size of Rhode Island. It pressed against his belly tightening his jeans until he wanted to squirm.

Other than yesterday when she'd arrived, it had been months since he'd had an erection. Why now when he was strapped up like a ball of twine? Just because she had the most perfectly shaped breasts he'd ever seen and a round little behind that could bring a saint to his knees….

Damn, he had to get his thoughts going in another direction. She must know how desperately he needed her now. The tables had turned on him. Even though he was still teed at her for the pancake episode, he was grateful she was there.

He really wanted to know why she was desperate for a job when she drove a car that cost what a family of five could live on for a year. But maybe he should try a friendlier approach.

"Did you get a chance to check on your car?" he asked, trying to slake his hunger with M&Ms that weren't even with peanuts.

She gave him a sideways look. "You still anxious to be rid of me?"

"I didn't say that. I just asked about your car."

"Why don't you say what's really on your mind? Like why I need a job when I drive a Maserati?"

"As a matter of fact I wasn't thinking about that at all," he lied. "But, now that you brought it up, that is a good question."

Her hands did an agitated move on the steering wheel. "Sorry," she said as though she wasn't sorry at all. "That's not open for discussion."

"Well, if there's going to be some rich bad-tempered bastard pounding on my door looking for you I'd like a little advance warning. I'm a little out of action here, in case you haven't noticed."

She actually laughed. "No need to worry about that. No one cares where I am."

"Good. Then let's get back to the status of your car."

She signaled to make a turn off the main highway and headed up the gravel road that led to the farm. "It could take two to three weeks to get the parts. That means I can be your slave until then."

"I didn't hire you to be a slave."

She shrugged. "Seems you didn't hire me at all yet. Why did you let me stay?"

Hell if I know. "Darren's my friend. I did it for him."

"Huh," she grunted.

"What's that supposed to mean?" he asked.

"You don't strike me as the kind to man who could be talked into doing something he didn't want to do."

"If you remember, I *was* looking for help."

"Why didn't you hire Wanda? She offered to help you?"

"She has a job."

"Sounded to me like she'd jump at the chance to be at your beck and call."

The snippy comment was delivered with an edge to it suggesting she *was* jealous after all. "I asked for an older woman. Someone who could keep up the house, cook a few meals, and go home at night." He wasn't going to tell her Wanda was the last person he wanted around. Let her be jealous, he thought satisfactorily. For some odd reason, he liked that idea.

She made that annoying *"huh"* sound again. It was even more annoying that he wanted to know what she was thinking.

"What's wrong with that?" he snapped when she remained silent.

She made a point of frowning thoughtfully and lifted her shoulders as though to say she didn't understand. "It's just kind of strange you'd avoid having a younger woman around."

He gritted his teeth and laid his head back. If she didn't know about his wife, he wasn't ready to explain now. The farmyard was in sight, and he was suddenly weary to the bone. The pills were making his head muzzy. He was still hungry but what he really wanted right now was to stretch out on his bed, close his eyes and sleep the effects of the medication off—with Ms. Patsy Bartlett lying beside him, preferably naked.

* * * *

They were on their second cup of coffee and had decided to order pie. Conner was having the time of his life. Debra was a delight. Except for the edge of sadness in her violet eyes, she was relaxed and easy to talk to.

"Willy is lucky to have a mother like you," he said.

She smiled. "No, I'm the lucky one. Willard—Willy— is so sweet. I know that's not a term boys like to be called, but…he's growing up so fast. He…he's so much like his father, except Sam was tall and strong."

Conner stuck his fork in to pluck a juicy piece of apple from middle of his pie. "Maybe Willy's like me. Give him a couple of years. Like I said, I didn't start my growing spurt until I was almost fourteen."

"At least you had an older sister to go to bat for you."

Conner threw his head back and laughed. "Did I forget to mention she's a year and a half younger than I am?"

For a second, she stared at him in shock, then for a moment, the sadness left her eyes, and she laughed with him. "That must have been awful for you."

"No kidding. But it wasn't just the karate thing. People were always making rude comments about my size and comparing me to my *little* sister—and I don't mean just kids."

"How did you handle that?"

He grinned. "I said I could run faster."

"Was that true?" she asked cutting a dainty bite out of her blueberry pie.

"Yup, I had an edge over the bullies there. I could outrun all of them. I was the shortest kid on the track team, and I took all the first place medals."

Her soft laughter was so utterly genuine. "Good for you. I wish Willy had a talent like that."

"He can. The nearest karate classes I could find are about thirty miles away in Alexandria. First, you'll have to ask him if he's interested, though. I balked at the idea when I was his age."

Debra smiled. "Oh, he's interested all right. That's all he's been talking about."

"Great. I'd even offer to drive him once a week. I just got here four days ago so I don't know anyone in town other than you and the kids, and a couple of other parents. I don't have much of a social life at this point."

"Let me get back to you on that."

Conner reached across the booth and touched her hand. "We could even do dinner where nobody knows us if you like."

She pulled her hand away, an adorable blush reddening her ears. "I—I'll have to get back to you on that, too."

Glancing at her watch she said, "I better get going; I need to get back to work. But it's really been fun. Thanks, Conner." She picked up her purse then hesitated, her brows drawn into a frown. She lowered her voice as she looked over Conner's shoulder. "There's a man behind you who keeps staring at us. He came in right after we did. Do you know him?"

Conner went on instant alert. Ever since he'd received the message from Patsy earlier saying she thought she was being followed, he'd been wary of anyone looking sideways at him. Of course, in his case, that was just about every person in town since he was the *new teacher.*

He turned to make a point of looking at the big clock he'd seen on the wall and, in doing so allowed, his gaze to flick over the lone man seated behind him.

No surprise; he didn't have a clue who the man was. "Don't you know him?" he asked Debra. "I'd have thought you knew everyone in town."

"No," she said, shaking her head. "That's why I was curious, because I didn't recognize him. Let's ask Teja." She waved the waitress over and quietly asked if she knew the stranger.

"Nope, can't say I do," Teja said. "But I call him Mr. Creepy. He sits there every day where he can watch the school across the street. I'd think he's stalking kids except that there's no one there this time of year. Well, except for your little class," she added, giving Conner a broad smile.

"You said he comes in every day," Conner replied. "You mean recently or like maybe he lives here?"

"About four days, I'd guess. He's probably one of those weird traveling salesmen. I just don't like him, especially given the fact that he sits there talking on his cell phone all day and chugging down one cup of coffee after the other and never bothers leaving a tip. Big-time jerk if you ask me."

Four days was exactly how long Conner had been there.

Conner gave her his famous Bartlett smile. "Thanks, Teja." He pressed a ten-dollar bill in her hand. "Keep an eye on him for me, would you? Let me know if he does anything suspicious."

Teja's eyes widened. "Wow, are you an undercover cop or a spy or something? I thought you were a teacher."

"I *am* a teacher." What would she think if he told her he was just a temporary teacher trying to last three months to save his inheritance? "I just get uneasy when men stare at me; although, he's more likely watching my lovely companion."

Teja giggled. "Or maybe it's the two of you together." She gave Debra a mischievous wink. "It's good to see you getting out."

"We're just having coffee," Debra stressed.

"And pie," Teja cooed in a singsong voice as she sashayed away.

Debra gave Conner a disbelieving smirk. "All you had to do was flash that killer smile of yours and she turned to putty."

"That's interesting," he said. "Why doesn't it work on you?"

"Who said it doesn't?"

* * * *

Patsy stood in the doorway of Luke's bedroom, watching him sleep. Even injured and medicated, he was an impressive figure of a man. The hard lines of his face were softened in slumber, and she wondered if it was the death of his wife and children that had put them there. She didn't know how long ago it had happened, but maybe tomorrow she'd ask him about it. All he could do was refuse to talk to her. But maybe he'd be relieved to know she'd heard about it in town.

She'd offered to help him get undressed after he'd eaten his deli sandwich but he'd flatly refused. Said, since it was only two o'clock, he was going to take a short rest and didn't need to take his clothes off to do that.

Surprisingly, he didn't argue when she handed him another two pills. He looked like he was miserable and the bottle said, "Take two tablets every four to six hours as needed for pain, not to exceed eight tablets in a twenty four hour period."

Actually, she'd only come up the six steps to his bedroom to make sure he was sleeping because she'd wanted to explore the house. Satisfied he was out, she gently eased the door shut and looked around.

There were three other doors. One, smaller than the others, proved, as she'd expected, to be a linen closet. The door next to it was a spare bedroom, nicely decorated but void of any personal effects with both the closet and the dresser drawers empty. Strange, she thought. If she had a big house with extra space she'd surely have things to put in it. The door made a soft click when she closed it, but certainly not loud enough for a heavily drugged, sleeping man to hear.

Drawing a heavy sigh, she walked across the hall to the next door, only to find it locked. After glancing toward Luke's bedroom to make sure he'd stayed put, she reached up and ran her fingers along the top of the doorframe. Sure enough, the key, along with an accumulation of dust, was there.

Shoving aside any feelings of guilt, she pressed the key in the lock with slightly shaking fingers and turned it. When the lock released, she quickly opened the door and slipped inside, softly closed the door her.

Unlike the other bedroom, this one was chaos. Pretty pink twin beds on each side of the room looked hastily made, dolls and toys were scattered about, even the book shelves were disorderly with children's books stacked every which way. It appeared no one had been in this room for a long time. Perhaps since the girls had died? A shiver ran up her spine as she wondered again how long it had been.

Hanging on the walls were labeled photos of two adorable little blue-eyed blondes at different ages in their lives. The youngest girl was Lola, the older one Betsy. Putting names to the faces somehow made it more real and more horrible. A feeling of intense sadness engulfed Patsy as she examined them closely. They were both happy, smiling children… What kind of monster did it take to harm them?

On the dresser, which was cluttered with childhood mementos, stood a framed informal wedding picture. The bride, exceptionally beautiful, held a bouquet of lavender lilies. Her beauty was so vivid, so exotic. She reminded Patsy of a young Elizabeth Taylor. She wore an exquisite white gown that had to be either a designer replica or the real thing. The man was decked out in a white tuxedo, his shirt matching the color of the flowers. Each of them held a child who appeared to be about two and four. Not until she picked up the picture to look at it more closely did she realize the groom partially hidden by the older child was Luke. A shocking realization hit her.

They weren't his biological children?

"Are you finding what you were looking for?"

Patsy whirled around to face Luke, a scream caught in her throat. Guilt washed over her, coloring her cheeks and spiking her heart rate into overdrive. He leaned against the open door frame, glaring at her with hostile eyes. His broad, muscular shoulders and upper chest above the bandaging were bare, his face a cynical mask of anger. He obviously expected an answer.

She closed her gaping mouth and said, "I…I was just…"

"Curious?" he finished for her. "Apparently, somebody in town clued you in."

"I…yes," she muttered backing up a step, suddenly nervous.

"Oh," he snarled, "so now, you're afraid of me. All afternoon, you've known, and now that you've been caught snooping around, you think I'm going to attack you."

"I'm not afraid," she said, a bit too quickly.

"The hell you aren't!" He said it so forcefully, she backed up another step. "Go pack your bags. I'll call Darren to come and get you out of here."

"I'm not leaving."

"You want to stay when you believe I'm a murderer."

She lifted her chin up a notch and squared her shoulders. "If I believed that, I wouldn't have come home with you today."

He looked at her for a long time then said, "Thanks for that, I appreciate it. Now, what are you doing in this room?"

She grimaced. "I suppose if I say I came in to dust, you wouldn't buy that?"

For a second, she thought he was going to laugh. "I wouldn't pay a plug nickel for that explanation. I would say you have an outrageous sense of humor though."

Her lips stretched into an exaggerated grin. "So I've been told." Setting the wedding photo back on the dresser, she sighed. "Look, I'm sorry I came in here without asking, but when Gertie told me—"

Luke interrupted her making a rude sound. "Gertie, huh? I wondered who you'd talked to. Did she also mention that her own husband died a year ago from some mysterious poison?"

"Ah, no, she didn't bring that up. But as I was saying— she checked out behind me at the grocery store. Not by accident, I suspect, but because she couldn't wait to warn me about staying with a man who murdered his wife and butchered his children. Rudy, by the way, stood up for you and informed her, and me, that you were released for lack of evidence."

"Rudy's one of the few who believes I'm innocent."

"Seems to me there are a lot of people on your side: Dr. Flanders and Wanda, Darren, Martin Bower at the service station, David, who said he'd worked for you, and a whole lot of his friends."

Luke's brows rose farther with each name she called off. "You certainly have been busy."

"Except I haven't heard from the main person, you. Would you care to tell me what happened? Since you didn't kill your wife and those kids, who do you think did?"

"My wife, I don't know, but I don't believe *anyone* killed Lola and Betsy."

Patsy frowned. "I don't understand. I hate to be graphic but Gertie said *butchered.* To me that implies a lot of blood. What am I missing here?"

"Nobody killed them because I don't believe they're dead."

Chapter Eight

Patsy made coffee while Luke sat at the table silently watching her. Since she'd paid attention when he'd made it that morning, she pretty much knew what to do it. Although, she had to guess at the amount of grounds to add. Asking him would only have shown her ignorance.

Sitting at the table across from him, she drew a ragged breath and folded her arms in front of her. "You look a little pale," she told him. "Would you like a couple more pain pills?"

"Stop mothering me."

"It's been almost four hours since you took those last two, you can have more."

He reached into his pocket, drew something out and threw the two she'd given him earlier on the table. "You mean these?"

"You didn't take them? No wonder you didn't sleep longer."

His features tightened into a scowl. "Were you trying to drug me so you could check out the house?"

"Don't be ridiculous."

"You know, all you had to do was ask. What happened is hardly a secret. I'm surprised Darren didn't enlighten you before he dropped you off."

"He never said a word, but he did have a suspicious smirk on his face. I wondered what he was up to. I guess this explains it. So, okay, now I'm asking."

"Coffee first. I need to clear my head. Those damn pills have my brain in a fog."

"Are you still in pain?"

"Not bad, I can handle it." He motioned toward the coffee. "I think it's done."

She jumped up, took down two cups, and filled them. She didn't remember coffee being that dark but maybe it was the brand he used. She set the cups on the table then went to the fridge and got a pitcher of milk to add a bit to the dark brew. He pushed his cup forward, indicating he wanted some too.

She put the milk away and sat back down ready to hear his story. He took a long pull of coffee and came up choking. "Hells bells, this taste like hog slop. What the hell did you put in it?"

"I…just coffee. You saw me. I made it just like you did this morning."

He gave her a long hard stare. "Are you telling me you've never made coffee?"

She opened her mouth to speak but couldn't find the right words. Finally, she shrugged and said, "Well, actually, I guess that would be a yes."

He shook his head muttering under his breath. "Where did you come from anyway, another planet? Can you even cook at all?"

Squirming in her seat she made a pained face. Conner called it her oh-oh-busted look.

She flinched when he got up and walked past her to the coffee pot. He dumped the dripping grounds into the trash can. "This thing is full. How much did you use?"

"Not a lot, there were still some left in there so—"

"You didn't dump the old grounds from this morning?"

When she didn't answer, he swore then finished making fresh coffee, working one handed. He reached past her for his cup, dumped the contents down the drain, and thoroughly rinsed it out. When he sat back down, he was breathing heavily. She wasn't certain if it was from anger or exertion.

After a moment, when he seemed to have calmed down, he asked in a low voice, "Is there anything you can do effectively?"

Patsy wanted to tell him about all the recipes and advice she'd gotten from her grandmother but this didn't feel like the right time, so she simply said, "Yes. I can learn."

Amazingly, that seemed to satisfy him. Before he could point out any of her other shortcomings, she decided to get him back on track. "You said you'd explain about why you believe your girls are still alive. I'm anxious to hear your theory, but maybe you could start at the beginning to help my slow brain comprehend."

"I don't think your brain is slow at all," he said. "I think you grew up in a cloistered nunnery and just recently escaped with a sugar daddy who bought you a Maserati and some sexy new clothes. Then, when you decided you weren't going to take any orders from him, you ran away to North Dakota to look for a hick farmer who could give you what you wanted with no strings attached."

Patsy forced herself not to roll her eyes and ask if he wrote books on the side. He certainly had the imagination for it.

"Wow," she said. "You're good. I'm impressed. It took the last two farmers a week to figure all that out. But now, I'm curious. How did you know my sugar daddy bought my clothes?"

He shrugged as though it were obvious. "You know how to *look* like a sex kitten but you don't know how to act like one."

It took a second for Patsy to fix her mind on whether that was an insult or a compliment. An insult, she decided. It raised her ire. "Why, because I don't purr all over you like Wanda?"

"Exactly. And, just for the record, that's the only reason I let you stay yesterday."

Speechless, Patsy gaped at him, realizing he wasn't just coming up with this stuff off the top of his head. He'd actually been thinking about it. His assessment of her, though not accurate, was a little disconcerting.

"So then," she said slowly. "How did you know about the nuns?"

"Easy. You don't have any tattoos."

She gave a short laugh. "How can you be so sure about that?"

"There's a surveillance camera in your bedroom," he said, punctuating his words with a cheeky grin.

When she laughed, he did, too, until his ribs started hurting. He had a nice robust laugh, deep and husky. It made her tingle in places she liked to ignore. It also made her aware of the smattering of dark hair on the part of his chest she could see. Whenever he moved, muscles rippled in his shoulders. At least on the side he was able to move.

She noticed the instant a serious expression replaced his smile. He had a look that implied he wasn't allowed to laugh. Clearing his throat, he said, "Now that I know all about you, if you'll please pour me a fresh cup of coffee, I'll tell you about Lola and Betsy."

She did as he requested then sat back down and waited.

Luke decided to start from the night Kelsey died. "It all came to a head on March seventeenth. Kelsey and I had a serious argument. She hated it out here. Too secluded. Too far from a mall. Too much of everything she didn't like— and not enough of the things she *did* like. She wanted to take the girls and go back to Bismarck, and thought I should go with her if I loved her.

"All I know is farming. I told her I couldn't make a living doing anything else. When she actually started packing, I stormed out of the house. I ended up at the Ashville Bar and proceeded to get very drunk. Since it was Saint Patrick's Day, the bar was crowded. I wasn't in the mood to party, but I was in the mood to drink. By ten-thirty, I'd already had about five drinks, and that's when Wanda came in and started rubbing around on me." He noticed Patsy raise her eyebrows at that but went on with his story. "When I got up to leave, Mel—he owns the bar— said I was too inebriated, he wouldn't allow me to drive home. After a weak protest, I let him call Glen to come and get me.

"When Glen finally got there, we had a drink together. Glen had a green beer; I had a Scotch and soda. At least I think that's what it was. It must have been pretty watered down because it tasted like crap. I went to the can, and by the time I came out, Glen had rounded up Rudy to follow us home with my truck. I finished my drink, and we left."

Luke was coming to the part he hated the most. He drained his coffee cup and motioned for a refill. Patsy obliged silently. In fact, she'd been amazingly quiet through the whole thing. Most women would be rattling off comments or asking questions every time he stopped to take a breath. She did neither, listening intently instead, like she was taking notes in her head.

"The drinks really hit me on the way home, and I was totally wasted by the time Glen dropped me off. He offered to help me get in the house. Of course, I refused. It was so damn cold outside, though, he was worried so, he told me later, both he and Rudy waited until I was inside before they left."

He put his free hand up to rub his face. He wasn't proud of himself for anything he did that night, least of all for his lack of memory. He rested his face in his hand, telling the rest while staring at the table.

"I must have blacked out at some point because going into the house was the last thing I remember. I woke up the next morning about nine-thirty and was surprised to see Kelsey still in bed. Sometime during my drunken binge, I'd decided to tell her I'd sell the farm and move with her. The truth is, I would have done it for the girls. I didn't want to lose them. I reached over to touch her, tell her about my decision, and her body was cold. I totally freaked out, trying to revive her. Of course, at that point I didn't know she'd been murdered. I thought she died of a heart attack or something. Whoever did it left her laying right in bed like she was sleeping."

He lifted his head and could tell by the shock on Patsy's face that she realized he'd spent the entire night with a dead woman. Swallowing the convulsive lump in his throat, he went on. Finally, I ran in to check on the girls. Their beds were empty, and initially, I thought they just got up and went downstairs. That's when I noticed the blood. Not a lot of it, it could have been from a nosebleed, except that it was on both beds.

"I raced through the house, looking for them, calling their names but they weren't there. Finally, I called nine-one-one. The next thing I knew the ambulance was there along with Sheriff Wilson, and I was in handcuffs and being hauled into jail."

"That's awful; how did she die?" Patsy whispered, speaking for the first time.

"She was strangled."

"Surely, they released you right away."

He gave a bitter laugh. "I couldn't even defend myself because I thought I might have done it. Problem was, even if I had killed Kelsey, there was no possible way I would have harmed those girls. I don't care how drunk I was. The fact that I didn't call in until ten o'clock the next morning didn't help my case any."

"What about the girls, Lola and Betsy?"

"They tried to say I stabbed them and buried them out in the field since I had half the morning to do it."

"But...wasn't the ground frozen?"

"Yes, but they still took cadaver sniffing dogs out. I have two thousand acres. It took them a couple of days to go over it all. They never found anything. So then, they decided I must have dumped their bodies in some trees or driven all the way to the river to dispose of them. Rudy couldn't remember how much gas I had in the truck or what the mileage was on the odometer so anything was possible. Both Rudy and Glen, however, insisted I was far too intoxicated to carry out a plan like that."

"But then again, you had a lot of time to sober up by morning," Patsy supplied morosely.

He nodded. "They moved me up to Bismarck and held me there for two months. Fortunately, between Glen and Darren, my farm was tended to. Since I didn't know if or when I would get released, I had Glen haul most of my cattle to market."

"So what was the deciding factor to release you?"

"It took that long to prove that Kelsey died an hour before I got home, and again, both Glen and Rudy knew exactly what time that was."

"And let me make a guess. They never looked for another killer."

Luke shook his head. "By then, the trail was cold. They still expect Lola and Betsy's bodies to show up. Their winter coats and boots were still in the closet. That, along with the blood that proved to be theirs, has everyone convinced they're dead. I'm the only one who believes they're still alive."

"So…what are you basing that assumption on?"

He paused a moment before going on. "This may sound trivial but Betsy had a grubby old yellow rabbit she'd named Binky. She never went anywhere without Binky. It wasn't here. I searched the house and even the yard and barn, everywhere…"

Patsy looked at him incredulously. "That's it?"

"Yes, you tell me what cold-blooded killer would take time to grab a child's favorite toy if the child was already dead."

"There was a yellow rabbit up on the bed, Luke. I saw it."

"That's one of the reason nobody else supports my theory. Kelsey bought that one for her because the other one was so ratty. She even threw the old one in the trash, and Betsy dug it back out. I myself didn't realize it was missing until three weeks ago." He drew a deep breath and waited for her to tell him he was crazy. "Have you ever torn the house apart looking for something you didn't want to find?"

"No, I guess not. I don't understand."

"When I couldn't find that rabbit in their bedroom, I did just that. I'm fully convinced it's not on this farm."

"Have you done anything to look for them?" she asked surprising him.

"Like I said I didn't suspect they were still alive until three weeks ago. I don't know where to start."

"What about the girls' father? Could he have taken them?"

He frowned at her. "You believe me?"

"I certainly believe it's a possibility. What you're saying makes sense."

For a moment, he gaped at her, stunned. He wasn't prepared for her to believe him. He swallowed a lump that had been building in his throat. "Even Darren and Glen, the people closest to me, think I'm losing it. What makes you feel differently?"

Blinking rapidly, she gave him a pensive smile. "When I was little, I had a blue bear. I was very limited to what I could bring with me in that cracker box of a car. But my blue bear is downstairs packed in one of my suitcases. Now, how do we get started?"

"You want to help?"

She slanted him a grin. "Didn't I say I was willing to do anything that needs doing?"

Luke was taken aback. Chest tightening, he stared, with renewed respect, at the woman with the wild red hair watching him expectantly. She not only believed him, she was willing to help. Right now, he didn't want to think about how much that meant to him. She was, after all, planning to leave when her car was fixed. He didn't want to think about that either.

His stomach growled and he decided it was safer to think about food.

"I don't function very well on an empty stomach. It's after seven, and we haven't eaten since that deli sandwich? Is it too much to hope for that you have a supper plan?"

Patsy held up the notebook she'd been studying earlier. "Thanks to Grams, I do." She jumped up, hunted in the cupboards and found a large pot. Filling it half full of water, she set it on the stove to boil then headed for the pantry for the Ragu sauce and garlic bread she'd purchased.

While the sauce was heating, she added some frozen meatballs and chatted excitedly about the simple recipes and cooking instructions she'd received during her visit with her Grams.

It only took her twenty minutes to set a plate of steaming spaghetti with meatballs, and buttery slices of bread in front of him. She stood back nervously, holding her breath as she waited for him to taste it. Luke glanced up at her then dug his fork in and took a bite. He chewed swallowed and took another bite.

"Well, how is it?" she demanded impatiently.

Grinning, he said, "Just like good old mom used to make." After another bite, he looked up at her, frowning. "Why aren't you eating?"

She let out a whoosh of air. "I am," she said, quickly grabbing a plate and filling it. "Is it really okay?"

"Yes," he said, chuckling. "But I'll like it better if I see you eating, too."

She rolled her eyes and sat across from him. "You're never going to let me forget about those pancakes are you?"

He popped a meatball in his mouth and talked around it. "I may never eat pancakes again."

"For crying out loud," Patsy said swirling pasta around her fork. "I was desperate. I'm sorry." She put the spaghetti in her mouth, suddenly very hungry. "Oh my gosh. This is actually good."

Luke laughed. "Patsy Bartlett, you are an interesting piece of work."

Patsy smiled, enjoying her first prepared meal with Luke. She could tell he was in pain so she avoided talking about the girls, keeping their conversation light instead.

Were Betsy and Lola really out there somewhere, still alive, waiting for their father to rescue them?

For Luke's sake, she prayed they were.

Chapter Nine

Patsy woke up early, anxious to get started on the mystery of Luke's missing little girls. Last night, she'd made him go to bed after supper. He'd looked like hell, and she'd been afraid he was going to collapse right there at the kitchen table.

Now, before Patsy could do anything else, she'd have to get through breakfast. She couldn't believe she was actually looking forward to cooking and trying new recipes. Unfortunately, her repertoire would run dry in a hurry. Soon, she'd have to make another visit to Grams.

Patsy stared in the open refrigerator, wondering if they could eat leftover spaghetti, when Reggie gave a low growl behind her.

She slammed the fridge shut and turned to glare at him. It was time she established her dominance with the smart-assed dog. But he didn't seem to be growling at her; he was looking toward the door.

Frowning, she walked over and peeked out the window, wondering if Luke had gotten up and gone outside already. She saw a sheriff's car parked in front of the barn, and a man in a brown uniform standing over the ladder. Given the conversation she'd overheard in Doc Flanders' office, it was unlikely Luke would have reported the accident to the local sheriff. The sheriff picked up the bottom end of the ladder by the twisted foot and was examining it.

"What are you looking at?"

Patsy jumped at the sound of Luke's voice behind her. Man, she had to talk to him about sneaking up on her like that. Before she could get her breath back to answer him, he pressed against her to look over her shoulder. She could feel his heat, and it wasn't totally uncomfortable. He backed away in a hurry.

"Dammit! What the hell is he doing here?" Luke jerked the front door open and strode angrily toward the sheriff, Reggie following at his heels and Patsy close behind. She had to take two steps to Luke's one to keep up. Patsy noticed he'd changed clothes and had somehow managed to dress himself, except for the buttons on his shirt.

When the sheriff saw Luke bearing down on him he dropped the ladder. Patsy thought she actually saw fear in his eyes, which was ridiculous considering Luke's condition.

"Get the hell off my property, Wilson."

"Take it easy Luke. I'm here to investigate your accident." He spoke to Luke but his gaze was fixed on Patsy as she came to stand beside Luke.

"It looks to me," Patsy said, indicating the ladder, "like you came to contaminate the evidence. What if we were going to have that ladder fingerprinted?"

Sheriff Wilson's face turned a vivid shade of red. "Well, if it isn't Miss Maserati," he sputtered, giving her an insolent bodily once over. "What? Are you his attorney?" His sneer suggested he didn't believe that for a minute.

"I can see where your son got his manners," Patsy snapped. "And you're lucky I'm not a lawyer because you'd be in deep doodoo if I were, since messing with evidence makes you the number one suspect."

"For your information, more than half the townsfolk are suspects. Most people believe he belongs in jail, including me."

Patsy put her hands on her hips and walked up in front of him. "Then what in the world are you doing here? Why do you care if somebody is trying to kill him?"

The sheriff gaped at her a moment as though he didn't quite know what to make of her, then with an angry glare at Luke, he got in his car and sprayed fifteen feet of gravel getting out of the yard.

Luke turned an incredulous stare at Patsy. He felt like he just got hit with a lightning bolt. "Are you a lawyer?" he asked.

"Of course not. I'm a cook. He's a big dink, and he made me angry. You look much better this morning, by the way."

When she headed back to the house, he followed. "I think you'd make a better lawyer than a cook. What's for breakfast?"

She laughed. "We can either have spaghetti or between the two of us figure out how to make an omelet. Grams said it was easy."

The omelet they created looked like mush but tasted quite good. "I think you're getting the hang of this," Luke told her as he hungrily shoveled the concoction into his mouth.

"Hey, I even made good coffee this morning," Patsy said, refilling their cups, laughing. "Apparently, whoever said presentation makes the meal is full of crap."

When Luke laughed with her, he realized he'd laughed more in the last two days than he had in several months. It felt good. She not only brought humor into his life she'd championed him like a tenacious pit bull. Watching Harvey Wilson's face when Patsy laid into him was priceless.

"How do you think the sheriff found out about your accident?" Patsy asked as if she'd sensed his line of thought. "I didn't tell anyone, and you didn't see anyone outside the hospital."

Luke snorted. "That's easy. He's Wanda's brother."

She looked up at him, wide eyed. "Holy cow, talk about a small town. Is everybody related?"

"Yup, in one way or another. How did you know about Harvey's son?"

"He was one of the kids ogling my car when I stopped to check on the repairs. The little twerp gave me a wolf whistle then asked if I was the killer's new whore."

She must have seen the anger flash in his eyes because she quickly added, "Don't worry the other kids defended you, and so did Martin then he chased them all away. Except David, who helped me load my things in the back of the truck. He told me you weren't a killer and that you really loved your little girls."

Patsy shoved the dishes aside, noting happily there were no omelet leftovers, and pulled out the notebook she'd used to copy Grams' cooking instructions. "We need to do a little brainstorming," she said. "Let's start with their biological father."

Luke stirred milk in his coffee and took a sip. "I'm afraid that won't be much help. Kelsey told me they had different fathers, and she wouldn't name either one of them."

Patsy didn't even try to hide her surprise or shock. "She told you that and you still married her?"

"I knew they had different fathers, but she didn't tell me she *couldn't* name them until six months after we were married."

"Okay, now, don't get impatient with me, but is it possible she lied?"

Scratching at the stubble on his chin, he said, "Anything's possible. Somebody killed her, and the court proved it wasn't me. So there's something going on that I don't know about."

She gave him a level look. "Since you told me you couldn't remember anything, are you comfortable with the court's decision?"

"Yes, because if I'd killed Kelsey, where are the girls? They searched the entire farm—and the neighboring farms." His chest tightened as the memories washed over him. Those painful days and nights sitting helplessly in jail while a search party walked over the frozen land, looking for the bodies of his two little girls. "Somebody set me up," he said gruffly.

Patsy observed him silently for a moment then tapped her pen on the notebook. "Okay, that tells me right there that those girls are alive. If whoever killed your wife planned to set you up, they'd have left their bodies close by where they could be found to point the finger at you. I'd say there was a reason the girls were spared. So who besides you has an emotional attachment to them and a reason to kill their mother?" When he didn't answer, she did. "A father, that's who. One of them must have a father who wanted Kelsey dead or wanted his daughter, or both. Maybe he was secretly paying her child support and wanted to end it. Why not kill the mother and grab the child. Results—he gets custody, no more support payments, and you take the rap."

After a few moments, he nodded. "You might be on to something."

"Do you have their birth certificates and do they have official seals?"

"They're in my safe but I've never had a reason to check the seals. The safe is in my office. I'll get them."

After he left, Patsy quickly cleared the dishes off the table and stuck them in the dishwasher. As she worked, she wondered what kind of woman could have two children and not know who their fathers were. And what sort of marriage did Luke have with Kelsey when he personally had to rely on the court to prove he hadn't murdered her?

David had implied Kelsey wasn't a pleasant person, and Patsy was getting the impression it might have been an understatement. Although for what it was worth, she appeared to love her children otherwise she might have just said adios and left them with Luke.

A moment later, when Luke walked in the room, she posed her question to him. "Why did you marry her?"

Instead of answering her, he burst out with, "What are you doing?"

She gesture to the soap in her hand. "I'm going to run the dishwasher. It's full."

"You've never run a dishwasher, have you?"

She looked down at the dishes. They seemed to be stacked properly, after all, how hard could it be. A dunce could load a dishwasher. "No," she admitted reluctantly, "but what's the problem?"

He gave her a long-suffering look, put the papers he was holding on the table, then walked up to her and took the soap out of her hand. "This is soap for washing dishes in the sink. If you use that in the dishwasher, you'll flood the whole kitchen with suds." He reached under the sink, took out a green bottle and handed it to her. "Here, use this."

She looked at the label on the bottle, frowning stupidly. "Huh. Go figure, two different kinds of soap just to wash dishes. How was I supposed to know that?"

He gave her the same look he'd used when she'd forgotten—well, maybe not exactly *forgotten*—to take the old grounds out of the coffee maker. Then, he rolled his eyes and looked skyward. "Lord help me. She *is* from another planet."

She gave him her famous Cheshire grin. "Yeah, and we don't need dishes there. We just eat these little square cubes for nourishment. It's great because it even eliminates the need for toilet paper. Now—where do I put this stuff and how much should I use?"

With exaggerated patience, he pointed to two little dispensers. She obediently filled them, then he slide one shut, closed the door firmly until it clicked, and pointed to a start button. "Push right here and you're good to go."

She followed his instructions and the dishwasher immediately hummed to life. "Voila," she purred happily. "My sugar daddy always said, 'It's a sad day when you don't learn something new'."

"In that case," Luke mumbled, "I doubt you have many sad days."

"Be nice." She chuckled. "I told you I was a good learner."

Luke shook his head and sat back at the table. He pushed the papers he'd brought with him over to her. "Here are the birth certificates, including Kelsey's. Hers and Lola's have seals; Betsy's doesn't. Both have the father listed as unknown."

Patsy sat to examine them. "Betsy's seems to be photo copy. The father is listed as unknown but look at this." She turned the document and slid it across to him. "The word *unknown* appears to be a different type than the rest of the document, and so is the last name. Is there some reason Kelsey didn't want anyone to know who Betsy's father was?"

"Beats me," he said. "But you're right. It does look falsified."

"Seems like a good place to start," she said. "Now, back to my earlier question. Why did you marry Kelsey?"

"What does that have to do with anything?"

"Somebody killed her. If I'm going to help you find out who it was, I need as much information as I can get. And why didn't you simply answer, '*because I loved her*'?"

She must have caught him off guard with that question because his cheeks took on a reddish hue. Wow, a man who blushed—go figure. Not ready to let him off the hook, she stared directly at him, watching his eyes, as she waited for him to answer.

"I guess I did love her," he said clumsily.

"You guess!"

His eyes narrowed defensively. "Why else would I marry her?"

"I don't know, you tell me."

He didn't answer.

"All right, let's try something else. Did you legally adopt the girls?"

He got up, took a glass out of the cupboard, and filled it with milk from the refrigerator. She got the feeling he was stalling. When he sat back down he said, "She wanted me to adopt Lola but not Betsy. I said it wasn't fair to them. It had to be either both or nothing, so she wanted to wait. She even approached me about three weeks before she died, wanting me to adopt Lola."

"That's ridiculous. Why would she let you adopt one but not the other? And wait? Wait for what?"

"I don't know. Sometimes I got the feeling she wanted to see if our marriage would last."

Patsy was confused. "How long were you married?"

"Not quite three years."

"Did she love you?"

He shot her an angry look but it dissipated quickly. "She said she did—all the time."

"It seems to me," Patsy said, "that if she really loved you, she'd have been willing to stay here and make it work. Isn't that what marriage is about?"

"That can work both ways," he countered. "She said if I loved her, I'd be willing to move back to Bismarck with her."

Patsy tapped her pen on her paper, thinking. Something wasn't adding up, but she was good at figuring out problems—as long as they didn't involve her. She rarely read a book that could hit her with a surprise ending because she always figured it out.

"She must have known you wouldn't do that when she agreed to marry you and move out here." When Luke didn't comment, she knew she'd guessed right. "Okay, bear with me," she said. "Let's just say she didn't love you. What other reason could she have for wanting to marry you?"

Luke simply stared at her. She wasn't sure if she was hitting pay dirt or if he was getting weary with her line of questioning. Maybe she just hadn't found the right question.

"There's been a big hubbub about oil in North Dakota. Any chance you have oil on your land?"

"No, the oil fields are all a long ways northwest of here."

"Huh. Okay. She wasn't from around here," Patsy continued. "Maybe she didn't know that."

"No chance. She lived in Bismarck. She'd have known where the oil was."

"How did you meet her?"

"Glen and I were at a weekend farmer's convention in Bismarck. He wanted to go so I went with him; Darren went, too, as well as a few others from the area. On Saturday night, we went to the hotel bar for a couple of drinks. Kelsey was sitting at the bar, drinking a glass of wine. We made eye contact, and she came over to me. All the other guys were playing pool, and I was the designated table holder. The bar was full of men attending the convention, but for some reason, she singled me out. She was a looker and a great conversationalist so I guess I was flattered that she chose me over a lot of better-looking men."

"I doubt that," Patsy muttered emphatically before she could stop herself. He raised an eyebrow at her, and she shrugged. "Sorry, I didn't mean to interrupt. Go ahead."

"That's about all there's to it. I started going to Bismarck to see her, and when I couldn't make it up there, she came to the farm with her daughters, gave me the impression that she loved it out there. We dated that way about six months, and then, I asked her to marry me. The girls were a bonus."

"You had no qualms about getting a readymade family?"

"None whatsoever. I was thirty-one years old. I wanted kids. That's why I was so disappointed when she wouldn't let me adopt Betsy."

"Is it possible she was still in love with Betsy's father?"

"I have no way of knowing that. She never gave any indication that she was. But... Come to think of it, she did drive to Bismarck once a month. She said it was to go shopping, and she enjoyed taking the trip alone."

"Did she take the girls along?"

"Yes, almost always. But..."

"But what?" Patsy prompted.

Luke got a strange look on his face. "Sometimes, she only took one of them. She said they needed some mother-daughter time together."

Patsy picked up Kelsey's birth certificate. "She was born Kelsey Anne Kempler. Did she have any relatives up there she could have been visiting?"

"None that I know of."

"After spending three years together, I would think you'd know if she did. Any brothers or sisters anywhere?"

"None that she told me about."

"Oh, for crying out loud," Patsy bellowed, throwing her hands in the air. "Did you even talk to each other? What kind of a marriage did you have?"

For a moment, she thought he was going to lash out at her, defend his marriage, then he gave a sigh of resignation. "Obviously, not a very good one."

Patsy felt empathy for his sadness. "There must have been something that drew you to her?"

"Oh yeah." He smiled reminiscently. "There was. The sex."

That answer caught Patsy off guard, and for some reason, it didn't please her at all. She gritted her teeth and drummed a beat on the table with her pen. "That's it? You married her for the sex? From what I understand, sex is free on every street corner."

"Not in Ashville. You have sex around here with someone who isn't your wife, and it's published in the local paper."

"No kidding," she murmured.

"So how is all this going to help me find my girls, which, by the way, is probably the main reason I married Kelsey. I loved those kids from the moment I met them."

"Your case never went to trial, did it?" Patsy asked.

"No. It was all set to, until the judge threw it out for lack of evidence."

"But there was probably extensive news coverage, all over the state, especially when you were released. I wondered if the father of either one of the girls might have been there. Did you notice anyone hanging around that didn't belong? Or did anyone approach you, angry or otherwise, that you didn't know."

"I was pretty distraught, and there were a lot of angry people there. Some arguing that I should be in jail, and some insisting that I shouldn't—most of them I knew. Nobody who got in my face, though—at least nobody I didn't know."

Patsy blew out a huff of air. "Criminy, that must have been a nightmare for you."

"Yeah, but not as bad as walking into this house afterwards. At least Glen was with me. It was hard for him, too, because he cared for Lola and Betsy, too."

"How about Kelsey?"

"He was always cordial to her; all my friends were. I suspect some of that was out of courtesy for me. She didn't warm up to strangers easily."

"I saw her picture. She was an exceptionally beautiful woman. I imagine most of the men didn't have a problem with her." Patsy thought about Kelsey slipping off a barstool and approaching Luke. Was there a reason she'd singled him out, other than his rugged good looks? "Did Kelsey ever have a run-in with anyone in Ashville?"

"No, not to my knowledge. She wasn't very well received, at least not by the females. The townsfolk don't take to outsiders too well, especially since there were a few women in town who had their sights on me."

"Like Wanda."

"For one."

Patsy's eyes widened. "There were others?"

He shrugged sheepishly. "No one who'd kill my wife to get me. I went to high school here," he added by way of explanation.

Patsy massaged her eye sockets then looked up at him. "Let me guess—you were captain of the football team. Were you also the quarterback?"

He cocked his head, grimacing. "Yeah."

She snorted. "Well, that clears that up. Let's go back to the girls. Did you ever ask them what they did when they went to Bismarck with their mother?"

"I asked Betsy once. She giggled and said it was a secret so I never asked again."

"Well, I think that's where we need to start. I know someone who is an expert with computers. I'm going to see if he can find out whose name is listed as the father on Betsy's birth certificate. I have a problem using my cell phone here, though. There mustn't be any towers close around."

"That's why I don't have one," Luke said, combing a hand through is dark hair. "It may sound crazy but if you go out and stand in the middle of the yard close to the hen house it might work. That's what Kelsey had to do."

Patsy grimaced. "Oh, that must be fun in the middle of the winter."

"That was just one of the things that bugged her about living here. You don't need to go outside, though. I have a landline; feel free to use it. While you do that, I have a few chores to take care of—see if I can manage to feed the chickens and gather the eggs without a nursemaid."

Luke had barely walked out of the house when his phone rang. She hesitated only a moment then deciding to answer it with a simple, "Hello."

What did it matter anyway? Everyone in town knew she was staying there.

"Hello, Patsy. It's David."

"Hi, David. You have some information for me already?"

"You bet. The guy drives a car with a Minnesota license plate. I can give you the number if you need it. He's from Minneapolis, and his name is Ben Fontaine. Nobody knows why he's here because he doesn't do anything but walk around, eat in the café, and ask questions. The interesting part is all he wants to know about is what's happening with you."

Patsy thanked David and hung up, trying to decide if she should call Conner first or her illustrious s*ugar daddy*. Conner, she thought, Conner first. He might have an idea what to do about Ben Fontaine.

Using Luke's phone, she dialed Conner's cell. He answered on the third ring.

"Conner, it's Patsy. How are you?"

"Hey Pats, I'm good. No, actually, I'm great."

"Did I dial the right number?" Patsy asked. "Is this my brother who's dealing with preteens or some delusional space alien that's invaded his body?"

"Yup, it's me, and life is good. How about you?"

"Not too bad. My boss fell and broke some ribs so he actually needs me. I found out who the guy is that's dogging me. His name is Ben Fontaine. Can you find out if he's working for Dad or should I just call and ask him myself? It tees me off to think he put a watchdog on me."

"Heck, as long as you're obeying all the rules, it might be a good thing. He'll know we're working and holding our own. We have less than three months to go."

"Maybe you're right," Patsy said. "But still, I'd rather know if Dad hired this guy or if somebody is stalking me."

"Well, it's interesting," Conner said. "Because I'm pretty sure there's a man watching me too. He sits in the café across from the school and drinks coffee all day. Seems suspicious to me."

"You know something hit me the other day. Do you think Dad might be sick, and that's why he came up with this silly stunt?"

Conner hesitated. "I...don't know. I sure wish he'd level with us if that was the case. Maybe we should explore that. If he's sick, I'd sure like to know."

"Me, too," Patsy agreed.

"All I can say is it's turning out to be good thing for me. I met a woman."

"Already?"

"Uh huh. She's the mother of one of my kids."

"Holy cow. Are looking to get a readymade family?"

"You're jumping the gun," Conner said, laughing. "We just met yesterday. I practically had to go down on my knees and beg just to go to coffee with her. Tell me about you and the farmer."

"You won't believe it. I'm learning how to cook, and here's the best part, I'm enjoying it. I can't believe how ignorant I was. Maybe Dad was on to something when he ousted us."

"So you're getting along with the farmer?"

"Actually, he's one of the reasons I'm calling." Patsy gave him a brief overview of Luke Macalister's situation. "We need to know who Betsy's father is, hoping he's listed on the original birth certificate. To familiarize yourself with the case you can pull most of it up on the internet. I figured you'd be happy to have something to work on. But now, that you have a girlfriend…"

"Don't worry about that. I still have plenty of free time. So far, all I've convinced her to do is have coffee, and that was a battle. I really like her, though."

Before she hung up, Patsy gave Conner Luke's phone number so he could call if he learned anything.

Chapter Ten

Conner pressed the disconnect button on his phone, an uneasy feeling teasing his gut. He didn't like the idea of his sister living on a remote farm with a man who'd been accused of killing his wife and children.

She'd caught him at a good time, just as his kids were filing out of the classroom. He had the whole afternoon clear to check out Luke Macalister. But first, he punched in his father's number.

Charles Bartlett answered so quickly Conner thought he must have been sitting there waiting for the call. He experienced a brief stab of guilt for not calling more often.

"Conner, son, good to hear from you. How are you?"

"I'm fine," Conner said, thinking his father's voice sounded tired, strained. "Thought you'd be happy to hear I'm working."

"That's wonderful," Charles said, some of the weariness leaving his voice. "Congratulations. Anything you care to share?"

"It's a teaching job. I'm teaching computer skills to preteens, getting them ready for the school year."

"Are you enjoying it?"

The question surprised Conner. He'd expected his father to be more interested in how much he was making. "I've only been on the job a couple of days, but, yeah, I am. Maybe I found my niche, huh?"

He could almost see Charles smiling. "Well, son, I suspected you'd find it working with computers. You always were a whiz at it. I never could get the hang of anything beyond the basics." There was a slight hesitation. "And Patsy? I haven't heard from her in a couple of months. How's she coming along?"

Conner laughed. "You'll love this. She's a cook and housekeeper for a farmer in North Dakota."

"You're kidding, right?" Charles questioned with a disbelieving chuckle.

"Nope."

"Now, that's a surprise. I knew she went out there but never figured her for a cook. I can't even imagine her in a domestic role."

So he knew she'd gone to North Dakota. That left an opening for Conner's next question. He took a fortifying breath. "Well, Dad, that's one of the reasons I'm calling. How did you know she was in North Dakota?"

He heard a long sigh. "I guess there's no harm in telling you I've been keeping tabs on where you are."

"So you already knew I was teaching, and Patsy was staying with a farmer. Are you having us followed?"

"No, no, of course not," Charles stated quickly. "I just asked Morty to monitor your spending habits. One of Patsy's friends told me she was going to see her grandmother."

"How did you expect him to monitor us?"

"Cell phones, credit cards, banking activities. You must know I have access to all three since I've been paying your bills for years."

Conner mentally winced at that. "Are you saying you aren't having us followed?"

"Certainly not," Charles sputtered.

"Do you know a man named Ben Fontaine?"

"Ah…no, not that I recall. Why?"

"He's been following Patsy, and I'm pretty sure there's someone tailing me too. Could Morty be doing it without telling you?" Conner asked.

"Good God, I hope not. But I'll be sure to ask him."

"I'd appreciate that. And let me know what you find out?"

"I'll do that. And Conner?"

"Yeah, Dad?

"Please understand I dearly love both of you. I didn't do this to be mean. I was concerned for your future. I won't always be around, and you needed to get some experience being on your own."

"That brings up another question I have. Are you ill? Is that what precipitated this?" When Charles didn't reply, Conner's heart rate picked up. "Dad, are you still there?"

"Yes, son. I'm here. You don't have to be concerned about my health. We'll talk about that when the two of you come home after your year is up. Okay?"

"Sure, Dad. I'll talk to you later."

Conner hung up, frowning. His father was lying about his health. There'd been too much hesitation in his answer. But apparently, it wasn't anything urgent since he wanted to wait three months to tell them about it. Still, it concerned Conner, and he was a little distressed Charles hadn't confessed to any health issues at the time he ousted the two of them. But would that kind of information have made a difference in the way he and Patsy had gone about changing their lives?

Heaving a sigh, Conner packed up his briefcase and headed for his lonely little efficiency room. He had research to do for Patsy, and maybe, he'd call Debra later.

As he walked out to his car his phone rang.

"Hi, Conner, it's Debra. I'm putting some hamburgers on the grill and was wondering if you wanted to join us."

Just the sound of her voice had his heart humming; the invitation turned it into a full-scale orchestra. "That's the best offer I've had all day. What time do you want me?"

"Around six, okay?"

"Super, I'll be there. Can I bring a bottle of wine?"

"Sure. See you in a while." She gave him directions to her house and hung up.

Conner's step got a little lighter. In the last minute, he decided to make a quick detour to the café to see if his shadow was there. And if he was, maybe Conner would have a little chat with him.

* * * *

Charles Bartlett sat for a long time staring out at his high-rise office window at the rushing Mississippi River. The water was higher than it usually was in August due to all the rain they'd had. Sadly, the thought hit him that he may never see another August.

On his last visit to the doctor, he'd been informed that only a major surgery could prolong his life. For how long was undetermined, and there was a sixty percent chance he'd never survive the operation. Without surgery, he'd be lucky to be around this time next year. The choices were grim.

Why was he still working? Why didn't he retire and spend his remaining time with his children? He already knew the answer. He'd known it when he set his plan in motion to force them into belated adulthood. Amazingly, after nine months of disappointing news, they seemed to be coming around. This was not the time to level with them. He didn't want to disrupt their apparent successes.

Patsy cooking and housekeeping? In spite of his situation, Charles found himself chuckling. And Conner teaching preteens? It was common knowledge his son didn't like being around kids. Maybe, because at twenty-nine, he was still a kid himself.

As it turned out, both of his children were doing something totally out of character. Nothing Charles had expected of them or, more importantly, what they expected of themselves. And they were enjoying it. How strange was that? He could finally feel Mary Beth smiling down on him.

It had happened quickly, too. The last time he'd seen them had been on Father's Day over a month ago. At that time, they were both irritable, and neither had anything encouraging to share. He'd just about given up hope something positive would come of his little scheme.

Maybe it was time to call Morty and amend the last revision he'd made to his will. Granted, the year wasn't up, but they didn't have to know what he was doing. And, what if he had heart failure between now and November first?

Also, he had to find out if Morty'd taken Charles' instructions to another level by having Patsy and Conner followed. If so, why hadn't Morty reported back that both of them were now gainfully employed?

Charles dialed Morty's number, only to get an answering machine saying he was out of the office. Charles left a message explaining what he was planning to do then disconnected the call. His defective heart was lighter than it had been in a long time. Tonight, in his dreams, he'd have an extended conversation with Mary Beth.

* * * *

There wasn't much more Patsy could do until she heard back from Conner so she busied herself emptying the dishwasher and straightening up the kitchen. Since she'd bought hamburger buns, she took a large package of ground beef out of the freezer to make hamburgers for supper because that was one of the easy ideas from Grams.

At two o'clock, Luke still hadn't come back in the house so she thought she might as well vacuum the living room since it looked like it hadn't been done in a few weeks. But, when she heard Reggie barking, she decided instead that she'd better check on Luke and make sure he wasn't doing anything against doctor's orders, which would be so like him—Mr. Macho Man.

Patsy walked to the front window and watched as a pale blue Ford pickup came up the drive. It stopped in front of the barn, and Glen, Luke's brother, got out. Luke came out of the chicken coop, and they clapped each other on the shoulders. Glen stood back to examine Luke's bandaging.

Patsy couldn't hear their conversation, but it appeared to be genial so she went in search of the vacuum cleaner. She found it in the hall closet. Since she'd never run one before, she was glad Luke wasn't there to observe her ignorance again like the dishwasher episode. This was one thing she'd seen the maid doing, so it only took her a few minutes to figure out all the levers and have it humming—well, actually growling—to life.

This, she smiled to herself, was easy. All she had to do was push the silly thing around the room, and it did its job. While she worked, she thought about Glen Johnson. He seemed different than he did the other night. Could it be possible he was rude to her out of concern for his brother? She imagined how Conner would react if some guy, or anybody, tried to take advantage of *her*. Maybe Glen and Luke's brotherly bond was stronger than she'd first thought.

Deep in concentration, Patsy suddenly saw a shadow move across her path. She jumped back with a shriek, dropping the vacuum handle on the floor, its roar loudening as the whirling brush became exposed.

A beautiful blonde woman stood just inside the door, staring at her apologetically. "I'm sorry," she shouted over the noise. "I didn't mean to startle you. I knocked and..."

Patsy quickly picked up the noisy machine and hit the off switch. The sudden silence had her ears ringing, and she immediately jumped to the conclusion that this gorgeous female had to be one of Luke's followers.

"I'm so sorry," she was saying, "I knocked, but when I heard the vacuum, I decided to just walk in."

Humiliation flushed Patsy's cheeks at being caught doing menial housework. This was not a state of affairs she was familiar with and found herself momentarily speechless.

The pretty lady held out her hand. "I'm Peg Marsh, Darren's wife. The men are busy outside, and I just couldn't wait to meet you."

Patsy wiped her palm on her jeans before she accepted Peg's hand.

"Hi. I guess you know then that I'm Patsy Bartlett?"

Peg's smile broadened. "Do I ever know. Darren's been talking non-stop about Luke's new *cook*. I'm delighted to finally meet you. I hope I'm not interrupting your work."

"No. No I just finished. Besides," she added, "this work needs interrupting." She quickly picked up the vacuum cleaner, wheeled it over to the closet, and stuffed it inside, thinking she could figure out how to deal with the cord later.

"My gosh," Peg said. "You're even more attractive than Darren described."

Patsy automatically put up a hand to smooth back what she knew must be a wild hairdo. She made a snorting sound. "Yeah, right. I'm sure he had a good story to tell you about the redheaded bimbo who ran into a deer."

Peg laughed. It was a warm and friendly sound. "That's not what he said, at all. Do you have any coffee? I really want to get to know you."

"Come on, I'll put a pot on." Patsy led the way into the kitchen, taking strange pride in how spotless it was—and in the fact she knew how to make coffee.

Peg took a seat at the table and said. "Patsy, you must be some kind of a miracle worker. This is the first time in months I've seen Luke laugh—and with broken ribs to boot."

"Seriously?"

"Absolutely. He's been awfully depressed. When Darren told me what he'd done—bringing you here—I was worried about you, but Darren insisted you could hold your own against the formidable Luke McAlister."

That made Patsy throw back her head and laugh. "You know, that's exactly what I thought when Darren dropped me here."

Peg gave her a perceptive smile. "Darren has a bit of a rascal in him, but then, you've probably figured that out by now. Okay, now," she said, leaning forward. "Darren mentioned you might need some pointers on cooking. How can I help you?"

Patsy found Peg to be a delightful conversationalist. They sipped coffee and discussed simple, ordinary ideas Patsy found invaluable. When she told Peg about the pancake incident, she thought the woman was going to wet her pants she laughed so hard. Then Peg set her at ease by telling her about a few of the faux pas she'd made as a novice bride—like setting the stove on fire by getting the oil too hot while trying to fry chicken and making gravy that was so hot and greasy it melted a plastic bowl. Granted, Peg had been a lot younger than Patsy was now, but the experiences were no less humorous.

They were coming out of the small laundry room next to the pantry where Peg was showing her how to run the washer and dryer when the front door opened and two little boys burst in followed by Reggie with Luke, Darren, and Glen close behind.

"Hey, it smells like coffee in here," Glen said, heading straight for the kitchen where he set a basket of eggs and a jug of milk in the refrigerator.

Peg rounded up her two boys and introduced them to Patsy. "This is Scott," she said putting a hand on the oldest towhead. "He'll be five in a couple of months and this little guy"—she snagged the younger child to give him a hug— "just turned three. His name is Mark. Say hi to Patsy" she instructed.

Both boys mimicked her "hi" then went charging off to the newly vacuumed living room to wrestle with Reggie. Their dad had taken a place at the table, and Glen pulled three mugs from the cupboard.

Glen held up the nearly empty glass carafe to Patsy. "Hope you don't mind we're helping ourselves." He was so friendly Patsy didn't recognize him as the same man she'd seen just a couple of nights ago.

She shrugged. "Go ahead. I'll make some more." Before she could move, Luke, who had taken his usual seat at the head of the table, met her gaze. The look in his eyes was so intense it stole her breath. It was beyond appreciation, more like…sexual? A lightning bolt of heat spread from her face to her center core.

Quickly giving her brain a mental shake, she reminded herself she was about to make coffee. Flustered, she walked past Darren, caught his eye, and received a mischievous wink. It said he'd observed the exchange and was tickled with what he saw. "I'd prefer a beer," he said drolly. "Any chance you have one?"

Not only had Patsy's body responded to Luke's perusal, she was overcome by a warm homey feeling and a strange sense of pleasure at having all these people gathered in her kitchen.

Her kitchen? Now wouldn't that just shock the tailor-made money belt off of Charles Bartlett, aka, sugar daddy.

Luke tried to ignore the growing throb in his groin, which was bothering him more than his ribs, as he watched Patsy putter around the kitchen. For someone who didn't even know how to make coffee twenty-four hours ago, she certainly seemed to be at home there. Of course Peg was hovering over her like a mother hen, and since Peg pointed out Patsy had thawed enough meat to feed everyone, they decided to make supper— under Peg's guiding hand. She sent Darren out to start up the grill while the two women raided the pantry.

They came out with three large cans of baked beans and a couple of onions. While Peg opened the beans Patsy, tackled the onions. Apparently she was surprised that onions actually could make you cry, so she was snuffling and laughing at the same time. Peg turned to look at Luke with raised eyebrows, and he swore under his breath when he felt his face color. Then, he realized Glen had been talking to him.

"So who do you think messed with your ladder?" Glen was asking.

Luke forced his attention away from Peg and the sobbing sex kitten and forced himself to focus on his brother. "If I had to make a guess, I'd say it was Harvey."

"The sheriff?" Glen quipped nearly choking on his coffee. "Are you serious?"

Luke shrugged. "He's hated me since high school."

"Man. Luke, that's what? Sixteen years ago. Could he hold a grudge that long? I mean, granted, you aced him out of every sport you played but there comes a time to move on."

Luke shook his head. "I agree, but I just don't know who else would have the nerve to come in the yard and do something that's likely to kill me."

Darren came in and stepped into their conversation. "When's the last time you used that ladder, Luke?"

"Not since last fall, unless one of you used it while I was in Bismarck?"

Both men shook their heads.

"So…realistically anyone could have done it," Glen said. "Anyone who has a vendetta against you."

"Well, that narrows it down," Darren commented dryly. "It only covers half the county."

"You know," Glen reflected. "It could have been me up on that ladder; seems like I offered to help you fix that damn pulley."

While they talked, Patsy moved between them, setting plates and silverware around the table. When she finished, she stood back and put her hands on her hips. "I think you're all barking up the wrong tree. It's clear to me that whoever killed Kelsey set up that ladder because they don't want Luke digging into the truth."

Chapter Eleven

Morty Chambers gritted his teeth angrily when he listened to Charles' message. Charles must have talked to one of his irresponsible children and found out they were both employed. If they continued as they were, they'd easily make it through October. He could stall Charles for now by taking his time redoing the will, and if Charles became impatient, he'd have to do and not record it. In the meantime, the way Morty saw it, there were only two options. Either both Patsy and Conner had to lose their jobs or he had to make sure Charles Bartlett had an unexpected demise before November first.

He picked up his phone to call his men in the field.

* * * *

The following morning was Sunday. Dark clouds hung low, making it look like a dreary day was in store. Even after a refreshing shower, Patsy moved around the kitchen only half-awake, waiting for the coffee to brew. When Luke's phone rang, she glanced at the clock. It was eight-thirty, and he was certainly out doing his chores by now. Besides, wasn't answering the phone part of her job? She picked it up in the kitchen.

"Hello, Patsy. It's Conner."

Patsy's heart took a jump. He couldn't possible have researched Luke's case by now. "Conner? Is everything okay? Did you talk to Dad?"

"As a matter of fact, I did," Conner replied. "Dad said he had nothing to do with having us being followed. I believe him."

"Then who is?" Patsy asked, becoming more alarmed by the minute.

"He said he asked Morty to monitor our whereabouts and spending habits but told him specifically not to have us tailed. Dad said he'd talk to him."

Patsy was confused. "How was he monitoring us then?"

"In Dad's words," Conner explained, "cell phones, credit cards, and banking statements. And before you get bent out of shape over that, he mentioned he had access to all three since he's been paying our bills—like forever."

"Huh. No wonder he offered to keep paying for our cell phones."

"We both had the option of turning that down and getting our own phones."

Patsy made a rude sound. "Yeah, like that was going to happen with our measly allowance. So, Morty's been the one keeping tabs on us? I never did trust that man. He seems like such a weasel."

"I'll second that," Conner agreed. "Anyway, I also asked Dad if he was sick and he sidestepped the question saying we'd talk about that when he sees us presumably in the fall when our time is up. So whatever it is, it mustn't be too urgent."

"I hope not. I don't suppose you had time to look into any of the other stuff I was asking about."

Conner chuckled. "I have been a little busy. Debra invited me over for burgers last night."

"Oooh, lucky you. Anything interesting happen?"

"We had a very nice evening. She owns a cute little house on a cul-de-sac and has a big backyard with a garden and flowers. The woman has a marvelous green thumb. And that's all you need to know right now."

Patsy sighed. At least somebody was having a love life. She was happy for Conner but…"All right fine, I'm not interested in your love life anyway."

Conner laughed. "Liar, liar pants on fire. But, in answer to your other question, I haven't had a chance to read any of the media information or what was published in the papers, but I found out who is listed as the father on Betsy's birth certificate. His name is Jerome Parker. He lives in Bismarck. Get a pen, and I'll give you his address."

Patsy grabbed a pen and paper lying beside the phone and wrote down the address Conner repeated to her. She thanked him, and he hung up, promising to get to the murder case later in the day.

Patsy hung up the phone just as Luke walked in the front door, followed closely by Reggie.

"Did somebody call? I thought I heard the phone ring."

"How in the world could you hear the phone from outside?"

He shrugged. "There's an extension in the barn?"

"There's a phone in the barn?" she asked dubiously.

"Sure. So who called?"

"My computer connoisseur. And—are you ready for this?—he found out who Betsy's father is. His name is Jerome Parker and he lives in Bismarck."

He stared at her, brows drawn. "It was that easy?"

She grinned. "Yup, not much harder than running a dishwasher if you know what you're doing."

Shaking his head, he turned away, muttering and hiding what she believed was a smile. Maybe he was getting acclimated to her quirky sense of humor. Even Reggie looked at her either smiling or wondering if he was going to be fed soon, she couldn't tell which.

She went to the pantry, got a scoopful of whatever the unappetizing stuff was he ate and filled his dish. He licked her hand and dug into his food.

Luke stared at her a hint of disbelief on his face. "You're feeding the dog before me?"

"Yeah, he appreciates me more. You've never licked my hand."

He grunted good-naturedly. "Not going to happen either—not until I die and come back as a rattler." He glanced at the counter where she'd set out the eggs. "Looks like you have something in mind for breakfast. I'm ready to head out for Bismarck after we eat. You game?"

"Try to stop me."

He went to wash up, and she quickly put some bacon in the microwave then cracked half a dozen eggs into a bowl. Peg had told her how easy it was to scramble them. You just whisk, add a little salt, pepper, and milk, then pour the mixture into a hot skillet with oil and stir continuously. Of course, Peg didn't explain how to do it without getting half the shells in with the eggs or tell Patsy the trick to getting the shells out of the slimy mixture.

Luke came back and looked over her shoulder. "Hmm, smells good, and looks good, too."

He didn't add "surprisingly", but she could hear it in his tone. He laid one hand on the counter and leaned past her with the other to take down two plates, brushing her upper arm with his chest. An unexpected odd shock wave soared through her body at the touch. She quickly moved over to give him better access to the cupboard. Unfortunately, by the amused look he gave her, he knew exactly why she did it.

"Why is your arm out of the sling?" she demanded, hoping to mask her jittery nerves.

He'd set the plates on the table then went to the silverware drawer. "Doc said I could take it out once in a while as long as I wasn't doing anything strenuous."

"Are you sure?"

"Yes, Mummy, but as long as you're concerned, there's something I need help with."

She gave him a suspicious look, remembering the butt wiping conversation they'd had on the way home from the hospital.

He laughed, apparently reading her mind. "I need a shower," he clarified quickly. "Don't worry, I can take it by myself but I'll need help getting the rib belt back on."

Patsy dished most of the scrambled eggs into his plate then put the balance in hers. "No problem." She smiled sweetly. "That's what you're paying me for." She set the crisp bacon in front of him. "You are paying me, aren't you?"

* * * *

An hour later, they were on their way to Bismarck. Luke sat in the passenger seat, smelling of soap and a light scent of aftershave. She'd waited outside of his bathroom, pacing nervously. The thought of seeing him in a state of undress had her hands shaking. What was wrong with her? It wasn't like she'd never seen a naked man before.

When he'd finally come out of the bathroom, she realized she'd worried for nothing. He had his pants on. Well, of course he did. He'd been dressing himself since the accident. He would have had to use both hands, which he'd obviously been doing rather than ask for her help.

When she'd wrapped the belt around him, she couldn't avoid touching him, feeling the warmth of his skin. Why should touching this particular man have her hands shaking? It was ridiculous. Maybe what Luke had said was true. She knew how to dress provocatively, but she was inept at acting the part.

She'd lost her virginity during her senior year of high school. It had been a disastrous, unsatisfying event between two clumsy teenagers. After that, she'd pretty much sworn off sex. Then she'd met Gordon Mandrill. They'd dated almost a year before she slept with him. Gordy was an okay lover, but there was never anything emotional between them. For three years, they'd had gratifying sex, but that's all it was—sex—nothing more. His touch never made her tingle; his kisses never took her breath away. And whatever they did, whenever they ate out, he'd expected her to pick up the tab. Because her daddy could afford it, Gordy continuously reminded her.

Now, Patsy had an employer who made her tingle without even trying, and she could only imagine what a kiss from him would do to her. But she had promised herself that the next time she became intimate with a man it was going to be for love. She couldn't see herself falling in love with a North Dakota farmer who'd been more in love with his farm than his wife. Not to mention he'd expect his wife to live on his isolated farm. Not that he'd even consider marriage to a spoiled rich girl. Or at least she *would* be rich if she got her credit card paid off and stayed solvent until November first. She couldn't take a chance deviating from the rules because she had the feeling Morty Chambers would be on her like a mosquito looking for blood.

"I'll plug it into the GPS."

Luke's voice drew her from her thoughts, and she realized he'd been speaking to her.

He gave her a strange look. "Your mind must have been on that planet you came from."

She laughed. "As a matter of fact it was. Sorry, what were you saying to me?"

"I said it looks like it might rain any minute. If you have Parker's address, I'll plug it into the GPS, so we don't drive around in a downpour searching for it. Just what they need up here with all the flooding, more rain," he muttered more to himself than to her.

"Oh, yeah, sure, good idea. It's on that little slip of paper in the front pocket of my purse."

Luke found the address, punched it in, then asked, "What were you thinking about anyway. You seemed to be lost in space somewhere."

"I guess I was," she admitted. "Another time, another planet."

"Anything you want to share?"

"No nothing important."

He gave a frustrated sigh. "Trying to get you to talk about yourself is like drilling for oil in a dry well."

"My life is boring, nothing to tell."

Luke made a disparaging hiss. "Give me a break. You drop out of nowhere, driving a Maserati, looking for a job. And you want to convince me your life is boring? Throw into the mix that you drink coffee but don't know how to make it—or run a dishwasher. What are you hiding? Did you steal the car and are on the run from the law? Escaping from an abusive rich husband? What brought you here?"

Patsy had no intention of telling him about her wealthy father who threw his twenty-eight year-old spoiled, lazy brat of a daughter out of the house. But she felt she had to tell him something…preferably without lying too much.

"I didn't steal my car, and I've never been married."

"That car costs well over a hundred grand. How did you get it?"

She looked at the Garmin, hoping they were nearing their destination so his barrage of questions would end, but it was still another twelve miles.

"You guessed it right when you asked if I had a sugar daddy," she said, telling a half lie. After all, Charles Bartlett *was* her father. It was a stroke of luck on her part Luke wasn't computer savvy.

"And you left him to come to North Dakota and look up your grandmother?"

His tone suggested he didn't believe it for a minute, but let him speculate, she thought.

"Yes," she answered.

"What about your parents. Couldn't they help you?"

"My mother died when I was thirteen."

"Ouch. That's rough. And your father?"

Okay, here's where it gets dicey. She took a deep breath. "I guess you could say my father had already helped me as much as he was willing to. Besides, I hadn't seen my grandmother for a long time."

"You have any brothers or sisters?"

"Just a brother. He's a teacher," she added truthfully. "We better watch the turns here. It's only a couple of miles."

Luke nodded. "I can help watch. And thanks, Patsy. I appreciate everything you've told me."

She could tell he wasn't totally satisfied with her answers, and why would he be? She hadn't told him anything that explained why she was reluctant to talk about her life. If he asked about her employment history, how could she tell him she was educated but had never held down a job of any kind? Well, she'd walked dogs if that counted.

That sounded awful even to her. Funny, she'd never thought anything of it before. Before she'd become a cook, housekeeper, and nurse for Luke McAlister.

"There it is." Luke said. "The green apartment house with the brick front."

It was a modest four-plex in a well-kept neighborhood with lots of flowers and neatly trimmed shrubs. A gardener was busy trimming rose bushes on one side.

She stopped on the street in front. "You have a plan?" she asked.

"Hadn't thought about it. There's a good chance he'll recognize me and slam the door in my face. Any ideas?"

"Yeah, try not to scowl at him like you did at me."

"I didn't scowl at you," he muttered opening his door to get out.

She stepped out of the truck and started up the walk beside him. "Oh, yeah, what would you call it?"

"More like deep frowning. I just wanted you to go away."

"And if I had," she said, "you wouldn't be here now."

"Okay," he admitted. "Maybe I did scowl a little."

She laughed as they entered a large foyer. They found one stairway going down and another up. Each seemed to lead to two separate apartments.

Luke looked at the mailboxes. "Huh, Jerome Parker is listed as the owner. He's in 201, upper left the way it looks." They mounted the stairs together. Luke and Patsy exchanged a glance before he rang the bell. When there was no answer, Luke rang it a second time then rapped his knuckles on the door.

From inside, they heard a man's voice. "Hold on, I'm coming."

Luke felt his heart rise to his throat. What if the girls where here? That didn't seem quite possible, but he still couldn't help but hope. Whatever else, at least he'd know they were alive.

He tried his best not to scowl as the door swung open. A man in his late thirties, wearing a sweat suit and slippers faced Luke. It took him a moment to realize the man was leaning heavily on a cane. About that same time, Jerome Parker recognized Luke.

"What are you doing here?" Parker sneered. "Haven't you done enough?"

Before Luke could fire back a retort, Patsy stepped in front of him, barring the door from being closed. "Mr. Parker, Luke didn't kill Kelsey or the girls. In fact, we have reason to believe they're still alive, and that's why we're here."

Parker stared at her as though she might be insane. "They're dead," he ground out bitterly. "They're all dead, and he killed them." He jerked his head toward Luke.

"What if they aren't?" Patsy said. "Can you at least entertain that possibility and hear what we have to say?"

"Who the hell are you?" Parker asked, glaring at Patsy.

Patsy held out her left hand, obviously in deference to Parker gripping the cane with his right hand. "Patsy Bartlett. I'm helping Luke investigate the disappearance of Betsy and Lola."

Suddenly, Luke had the horrible thought that maybe Patsy was a legitimate investigator, planted in his home to observe him.

Parker shook her hand and glowered at Luke, his gaze flicking over Luke's arm anchored to the rib belt as though noticing it for the first time. He stepped aside and allowed them to enter then closed the door behind them. That was when Luke noticed the wheelchair sitting against the wall behind the door. The glance Patsy gave him said she'd seen it, too.

Luke figured Patsy was wondering, as he was what kind of injury Jerome Parker had and did it have anything to do with Kelsey's death. On the other hand, if Jerome had been responsible for her death and the disappearance of the girls, why would he have let them in? Perhaps out of curiosity to see what they knew.

Luke made a quick perusal of the apartment, looking for any evidence of children. Seeing nothing that indicated it was anything other than a bachelor pad, he took a seat on the sofa beside Patsy. Parker sat in a well-worn recliner directly in front of the television. He turned to face them.

Luke didn't have a clue how Patsy intended to handle the situation so he decided to just let her go with it. She was, after all, by her own admission, *the investigator.*

She dug a pen and miniscule pad of paper from her purse. From Parker's vantage point, he couldn't have known it had an emblem of Porky Pig on it. She took a fortifying breath.

"Mr. Parker, I understand Kelsey brought your daughter up here to see you once a month."

Parker's gaze shifted from Patsy to Luke and back again. For the first time, he looked nervous. "How do you know that?" Parker asked.

Patsy pretended to scribble something on her pad, when in fact she'd drawn a smiley face. "That's not important. What is important is how much child support you were paying her. I could find that out by subpoenaing your records, but it would be a lot easier if you just told me."

Parker made light of it. "That's not exactly top-secret information. I'm surprised you don't already know."

"Like I said, I haven't looked into it yet. I was hoping you could just tell me."

"Betsy got six hundred dollars a month through my disability insurance."

Luke sat beside Patsy, trying not to look dumbfounded. He wanted to ask how Betsy was getting the money since he never saw any checks coming in the mail at the farm but he thought it best to let the *investigator* ask the questions.

"So," Patsy went on, "the checks came to you here, and Kelsey just picked them up once a month."

Parker took a sip of water from a bottle on the table beside him. "Yes." Tears suddenly flooded his eyes. "Betsy was such a delightful child. I can't tell you how much I miss her. When she lived here in Bismarck I got to see her two, three times a month—until Kelsey married *him.*" His moist gaze zeroed in on Luke.

"Tell me, Mr. Parker, why didn't you just have the checks sent to her home?"

"Two reasons. First, it forced her to come up here, and second, she told me *he* would take the money and squander it on the farm."

Moving forward, Luke opened his mouth to protest but Patsy snaked a firm hand to his thigh, signaling him to stay put and keep silent.

"Luke, you'll get your chance to talk. Right now, I'm speaking to Mr. Parker."

Luke took a deep, steadying breath and sat back, wishing at this moment he could get his hands around his dead wife's throat. He nodded, his admiration—and consternation— for his *investigator* growing. *Was* she really a lawyer like Sheriff Wilson had suggested when she accused him of contaminating evidence by touching the ladder? A slow irritation had begun to gnaw at his stomach. Granted, he wanted to know the answers to all the questions she asked, but the more professional she sounded, the more the knot in his belly tightened.

Obviously satisfied that he'd behave, Patsy continued, "Mr. Parker, this is off the record, and you're under no obligation to answer, but why didn't you marry Kelsey when she became pregnant with your child?"

Parker's gaze darted to the wheelchair, and he took what appeared to be a painful breath. "We were going to be married until I was diagnosed with an aggressive form of multiple sclerosis. She didn't want to be married to an invalid."

"I'm sorry," Patsy said. "Life can be so unfair. I'm glad she made it possible for you to continue a relationship with your daughter."

"I know now," Parker said, a bitter edge to his voice "it was only the money she wanted."

"Then you really don't believe Luke would have taken the money from Betsy?"

Parker stared at the blank TV screen. "No. It's what she wanted me to believe, and I let her because that meant she'd come to see me once a month."

Patsy looked down at her notepad then up at Parker again. "I hope you understand that Luke couldn't have killed her. He was released because the autopsy proved she died before he got home that night."

Luke was amazed at all the things Patsy remembered. If he couldn't see her blank note pad, he would have believed she was reading from it.

Parker visibly swallowed thickly. "I guess it was easier if I had someone to blame."

"Good, then let's get down to figuring out who did kill her and abduct the girls."

Parkers head shot up. "You really believe they're still alive?"

"Yes, we do. Now, do you know who Lola's father is?"

Parker rubbed his fingers in his eyes, massaging the sockets. "When Lola was born Kelsey tried to talk me into acknowledging her as my child, so she could get more money. That's why she put father unknown on the birth certificate—in hopes that I'd eventually change my mind."

"Is there any chance she is yours?" Patsy asked.

Parker gave a bitter laugh. "No, not with all the medication I'm on. And I don't believe for a minute that she didn't know who he was because I knew she was meeting a guy when she was up here. Especially since she'd leave Betsy with me and take Lola with her. She'd often be gone for several hours." He glanced almost sympathetically at Luke. "My senses are extremely acute since my illness. When she came back, I could smell…sex on her."

It was Luke's turn to grimace. "It sounds she was involved with him before she met me. Why didn't she marry him instead of me?"

Patsy shot him a concerned glance. "Maybe he was already married," she suggested then turned back to Parker. "I guess we can assume then, that since she took Lola along, Kelsey was meeting Lola's father."

"That's what I suspected. However, sometimes, Lola didn't come with her, and Kelsey still left and came back smelling the same way. I took a perverse amount of joy from those encounters. I knew she was married, and I was glad she was screwing around on him—" he indicated Luke—"because I was green with envy. God help me I never stopped loving the witch." He was silent for a moment then said, "Do you suspect it was Lola's father who murdered her and he might have the girls?" For the first time, there was a trace of hope in his voice.

Patsy glanced at Luke. "What do you think?"

"That sounds like the best possibility. But how do we find out who it is?"

Patsy turned back to Parker. "Did either Lola or Betsy ever give any hint of who she was seeing?"

"I'm not proud of it," Parker admitted, "but I did question Betsy once."

"What did she say?" Luke asked anxiously.

"Nothing that made sense to me," Parker said. "I can't even remember what it was. Something like Undygen or Umpygen. As I'm sure you know Betsy had a hard time pronouncing Ls. Even with that in mind, it just didn't ring any bells for me."

For the first time, Patsy actually jotted something down on her pad. Luke noticed she'd written *Undygen* and *Umpygen* as they sounded when Parker had said them. Might be important, he thought absently, but it also could be a child's babbling.

"What gave you the idea that the girls were still alive?" Parker asked Luke. "Tell me please, so I can be as enthusiastic about this as you are."

Luke told him about the missing rabbit and Betsy's adamancy about never going anywhere without it. He explained that he understood it was a weak theory but since no bodies had been found...

Parker's weary face brightened. "It's true. She was always clutching that stuffed rabbit. It gave me a cheap thrill because I bought it for her when she was born."

Patsy gave him a sad smile. "And it seems she treasured it."

Parker returned the smile, then his thin shoulders sagged, and he wiped a hand over his eyes. "I was there in the room with them during her birth," he said. "She was the cutest little peanut you ever saw…" His voice trailed off and he stared into space as if lost in a happier time.

Patsy nudged Luke's knee, and he nodded. It was time for them to go.

"Thanks for your help," Luke said, getting to his feet. Patsy followed suit.

"Thank you both for coming," Parker said. He handed Patsy a card he picked up from the end table beside him. "If you have any other questions or you learn something new, please call me."

Patsy quickly scribbled Luke's name and phone number on a sheet from her little pad and laid it on the table beside him. "Likewise. If you think of anything you may have missed that could help us with our investigation, please don't hesitate to contact us."

Parker asked if they wouldn't mind seeing themselves out as he needed to take his medication and go lie down.

Patsy thought the interview went quite well, but as they walked to the pickup in total silence, she began to wonder what she'd done wrong. She hadn't expected raving thanks for her efforts—well, maybe she did—but Luke's silence was unnerving and annoying. He was clearly agitated about something. Possibly because she hadn't allowed him to talk? She couldn't have, though; he was too hot headed.

They both got in the pickup, slamming their doors simultaneously. If there was one thing she couldn't tolerate it was silent treatment.

"All right, what the hell is bugging you?" she snapped. "I thought it went very well in there."

His head swiveled, and his glare pinned her with hostility. "Tell me the truth. There's no sugar daddy, is there? You're a high-buck attorney, aren't you? All I want to know is who hired you to spy on me?"

For a moment, she stared at him, speechless, trying to absorb his ludicrous accusation. The realization of what he was saying finally hit her. In his off-handed, ridiculous way, he was complimenting her.

So that he'd grasped the absurdity of what he was suggesting, she wanted to inform him she'd never held down any kind of a job in her life. Not counting , of course, walking dogs when she was thirteen. But, right now, that was far more information than she wanted to share.

If Luke hadn't looked so serious, and furious, she would have burst out laughing. As it was she had to struggle to contain herself.

"Luke. Think about it. If I was coming to North Dakota to spy on you by pretending to be a cook, don't you think I'd have learned how to cook first? And did I plan to hit a deer in front of Darren so he could drive me out to your house? Would I drive a Maserati to apply for your menial job and then deliberately smash it just so I could meet you?"

He stared at her a long time. Then, the anger slowly left his face and was replaced by a sheepish grin.

"Sorry," he said. "You were just so damn good in there. I guess it was when you threatened to subpoena his records to find out how much child support he paid. Hell, I didn't even know you could do that."

Patsy laughed. "Neither did I."

"You were bluffing?"

"All the way. My expertise comes from watching a lot of cop shows. Oh, and Harry's Law, my all-time favorite."

"Incredible. You had me so convinced I wanted to throttle you. Poor Mr. Parker didn't have a chance."

Patsy started the truck and pulled away from the building. "I can't believe you fell for it."

"Probably because there are so many things about you I don't know. Let's go find someplace to eat. It's a long shot, but I'd like to check those names Parker gave us in the Bismarck phone book. There can't be that many starting with Un or Um."

Large drops of rain splattered the windshield as she pulled into an Olive Garden parking lot. They dashed inside, just ahead of a downpour.

After they were seated, served iced tea, and placed their orders, Luke went in search of a phone book. When he returned, he started flipping through the pages. It only took him a moment to locate the one page he was looking for. He tore it then shoved the book aside. "I'll check these later but it doesn't look promising."

"I've been thinking," Patsy said, sipping her tea. "You told me you asked Betsy once what they did in Bismarck. and she said it was a secret. Why didn't you press her for more information?"

Luke poured two packets of sugar in his tea, and took his time stirring it. "This may sound crazy, but I trusted Kelsey. Besides, she always took at least one of the girls along. I had no reason to be suspicious."

"You didn't mind that she went up there once a month."

"No. She was a city girl, and I knew she missed it. Her monthly trip was a small concession. I thought, if it makes her happy," he shrugged, "why not?"

"I'm curious; did you ever offer to go along?"

"Only once. It was a rainy day, kind of like this, and I didn't have any work I could do so I suggested I could tag along…"

"And?" Patsy prompted when he didn't continue."

"She insisted it was her alone time with the girls. I never asked again."

"You have any idea what she did with the six hundred dollars a month she got from Parker?"

He shook his head. "No, I don't. She wasn't necessarily a spendthrift. I gave her anything she asked for, which wasn't a whole lot. I wonder now if she was squirreling it away so she'd have a nest egg when she left me."

"But wouldn't it have shown up after she died?" Patsy asked.

"No unfamiliar bank statements ever came, or any other suspicious mail, for that matter. Most of the time, I picked it up because the mailbox is at the end of the drive."

"Huh." Patsy thought a moment, trying to figure out what Kelsey could have done with it. "There could have been more, too," she said. "What if she was also getting money from Lola's father?"

Luke took a moment to think about that. "Holy crap. And if he was married, like you speculated, he might have paid her in cash."

"Let's see," Patsy said, calculating in her head. "You were married almost three years at approximately a thousand a month, maybe more, she could have accumulated in excess of thirty-five thousand dollars if she saved it all. Is it possible it's hidden around the house someplace?"

"Wow, is your real name Nancy Drew? You have an unusually cunning mind."

Patsy grinned. "Possible my only asset."

The waitress appeared with their meals, asked if they needed anything else, then quickly disappeared.

Luke slathered a wad of soft butter on a bread stick. "Dang, this looks good."

Patsy agreed. She hadn't realized how hungry she was, especially for something she didn't have to prepare. It was the first time she could remember that she actually appreciated eating out.

"In answer to your question," Luke said, taking a bite of his a breadstick, "I didn't find the money when I searched for Betsy's rabbit, but I didn't necessarily look for something that was deliberately hidden. So there's a good chance it could be there somewhere. Especially since, to my knowledge, she never made any unexplained extravagant purchases. On the other hand, she was packing up to leave that night so she might have had it on her."

Patsy made an oohing sound as she forked Fettuccini Alfredo in her mouth. Between bites, she said, "Maybe we should do a complete search of the house when we get home. If it's not there, we can assume the killer has it. And, if we're also assuming the killer is Lola's father, tracking him down is our next step?"

"That's a big step," Luke said with a deep sigh.

"You said you believed Sherriff Wilson was your main suspect in tampering with your ladder. That adds up, because when I was in looking at my car, the kids were bantering back and forth. One of them accused Gabe—he's

Wilson's son right?" When Luke nodded, she went on. "He taunted Gabe by saying that most of the kids in the next county were his half brothers and sisters. That makes him a known philanderer."

"I can give you another little tidbit to gnaw on," Luke said enthusiastically. "I just remembered Wilson owns a house he inherited from his dad on the Missouri river less than ten miles north of Bismarck. It's on a bluff, high enough so it's not in danger of flooding."

Patsy stopped chewing and stared at him. "For real?"

Luke nodded. "Yup."

"Okay," she said quickly. "How tight are you with Doc Flanders?"

Luke shrugged. "We're good friends. Why?"

"You said there was blood on the sheets in the girl's room. If we could get our hands on Lola's blood type, et cetera, maybe we could also get something from the sheriff and have Flanders compare the two."

"How do we get Wilson to give a blood sample? Ask nicely?"

Patsy licked the sauce off her fork and waved it at him, her eyes narrowed. "With all those illegitimate kids he's supposed to have, at least one of them must have filed a paternity suit."

Luke gave her a long look. "You're starting to worry me."

Chapter Twelve

By the time they'd picked up a few groceries, including a frozen pizza for supper, and got home, the rain had slowed to a drizzle. Patsy noticed Luke looked drained. He'd taken his arm out of the sling to eat, and she could tell by the sounds he tried to suppress that it was giving him some trouble. No sense telling him to take a pain pill, he'd just tell her to quit mothering him. He had his eyes closed, but when she turned into the drive, he opened them.

"Can you stop and pick up the mail?" he asked.

"It's Sunday," she reminded him.

"I know, but I haven't picked it up for two days. Just pull up close to the box; you even don't have to get out."

She did as he asked, pulled a huge stack of magazines, letters and what looked like junk mail out of the big box, and slid it across the seat to him. She then drove up the drive and stopped in front of the house.

"You go on in," she said. "I'll bring the bags." She expected Mr. Macho to argue but he let himself out of the truck and trudged up to the house, carrying his mail under his injured arm.

Patsy hopped out, grabbed a couple of bags from the rear seat, and hurried after him. He held the door for her, giving her a grateful smile.

"I'm going to go gather the eggs then take a short rest before supper. You okay for a while?"

Patsy walked past him, laughing. "Of course. In fact, let me get the eggs. I did it at Grandpa's place all the time."

She set her bags on the counter and started to put the frozen and refrigerated items away. He'd followed her into the kitchen, dropped his mail on the table then went to help her.

"Did I ever tell you I knew Hank Summers?" he said as they worked.

"No, you didn't," she said, turning to stare at him. "I'm certainly anxious to hear that story. Let me get the rest of the bags in before it starts raining again, then you can tell me about it."

"You need some help?" he asked.

She was already at the door. "No, I got it, thanks," she called over her shoulder.

He was sitting at the table, sorting his mail, when she came back in with the last two bags. She quickly put the rest of the things in the pantry then took a chair across from him. "Okay, now tell me how you knew Grandpa Hank."

He was staring at a small envelope, his brow creased into a frown. "This has your name on it," he said, passing it across the table to her.

"This didn't come in the mail," she said, examining the curious envelope. "All it has is *Patsy* scribbled across it."

"Obviously, somebody besides the mail man put it in there."

She reached for a knife from the rack on the counter and carefully slit the edge open. Inside was single folded sheet of unlined paper. It held one line of type it. Her heart slammed into an adrenalin rush as she read.

Leave now before you become his next victim.

"What does it say?" he asked quickly.

Numbly, she handed it to him. After reading it, he looked up at her, swearing. "This is a sick joke. Why can't people just leave it be?"

Initially shaken, Patsy now felt the same anger Luke did. "When do you think it was delivered?"

"It was in the middle of the pile, but it must have been today when we were gone. We can see the mailbox from the house so nobody would take chance putting it there while we were home."

"Unless it was done at night," she said.

"I'm calling Darren. Any car coming from Ashville has to come directly by his house."

He picked up the phone, dialed the number. One of the kids must have answered the phone because he asked to talk to their father. Moments later, he was asking Darren if he'd seen any cars on the road today. Frustrated with the one-sided conversation, Patsy raced to the bathroom. By the time she returned, he'd hung up.

She waited expectantly for him to tell her what he'd learned.

"Darren was gone yesterday all day but, this morning, he was out mowing his front yard before the rain hit. Given the size of it, even with his rider, it takes him about three hours. In that time, he saw four vehicles go by. One of them was Pete Cadowa, an old guy who lives with his off-the-wall wife Terry. He drives an old Buick, and their farm is directly on the other side of my property. The other three cars all returned within a few minutes, going back into town the way they came. One was the sheriff's cruiser."

"Any chance he noticed any of them stopping at your mailbox."

"He can't see the mailbox or my driveway because his trees block the view. Oh, but he was mowing the ditch when one went by, and he was close enough to notice it had a Minnesota license plate. Said the driver was ugly as sin."

Ben Fontaine! Patsy's heart suddenly slammed against her ribcage. She quickly took a deep breath and forced herself to remain calm.

Luke stared at her, his brow furrowing. "Sound like anybody you know?"

"Nope, I don't know anyone who looks like that." *Okay, so she knew his name but she really didn't know him.* She needed to talk to Conner. See what he'd found out.

"Not your sugar daddy?" Luke persisted.

Patsy forced out a laugh. "Ugly as sin? I don't think so."

"Is he having you followed?"

Patsy threw her hands on her hips. She had to end this train wreck quickly before she had to start inventing lies. "Look, he pretty much threw me out. I can't think of any reason he'd want to have me followed. Now can we get back—"

"He threw *you* out?"

"Didn't I just say that?" When he opened his mouth to say more, she stopped him. "I don't want to talk about him. Let's get back to this note." She waved the piece of paper in front of him. "I think you should call Doc Flanders and see if he'll come out here. I have a feeling he'd jump at the chance to check us out."

"There is no *us*." Luke said dryly. He stretched his back and rubbed a hand over his rib cage, visibly gritting his teeth and releasing a hiss of air at the same time.

He was obviously in pain from riding in the pickup and being active all day, but she knew better than to tell him to take a pill or lay down. "I know that, but Flanders seemed to think there should be. Ask him nicely to come visit, and when he gets here, we'll lay our plan him."

Luke nodded. "I guess you're right. Especially since we know Wilson was in the area this morning. He had a perfect opportunity to slip that note in with the rest of the mail."

"Darren didn't know who owned the third car, did he?" she questioned.

"Nope, said he was adjusting the mower blade to do the ditch when they went by."

Patsy's head shot up. "They?"

"Yeah, there was at least one passenger. It was a beat up old junker the way he described it. He mentioned it went by right after the Minnesota car and came back after it too."

She got up and poured some cold coffee leftover from breakfast in a cup then popped it in the microwave, ignoring Luke's frown. "Is this road a dead end?" she asked.

"No, it comes out on a gravel road that intersects with the highway going north to the small towns between Bismarck and Jamestown. It's in such bad repair and often under water, so it's rarely used except by farmers that live along here. Besides Cramdon, there are three others, plus Darren and me."

"So, someone could come that way and go back the same way without passing Darren's place."

"Yup. Even if there's water on the road, a four-wheel drive could probably get through."

Patsy heaved a heavy sigh. "I hate to say this but wouldn't it be awfully gutsy of the sheriff to come up this road in his patrol car, then blatantly drop a note in your mailbox and drive back out?"

"Our esteemed sheriff is well known for having more guts than sense."

Patsy had already come to that same conclusion. "Too bad we don't know who was driving the other car. They might have seen something."

"Yeah, and they might just have been the ones who put the note in there. There's too many people around, like Gertie, who'd like to see me doing prison time. And who knows, that note could even come from a do-gooder who thinks you're in danger here. It wasn't really a threat, more like a warning to get away from me."

"I'd still feel better if I knew who did it," Patsy said, glancing out the window when she heard a roll of thunder. "Oh well, I'm going to go get the eggs before it starts raining again. You have at least an hour before I put the pizza in the oven. If you want to sit back and rest, now's your chance. You're starting to look a little drained around the edges."

"I might just do that. By the way, there are plastic pails inside the door for eggs. I only have fifteen laying hens, but they lay enough eggs to supply the entire neighborhood including Glen. There's also a big metal trash can in there with food. If you could give them a bucketful I'd appreciate it. And I'm sure the chickens will, too," he added, chuckling. "I suppose we should talk about your salary sometime soon."

"Oh that'd be good," she said, heading for the door. "I hope I get extra pay for feeding chickens. I don't think that was bought up in your ad." She didn't mention that she had a Visa bill coming due and a thousand-dollar deductible on her car to pay.

She headed for the door then thought of something. With Reggie close on her heels, she stopped and turned around to ask Luke about water for the chickens. He had swiveled in his chair to watch her leave, except his gaze was fixed on her backside. When he realized she'd stopped, he quickly met her eyes, a rosy hue coloring his cheeks. Forgetting about the water, she smiled and walked out, presenting him with her little butt-wiggle display.

Halfway to the hen house, she commented to Reggie about how unique it was to see a man blush. When Reggie looked up at her with soulful sad eyes, she quickly chastised herself for enticing Luke. After all, when her three months were up, she'd be heading back to her life in Minneapolis.

Somehow, that idea wasn't as appealing as it had once been. Spending time here on the farm brought back a lot of happy memories from summers with Grandpa Hank and Grams. She hated to admit it, but she'd miss this place— and Luke— when she left. She frowned down at Reggie. "I'll even miss you, you wise-assed mutt."

Luke swore at himself for getting caught lusting after Patsy. Hell, he'd been hard all day, but he'd managed to behave himself. Even when he was accusing her of being a spy, he wanted to grab her, throw down on the seat and... Damn, what was wrong with him? He was acting like a randy teenager. She was poison—a sassy, good-looking woman who'd been catered to by a rich bastard who'd bought her expensive toys and probably indulged her in every little whim.

Luke couldn't begin to compete with that, and he had no intention of trying. She definitely wasn't his type, too much like Kelsey. But, in most ways, she wasn't like Kelsey at all. Kelsey wouldn't have been caught dead walking in the chicken coop. As far as she was concerned, you could buy eggs in the market. Why bother having chickens? He'd had to build a fence for them because she was afraid of the rooster.

Besides, he was certain as soon as her car was done, Patsy Bartlett would disappear from his life, never to be heard from again. Sighing, he got up and walking into the living room to his recliner. It was a lot less stress on his ribs if he relaxed in that—and easier to get up. Every morning, he'd gritted his teeth in pain just getting out of bed.

That thought served as a reminder that it would be some time before he'd be able to make love to a woman anyway, so why fantasize about it? Oh, but she'd be one hell of a ride, of that he was certain.

Trying to picture Patsy naked, he'd barely closed his eyes when she burst in the door screaming his name.

"Luke! Luke! The chickens!"

He charged to his feet so suddenly a river of pain shot through his midsection. For several seconds, he doubled over, gasping, trying to get his breath.

Patsy rushed up to him, her eyes wide first with fear then with concern. "Oh, my God, Luke? I'm sorry. Are you okay?"

Hell no. "Yeah…give…me…a sec."

"Sorry, I shouldn't have rushed in here like that. It's just that the chickens—" She stopped, obviously waiting for him to catch his breath.

He finally drew a deep breath and straightened. "Okay, I'm good. What's wrong with the chickens? Did one bite you?"

She looked at him, frowning. "No. They're sick or something. I think they're dying."

That got his attention. "Are you sure? Maybe they're just sleeping."

She gave him an exasperated look. "Luke, I may not know how to make coffee, but I do know the difference between a sick chicken and a sleeping one."

She actually had tears in her eyes—for chickens. This woman was definitely not Kelsey. "Let's go take a look."

She preceded him out the door and quickly led the way to the chicken coop. Once inside, Luke saw immediately that there was definitely something wrong. All the hens were sitting on the straw covered ground, heads drooping and looking basically lifeless. They were alive, but, just as she'd said, very sick.

He nudged one of the hens, and she got up and moved but only an inch or so. "This didn't happen on its own," he muttered angrily.

"You think somebody poisoned them?" Patsy asked, her voice husky.

"That would be my guess. Let's get a sample of their water then dump it and put in fresh."

Patsy grabbed one of the pails while he lifted the cover off the five-gallon metal water receptacle. He scooped half a bucketful out, handed it back to her then, with one hand, lifted the nearly empty container and carried it outside where he dumped it in the yard.

Patsy set her pail down, sternly warned Reggie to stay away from it, then walked outside the fence and turned the water on to the hose. Luke washed the watering can before carrying it back inside where he used the hose to refill it. They worked together in silence, and Luke was amazed to observe Patsy helping as though she knew exactly what he was thinking. When the water was nearing the top, she went out and switched the hose off.

She came back in and went straight to the feed can, got a bucketful of pellets, and filled the empty trough. As she did, she made little clucking sounds as though calling the sick birds to come and eat. Luke smiled, thinking she must have learned that from her grandfather. When a couple of hens wobbled to their feet and came forward, she looked up at him optimistically.

"Do you think they'll be all right?" she asked.

He shook his head. "All we can do is wait and see. With a little luck, some of them might make it."

When two hens that had been nesting jumped down and hurried over to the trough, he was convinced the water *had* been poisoned.

"Those two mustn't have drunk the water yet," Patsy said voicing his thoughts. "Who would do such a thing?"

Luke gritted his teeth. "The same person who fixed the ladder and left you a nasty note."

"Lola's father," Patsy said emphatically, brushing the tears from her eyes.

Meaning only to comfort her, Luke put his fingertips under her chin and tipped her face up. Her soft and pouty lips did him in. He lowered his head and kissed her. He wasn't holding her, so she could have back away, but instead, she reached up, put her arms around his neck, and leaned into him, not only accepting the kiss but encouraging it to continue.

When he lifted his head, she backed away and looked up at him. "What was that for?" she whispered, her voice low and throaty.

He gave her the only reasonable explanation that came to mind. "For caring about my chickens."

* * * *

Patsy stared out the moonlit window, unable to sleep. She shouldn't have let Luke kiss her, or more importantly, she shouldn't have kissed him back. If they got involved, things could get sticky when it was time for her to leave. Just when everything seemed to be going along so smoothly, he had to go ahead and ruin it. In spite of a rocky start, they'd even managed to develop a camaraderie, working together to find his missing girls.

That kiss did not fit into the equation. But why, she reflected, did he taste so damn good? And feel so right at the time? Her body had responded with a will of its own. Even now, after a cold shower, she wanted to march up to his room and demand he finish what he'd started.

She'd been so distracted she hadn't managed to call Conner. She didn't want to do it within earshot of Luke, and damned if she was going to stand out in the middle of the yard in the dark where her cell phone may or may not work. Especially when there was some crazy note writer, chicken poisoner, lurking about. That bought her mind back to Ben Fontaine. Could he have given her that note— and would he poison the chickens. If so…why? That was assuming there weren't two crazy people out there. She'd definitely call Conner first thing tomorrow. Maybe he'd found out who Fontaine was working for and if he was really following Patsy. Maybe he was someone hired to keep an eye on Luke and had nothing to do with her at all. But then, why would someone also be following Conner?

One thing she was sure of—that sheriff wouldn't hesitate to kill a few chickens to make some kind of a sick point. Lord, as much as she wanted to solve this case and find those girls alive, she sincerely hoped that reprobate wasn't Lola's father.

She leaned up on her elbow, punched her pillow and glanced at the green glowing clock on the nightstand. It was after midnight. Groaning, she pressed her face into the pillow, trying to think of something positive.

After supper they'd walked back out to the hen house to check the chickens—only three hens had died. She supposed that was somewhat positive.

Chapter Thirteen

Patsy awoke in a panic. It was almost nine o'clock. Dang, she was going to call Conner before he went to his class and before Luke came in from his usual morning chores, whatever they were. The wonderful aroma of coffee told her Luke was already in the kitchen. She hopped out of bed, dressed quickly, and headed up the short stairs.

"Good morning," Luke said from where he sat at the table, cradling a large mug in both hands—he wasn't using the brace, she noted. She also noticed his wind-blown dark hair and ruggedly handsome face. He looked more like a pirate standing on the deck of a ship, ready to wield a sword, than a farmer who handled a pitchfork. His inquisitive gray eyes followed her into the kitchen.

He was uncomfortably cheerful, she thought, wishing he'd turn back into his normal self so she could forget about that damnable kiss, the memory of which had kept her up half the night. She grunted a reply as she grabbed a cup and filled it.

"Flanders will be here in a little over an hour," he informed her.

"Well, that was quick," she said, trying to decide what they would have for breakfast. Maybe pancakes, she thought nastily. That would pull him out of his cheerful mood.

"The only free time he had was this morning. I explained what we needed from him, and he seemed to think he could help. Oh, you had a phone call from a kid who said he wanted you to call him. He didn't tell me his name, but his number's on the pad by the phone."

Patsy's heart skipped a beat. That had to be David, being secretive. He must have news to report about Fontaine. She didn't want Luke to hear her conversation with David. After breakfast, if Luke was still in the house, she'd go outside in the yard and see if her cell worked. Right now, the less importance she put on the call, the less likely he would be to ask about it. "I'll give him a call later after I decide what to do about breakfast."

"Sounded like he was pretty anxious to talk to you," Luke said, then added with a hint of humor. "I'd say you have an admirer."

Patsy rolled her eyes. "Just what I need, a fourteen-year-old heartthrob. How about scrambled eggs?" she asked. "We have a lot of eggs."

"Good idea. By the way, we lost two more chickens during the night. The rest appear to be back to normal. I guess that's not too bad. If you hadn't gone out there when you did, we'd have lost them all."

Patsy took the eggs out and started cracking them into a bowl. Luke's reference to "we" was both bothersome and endearing. She didn't want to be a *we* or an *us*, since she had no intentions of spending the rest of her life as a recluse on a North Dakota farm. Not that there was any chance of that happening.

After breakfast, she got her chance to call David and Conner when Luke said he had some bills to pay while he waited for Flanders to arrive. When he went into his office, Patsy grabbed her cell phone and headed outside. She had to walk around the yard and finally end up in front of the chicken coop to get her phone to work.

It was the wrong time of day to call Conner on a Monday, and there weren't any messages from him so she punched in David's number. A woman answered. Patsy assumed was his mother, so Patsy asked for him doing her best to sound like a teenager. David came on the line shortly.

"Hello this is David."

"Hi, it's Patsy. Luke said you called earlier."

"Oh yeah. I got good stuff for you. Yesterday, your guy, Fontaine, took a drive out of town. I was cruising around with my friend LeRoy—he's old enough to drive—anyway, we followed him, and he drove right out by Luke's place."

"Did he go into the farmyard?" she asked quickly.

"I don't know. When he stopped at your approach, we had to drive past so he wouldn't know we were following him. We waited about ten minutes then doubled back, and he was just leaving. He drove straight into town and was talking on his cell phone the whole way."

"You didn't see him put anything in Luke's mailbox, did you?"

"Not while we were watching, but we couldn't see what he was doing after we got by him a ways."

Patsy's heart sank. He wasn't giving her any information she didn't already know. Obviously, their car was the old junker with two people in it that Darren saw. "Did you see any other cars on that road?"

"Yeah, a Blazer came up from the back way, after we were turned around. It stopped beside the road about a quarter of a mile behind us and didn't move again, at least not that we could see."

What had Luke said? Only a vehicle with a four-wheel drive could maneuver that water-covered road. Wasn't a Blazer a four-wheel drive? She asked David, and he confirmed it was. "Did you recognize who was driving?" she asked.

"Nope. Too far away. But it was looked like it was gray."

Patsy thanked him and asked him to keep an eye out for the vehicle and see who drove it. She ended the call just as Glen's blue Ford pickup pulled into the yard.

He parked as before, in front of the barn, got out, and walked toward her, smiling.

"Hi, Patsy," he called. "How's my big brother getting along?"

Patsy hadn't really noticed before how much Glen resembled Luke—at least from a distance—especially the disarming smile and gray eyes, although Glen's were a little darker. Since they had different fathers, they must both take after their mother, she decided.

"He's doing fine," she said, snapping her phone shut.

He laughed. "Looks like you have the same problem with your cell phone as Kelsey did, having to stand out here with the chickens to make a call."

"Yeah. It's like stepping back in time. Luke's in the house, in his office, if you wanted to talk to him."

He shook his head. "God, I worry about him. I meant to tell you how much I appreciate you being here. I know I was a little abrupt with you that first night, and I want to apologize. I suppose it's natural for brothers to be little protective of each other. Especially with all the problems he's had."

She smiled. "Well, I'm learning how to cook at least."

Glen chuckled. "When Darren called me that night to tell me he dropped you off, I was so pissed at him, which is why I came over. I was concerned. Luke's a big tough guy but he's a little vulnerable right now. I'm happy to know I was wrong about you." He reached over and gently squeezed her shoulder. "Turns out you're a good thing for him, particularly since he got hurt." He took off for the house, saying, "I need to talk to him, maybe he won't be so grumpy today."

Patsy stared after him, understanding now why he'd been deliberately rude to her. He was just looking out for his brother. It also came as a surprise to her that Darren had called Glen. Both of them were looking after Luke's best interests, and yet, neither one of them believed his girls were alive.

Before she could ponder it further, her phone chimed. She glanced at the caller ID thinking it might be Conner, but it was the same number she'd dialed to get David.

She answered the phone, hoping he remembered something he forgot to tell her. "Yes, David."

"Yeah, Patsy… I like that name by the way. I don't know another Patsy."

Oh.boy. He was calling to tell her he liked her name. She was deciding how to best let him down when he said. "LeRoy, that's my friend who drives, wanted me to tell you that the grayish SUV we saw had a big dent in the right fender and bumper. Should make it easier to spot. We'll troll around looking for it."

"Gee, thanks, David—and thank LeRoy too. Oh, and, David, don't mention this to anybody other than me, not even Luke." *Especially not Luke.* That would mean she'd have to explain why she was having David spy on Ben Fontaine. But...somehow she'd have to tell him about the Blazer on the outside chance he knew who it belonged to. Maybe she'd give the boys a couple of days to find it before she did that.

"You got it, *Patsy.* We're on it," David chirped before he hung up.

Patsy closed her phone, smiling at the exuberance of teenage boys who were likely bored with an inactive summer. She recalled her own carefree days before her mother died. Life had changed for her after that. Her father, also grieving, had thrown himself into his work. Conner had been old enough to have friends with cars, which left Patsy basically left on her own. She'd learned to take advantage of her father's money, which he'd handed out copiously to both her and Conner, probably to appease his guilt for ignoring his children. The money had made it easy to make friends, or rather buy them. As she recalled, she'd had everything but happiness. Those days, even years, however, did not generate memories she cared to dwell on.

She blew out a huff of air and decided she couldn't stand in the yard all day waiting for Conner to call. She may as well go inside in case he called on Luke's land line.

Doc Flanders drove up just as she reached the house. She stopped and gave him a little wave as he stepped out of a shiny new powder blue Cadillac.

"Hi, Patsy. How are you, and how's our cranky patient?"

Patsy laughed. "I'm fine and Luke's doing better than the chickens."

"Ouch. He mentioned that on the phone. Who the hell would poison chickens?"

"Somebody with a sick mind and a vendetta against Luke." *Or me*, she thought.

Flanders scratched the back of his neck. "That would probably be the same person who killed Kelsey and her girls. He *or she* doesn't want Luke digging around in it."

Patsy realized Luke hadn't mentioned to the Doc about his theory about the girls being alive, or he had and Flanders didn't believe it.

"He's only trying to do the job the police should be taking care of," she told him.

Flanders sighed. "You're absolutely right. Problem is too many people, including the local authorities, still think Luke is guilty. And it doesn't help any that Luke can't remember anything about that night." Flanders hesitated. "He did tell you about that, didn't he?"

"Yeah, he told me the story. Do you think he was drugged?"

Flanders gave a sad shake of his head. "Problem was, it took so long for him to call in that, by the time he was taken into custody, the drugs would have worn off, but I don't think they even tested him. They assumed he was guilty, and that was the end of it. In answer to your question though, I've known Luke both as a patient and a friend for better than three years. I've never known him to even drink to excess, much less drink himself into a blackout stupor. Most people just pass out if all they've had is alcohol. So yes, I do think he was drugged. It's just my opinion, however, and doesn't count for a hill of beans in a courtroom." He nodded to the truck parked in front of the barn. "Is Glen here?" he asked.

"Yeah, just came a few minutes ago."

Flanders drew in a deep breath and huffed it out. "I'd as soon not have a witness to what Luke is going to ask me to do. Maybe if I say I'm here to examine him, Glen might clear out."

"We'll find out," Patsy said with a smile. "I'll go in and announce you."

"Thanks, Patsy, I'd appreciate that."

She went inside and found Luke's office door open. Glen was sprawled in a chair in front of the desk. The brothers were both sharing a laugh about something. She stuck her head in the door.

"Doc Flanders is here to examine you," she said to Luke.

Luke didn't skip a beat. "Okay, thanks, Patsy. Send him in." He looked at Glen. "Sorry. If you wanna to continue this discussion, you'll have to hang around until the doc is through with me."

"Naw," Glen said, getting to his feet. "It can wait. I have to go into town and drop off a mower blade to be sharpened. I'll see you later. I really just wanted to see how you were doing and if you needed help with anything. Looks like you're good."

Patsy stood back to let him pass. He winked at her and said. "Take care of him."

Luke asked Patsy to stay while he talked to Flanders. After all, she knew as much as he did about what they wanted from the doctor.

"I know this might be a little unorthodox for you, but I have a feeling we're on to something. We've done a lot of research," he nodded to indicate Patsy, "and I'm convinced that Lola's father killed Kelsey—"

"Why would he kill his own daughter?" Flanders asked incredulously.

Luke took a deep breath. He knew he was going out on a limb confiding in the Doc, but he didn't see any other way to convince him to go along with his request.

"I don't believe Lola and Betsy are dead."

Flanders eyes widened. "Okay," he said slowly, drawing the word out. "You're not the kind of man who would jump on something like this blindly. I'm assuming you have a reason for believing that—and since they never found their bodies, I'll go along with you for now."

Luke gave a brief explanation for his reasoning, and Patsy eagerly backed him up. Between the two of them, they told about their visit to Jerome Parker and their need to identify Lola's father.

"Since Lola was in to see you for stitches shortly before the girls disappeared, I was hoping you had her blood type on file. I want you to compare it with Sheriff Wilson's blood and see if she could be his daughter. I know it's confidential but I'm speculating Wilson had at least one paternity suit filed against him."

Flanders drummed his fingers on the arm of his chair and stared at Luke for a long time before he spoke. "Even if I can get my hands on both blood samples, unless we do a complete DNA, which could take weeks, all I could do would be a simple paternity test. That would only be useful by proving he *wasn't* her father."

"That's all I'm asking for right now," Luke said. "At least that would eliminate our prime suspect."

Flanders nodded. "And if there's a chance he is, we could then go with the DNA. That takes a while and it's a long shot, but I'd be interested in the result myself. I know they took samples of Lola's blood from her bed and the crime scene. I should be able to get my hands on that report. I'm curious, though. If she is his daughter, where would he be keeping her?"

Luke shook his head. "I don't know. But I'll deal with that when I have more information."

"You know you're both flirting with trouble here," Flanders warned. "First, the ladder, then the note and the chickens; what's this person going to do next?"

"The ladder incident happened before I even started looking into finding the girls. And I've only told four people about my theory, so my guess is this person is more worried about me finding out who killed Kelsey."

Flanders ran a hand through his short sandy hair. "Okay, but just be careful—both of you. And lock your door if you leave. Whoever's bold enough to come into your yard and contaminate the water in your chicken coop could just as easily come in the house and poison your milk or whatever. Put some sort of marker on anything that's open so you can identify if it's been tampered with. While we're at it, get me a sample of something from your refrigerator, like milk. I'll test that, too. We'll find out just how dangerous this guy is…and don't drink anything that's been opened until I call you with the results."

Patsy's eyes widened. "Wow, did they teach you that in medical school?"

Flanders laughed. "Not hardly. I watch a lot of CSI."

"That's one of my favorite programs," she said. "I must have missed that one. I'll get some milk, I know we have that."

Glancing at his watch when Patsy came back with the small container of milk, Flanders stood. "I need to get back to the hospital; I have two surgeries this afternoon. After I get the results on the water and milk, I'll give you a call. And I repeat, be careful what you drink until you hear from me." He paused and glanced at Luke. "A little exercise on that arm is good but don't use it on anything that causes pain." To Patsy, he said, "Make sure he follows doctor's orders."

She grimaced. "That's like asking Reggie to roll over and play dead when a car comes up the drive."

Chuckling, Flanders picked up the water bottle sample from Luke's desk, gave a short salute, and left.

Luke looked at Patsy and shook his head. "That's just great. Now, I have someone besides you to worry about poisoning me."

She picked up a throw pillow and flung it at him. With the reflexes of a cat, he deflected it with his good arm. "Hey, be careful. I'm injured."

She laughed at that. "You're like a bear when it's wounded—twice as snarly."

And twice as horny, Luke thought, giving her a wicked grin. Her eyes glittered like bright green emeralds when she gave him that hostile look even when he knew it was in good humor. What would she say if he suggested they spend the rest of the day in bed together? She'd probably throw more than a pillow at him.

He stood abruptly. "I haven't been out to the pasture in a few days, come on I'll show you my property. You drive."

Twenty minutes later, Luke held the swing gate open for Patsy while she drove through then, after closing it behind her, got back in the truck. It reminded her of driving out in the pasture with Grandpa Hank to bring the milk cows home. Sometimes, he even let her sit on his lap and steer.

"How many acres did you tell me you had?" she asked following a rutted path that led upward to high ground.

"A little over two thousand," he replied.

"Gosh," she said, "that seems like a lot. Grandpa Hank only had fifteen hundred."

"He lived down by the highway where it's flatter," Luke explained. "He had more cultivated acreage. It's only about sixteen miles, but the layout of the land changes dramatically up here. All these hills are good for is pasture and making hay."

She drove past a large herd of cows with calves frolicking alongside; a few were black but most were red and white. From somewhere in the recess of her brain, she remembered what they were called.

"Herefords," she said laughing. "I remember these cows are Herefords and the black ones are Angus."

"I'm impressed," Luke said, chuckling. "For a city girl, you know a lot about farming."

She ignored that statement because she didn't want him to get the idea she *liked* farming. "Are these all yours?" she asked.

He didn't answer for a moment. When he did his voice was husky with a hint of anger. "No, I had to sell most of mine because I wasn't here to tend to them. The Herefords belong to a renter. The Angus are mine. I'll run a full herd again next spring."

Patsy glanced at him and saw the deep sadness etched around his eyes. Kelsey's death and his brief incarceration, she realized, had affected him in more ways than one.

The road seemed to have ended so she drove where he directed her. He also warned her about avoiding large rocks.

"Where are we headed?" she asked.

"Up that hill," he said, gesturing to the highest point.

When they reached a rocky ridge, he told her to stop. "Come on, I'll show you the most spectacular sight in this part of the country."

She trudged up the rest of the hill beside him, gasping when they came to the rim of a deep gorge. A pristine lake glistened at the bottom.

Her mouth hung open in awe. "I never knew North Dakota had land like this."

"It gets even hillier north and west of here. But this spot is unique for this area. Only half the lake is on my side. See the farm on the other end?" When she nodded, he said, "That's were Pete and Terry Cadowa live."

"Oh, yeah, you mentioned them. He's the one with the wacky wife."

Luke laughed. "You have a good memory. I grew up on this farm, and they've lived there for as long as I can remember. They're pretty much retired now; their son Seth does the farming. He's the one who rents my pasture."

Patsy bent down and picked up a colorful shiny stone the size of her thumb. She polished it off and stuck it in her pocket. "So what kind of things does Terry do?"

He snickered. "Well, one time, she asked me over for supper, and when I got there, she asked me what I brought to eat. Apparently, she thought I was bringing fish for her to fry. Pete has to hide the car keys because she takes off and goes places and forgets to tell him she's leaving."

"She sounds like an interesting character."

"Perfect description," he said. "But harmless as a butterfly." He laughed and added, "Flighty like a butterfly too."

They were silent for a few moments when she got to thinking. "Did they ever drag—" She stopped when she realized what she was asking.

Luke gave her a dejected look. "Drag the lake for Betsy and Lola?" he finished for her. "No, except for that small spring just below us, it was frozen over at the time. There was probably two or three feet of ice on it, so there was no need." He sighed. "Sometimes, I think I should just sell out and get away from here, away from the memories."

Patsy was shocked to hear him say that. "But you love it here."

"I used to," he said, a faraway look on his face as he stared out over the hills.

Luke belonged here. This farm was as much a part of him as his vital organs. Patsy couldn't imagine him going anywhere else. "What would you do if you sold your farm?" she asked. "Where would you go?"

He slowly shook his head. "Hell if I know."

Chapter Fourteen

"Let's search the house for Kelsey's money," Patsy suggested after their late lunch. "Maybe there's a clue with it. Like an uncashed check or something."

She had to get Luke's mind off of something besides sex because the looks he'd been giving her, the way his eyes had been following her around all day suggested he was ready to jump her bones if she got within five feet of him. Not that it would be such a bad thing, especially when his intense gaze heated her up in all the right places, but she wasn't sure she was ready to take that step. Ever since that kiss yesterday, she'd even stopped doing her wiggle-walk in front of him.

"Sure, I can't think of anything else we can do." *Now that was a bald assed lie if she ever heard one.* "So we might as well give it a try. There are a couple of places she'd never hide anything. One is in the basement—Kelsey was deathly afraid of spiders—and the other is in the barn. Three years she lived here and I think she was in there four or five times, always to hunt for Betsy who kept sneaking off to play with the cats."

"All right," Patsy said. "I'll look upstairs; you look down here—but don't be abusing your arm." She hesitated on the stairway. "Okay if I search your room or is there something private you don't want me to see?"

"Just dirty laundry," he said, grinning up at her.

Patsy groaned. Sometime soon she was going to have to wash clothes. Fortunately, Peg had shown her how to run the washer and dryer.

She started with the easy room—the spare bedroom. That took very little time since, except for furniture, it was basically empty. Next, she did Luke's room, going through drawers, under the bathroom sink, the upper shelves of the closet. There were no female things anywhere so she figured someone had cleaned out Kelsey's clothes and toiletries, and any other evidence a woman had ever lived there. In the back corner of the closet, she found a guitar and the memory of her first night there came back to her. She'd heard a familiar song accompanied by a guitar. She hadn't recognized the singer but it had sounded like Vince Gill. There was no stereo in the room, so she realized it must have been Luke singing.

Intending to explore that discovery later, she moved on to the hallway linen closet, where she carefully emptied every shelf and opened every box. She found old photos that she glanced at briefly. Some were of a young Luke and his parents, both of whom were striking looking people. Luke did resemble his mother with her full head of brown curls, but it was his father whom he'd inherited the arresting gray eyes from. She then found other pictures with another man who strangely enough also had gray eyes, which she supposed is why the brothers looked so much alike. There were family shots showing Glen as a baby, and Luke who always had an arm around his little brother.

"You finding anything?" Luke called from the bottom of the stairs. She quickly stacked the pictures back in the box and stuck it on the top shelf where she'd found it.

She walked to the top of the stairs and looked down at Luke. "Nothing and all that's left to go through is the girls' room."

"I'm ready to make a bet that whoever killed her has it."

"You said she started packing her suitcases when you left the house. Were the suitcases still here?"

"Huh, not when I got home. Of course, that was two months later."

Feeling a little weary, Patsy plopped down on the top step. "So who cleaned all her stuff out of your closet and took the suitcases?"

"Far as I remember, Peg and Darren. Glen might have helped. If any of them had found money, they'd have told me."

"Well, let's talk to them, because she must have also packed clothes for the girls. Did they find those suitcases?"

When Luke ran a hand through his already mussed hair, Patsy had an odd urge to walk down and straighten it out.

"That's an excellent question, Patsy. Why don't we go ask them?"

"I still have the girls room to go through."

"That can wait. It's highly unlikely Kelsey would put money in their room anyway. Betsy was as curious as a cat. You couldn't even hide a Christmas present in the house around her."

A distant smile appeared on Luke's his face when he talked about Betsy. There was no doubt in Patsy's mind about how much he loved her and Lola.

Assuming he wanted to go over to the Marshes' right now, Patsy decided that after almost two hours of digging through dusty closets, she better at least go wash her face and comb her hair.

She got up and came down the steps, but Luke stood at the bottom blocking her way. When she stopped on the last step, her eyes were almost level with his. Their bodies inches apart. If she'd had any sense at all, she'd have stopped before she got that close to him, but she'd expected him to move.

He put his hands on her waist, both of them since he wasn't using his brace, and pulled her toward him. Her mind slipped into some bottomless abyss, abandoning her entirely. She put her arms around his neck and pressed her mouth down on his inviting lips.

She'd heard of people claiming to see fireworks when they kissed, but she'd always pooh-poohed that idea away as someone's silly romantic imagination—until this moment. Lights flashed in her head as she pressed her body against him. His arms, at the same time, encircled her waist. Apparently, he noted her surrender, because his kisses suddenly became urgent. He kissed her neck then her shoulder where her sensitive skin was exposed. His injured arm slid up under her top to cup a breast. The sensation streaking through her body forced her to concentrate on staying on her feet instead of melting into a puddle on the step.

She vaguely had thoughts about him not using that arm to do anything painful but the only painful thing she could think of was if he pulled it away.

"I want you Patsy. I need you." His voice was deep and husky and shivered through her veins like scorching lead.

She was beyond words and couldn't remember another time in her life when she wanted a man more than she wanted Luke, right now. Sex for her had never been a hungry aching need like the words in *The Rose*—until now.

"I'd carry you up the steps to my room if I could," he murmured in her ear. "Will you walk with me?"

Silently, she took his hand, turned, and led the way. In his room, she helped him remove her blouse, then she helped him remove his shirt. He unsnapped her pants, and she undid his. Simultaneously, they kicked free of them, and he pulled her onto the bed.

Mindful of his rib brace, she went to him. The passion in his hooded eyes stole her breath away—another first for her. His gentle hands moved over her body as he whispered words she could barely hear over the drumming beat of her heart.

No man had ever expressed such a raw need for her, and never had she wanted to give of herself and at the same time return the sensations she was receiving. Her pulse quickened, pounding in her chest, blinding her to anything but Luke. His breath came in strained gasps, and she realized he was trying to ignore the pain in his ribs and turn toward her. She pushed him to his back.

"Lay still," she whispered. "Let me do it."

"You're asking an awful lot of a starving man," he whispered, his voice raspy. His gaze held hers in a look so intense it might have penetrated steel.

She put a finger over his lips. "Shh. Doctor's orders."

Separating from him, she quickly removed her underwear then, with his help, worked his down over his hips and legs. When his erection sprang free, she gasped. He was magnificent. His long, lean body excited her beyond her wildest dreams. Moving over him, she straddled his torso and bent down on her elbows to kiss him. His hands held her face and pulled her toward him, holding her to enjoy the most exotic kiss she'd ever imagined. With quick darting stabs, his tongue played havoc with her mouth, making her moan with pleasure. She could feel the moisture pooling between her legs, but was suddenly too shy to tell him she was more than ready for him.

Clumsily attempting something she'd never done before, she lifted herself over him and slowly slid down on top of him taking the entire length of him inside her. She gasped for air trying to absorb him, while his hands clamped onto her hips. Rasping, animalistic sounds came from his throat. His smoky eyes locked onto hers until they began to glaze over as he started to move inside her. She sensed each upward thrust he made caused him pain, but he still didn't stop. She tried to match his efforts, hoping to alleviate his necessity to move, but the need for her own pleasure took control and she was forced to forget about what he was doing and concentrate on getting the release she so desperately craved.

When it finally came, she threw her head back and moaned, making sounds that had never come from her before. Only when she'd collapsed on top of him did she realize he'd stopped moving, and she remembered hearing the growl of his release coming simultaneously with hers. Yet another first for her.

She felt his heartbeat racing to keep time with her own. When his breathing became obvious groans of pain, she lifted to her elbows guiltily, trying to ease the pressure she was putting on him, but when she would have allowed him to slide out of her, he grasped her hips with an amazingly strong hold.

"No, don't move just yet. Give me a minute to savor this."

"You're in pain, Luke."

"Not as much as I will be if you eject me right now."

Laughing, she went down on her elbows to nuzzle his neck without putting pressure on his ribs. "You wore me out, Luke. If you had been in your prime, I may not have survived."

He tried to laugh but it turned instead into a grimace of pain.

In one swift movement, she pulled away from him and dropped to the bed on his left side, avoiding his sprained shoulder.

"Awe, now that hurt," he grumbled.

"Doctor's orders," she said. "If it's painful, stop doing it."

He put his arm down to pull her against him, and she snuggled into his embrace, more content then she'd ever remembered being. With a long, happy sigh, she slept.

Two hours later, Luke awoke with a start and a woman's name on his lips.

"Kelsey!" he shouted, shaking the woman pressed to his side. "Kelsey! Wake up!"

The woman who sat up rubbing her eyes, a confused look in her face, was not Kelsey. Her flaming red hair hanging in wild array around her head brought him out of his dream.

"My God, Patsy. I'm sorry, thought you were…"

"Kelsey?"

"Yes. Sometimes, I'm afraid to fall asleep; I have that dream so often."

She lay back down beside him, gently putting her arms around him. "It's okay," she said quietly. "It's going to be okay."

Heart hammering, he closed his eyes trying not to think, to remember. It was no use. Finally, he nudged her. "I'm hungry," he said. "Do you think we could scare up something to eat?"

"Is it morning already?" she asked sleepily.

He laughed. "It's seven o'clock—in the evening."

"Oh." She sat up quickly. "And here I was thinking we could have scramble eggs again."

He groaned. "Let's see what else we can find." He pulled her head down and gave her a long, deep kiss. "I just figured out what I'm hungry for," he mumbled into her mouth.

"That's fine with me," she murmured, "as long as you're not going to want to eat afterwards."

He released her, sighing. "All right, food first, then sex."

She gave him a quick kiss then jumped out of bed and started looking for her clothes, quickly putting them on as she found them.

Luke gazed at her, enjoying every minute of her scramble. She appeared to be nervous about parading around in front of him naked. Granted, they'd only known each other a few days, but the way she dressed and wiggled her butt, he'd expected her to be a little more at ease. She was an enigma, all right. A city girl asking how much land he had wasn't so unusual, but unlike Kelsey, Patsy understood acreage. Kelsey had an uncle who farmed twenty miles south of Bismarck; surely she'd spend time there with her cousins. She'd never talked about it, though. It was almost like she was ashamed of being associated with them.

The big question then, was why had she married Luke? He didn't have enough land to be considered wealthy.

There was no immediate promise of oil this far southeast. Maybe he'd been too anxious to get married when he met her. She was beautiful, good in bed—now, there'd been a woman with experience. Kelsey had known all the right moves and had used every one of them on him.

Even after their marriage, she'd regularly expressed her love for him, and she'd wanted to get pregnant right away. The fact she hadn't was clearly a disappointment for her.

What he knew of Patsy's background wasn't much. But being pampered by a sugar daddy didn't make her good farmer's wife material.

So they'd great sex—no, make that terrific sex—even though with his injury he was unable to fully participate. One thing confused him. She'd almost seemed awkward, like she was one step away from being a virgin. And yet she'd come to him so willingly. Was it an act? Wouldn't be the first time he'd been duped by a woman. This time, he'd be more careful—keep a check on his emotions until he knew a little more about Patsy Bartlett.

Reflecting on the past, Luke realized that, in all their years together, he'd never enjoyed Kelsey as much as he had Patsy, who'd somehow wormed her way under his skin. But he didn't dare let her get any deeper.

* * * *

Patsy hummed a little tune while she opened a couple of large cans of vegetable soup she'd found in the pantry. She dumped them out into a pot and set it on the stove to heat, priding herself on her resourcefulness. Setting out bowls and crackers, she made a deliberate effort not to think about what had gone on upstairs in Luke's bedroom. How could she so easily have thrown her plan to avoid attachment out the window and jump into bed with a man she hardly knew? *A farmer yet,* who lived in the middle of *North Dakota,* a hundred miles from the nearest mall. What was she thinking?

And she had to spend another two and a half months here. Good grief, what if he fell in love with her?

Between her car and her credit card, she'd have to use up every dollar she had. Why hadn't she listened to Conner and spent her twenty-five thousand dollars more wisely?

Conner! She'd forgotten to call him. Okay, so she'd been a little distracted having mind-boggling sex with Luke

McAlister, which was a complete no no. But every minute in bed with Luke had been worth…what…giving up her inheritance?

She had to talk to Luke. Explain there would be no more sex because—

A pounding on the door pulled her out of her musings. At the same time, she noticed the soup was boiling at full speed. She quickly turned the burner off and hurried to the door as the pounding persisted, keeping time with the erratic beating of her heart. Holy cow, was the barn on fire or what?

She flung the door open and faced a frantic Darren Marsh.

"Peg is having an appendix attack or something. Can you keep the boys while I drive her in to the hospital?"

Without thinking, she nodded and said, "Of course."

He raced to his running car, hauled the distraught boys out of the back seat, and ushered them into the house. He then thrust a bag at Patsy and ran back to his car, saying over his shoulder, "Thank you so much. I'll call."

Dazed, she held the bag he'd given her and stared after the receding taillights, unaware Luke had come up behind her.

"What in the world is going on?" he asked.

She jumped, then turned to face him, noting he'd slipped his pants on, but left them hanging loose, unsnapped. Tearing her eyes away from his half-dressed body, she gave him a brief explanation, then set the bag aside and knelt down to gather the sobbing, frenzied boys in her arms. That's when she noticed each one was clutching a toy. Some secret mothering instinct must have kicked in because she could not for the life of her, ever remember touching a child before.

Luke somehow managed to get to his knees beside her. He put one arm around Patsy and the other around the boys. "Come on, guys. It'll be okay."

He caught Patsy's look over their heads. She hoped he couldn't see how terrified she was of having these kids under her care. At least, she thought, Luke knew how to entertain children.

"Did you guys have supper?" Luke asked. Patsy's heart took a nose dive until they nodded. Luke raised his brows at her then used her shoulder to boost himself to his feet. The boys had stopped crying and were looking around the room.

"What would you like to do?" Luke asked them.

Scott, the older of the two, still sniffling, answered, "Can we watch your big screen TV?"

Patsy admired Luke as he settled the boys on the sofa and asked them what they wanted to watch. In minutes, he had them entranced in an animated action movie. She guessed he had knowledge of kids' shows after having Lola and Betsy around.

Wondering if having Scott and Mark there was a painful reminder to him, she looked at his eyes. They were clouded over with moisture.

Silently, she went to the kitchen to pour the soup into bowls.

* * * *

Darren called at ten o'clock to inform them Peg had gone into surgery for an emergency appendectomy. He asked if they would keep Scott and Mark overnight. Together, Luke and Patsy reassured the boys everything would be all right and put them to bed in the spare room.

Patsy could tell by Luke's expression that he appreciated her not settling them into the girls' room. When she walked past him, intending to go downstairs and sleep in her own room, his fingers wrapped around her arm, stopping her.

He gave her a haunted look and said, "Stay with me."

The sadness in his eyes was so palpable she couldn't refuse. Not that she wanted to anyway. Having the boys so near, next to where his girls slept, was taking its toll on him. Scott had asked to sleep in *Betsy's room* but Patsy had vetoed it immediately, telling him the room wasn't cleaned.

"I'll be right back," she told Luke.

When he nodded his understanding, she hurried down to her room to get the shorty pajamas she liked to wear. She wanted to have something covering her in case one of the boys woke up and needed her. Then, grabbing her toiletries kit, she hurried back to Luke's room, where she found him in bed, waiting for her.

Patsy didn't know if he wore anything beneath the covers, but from the rib brace up, he was bare-chested. He had exquisite arms and shoulders. Giving him a tremulous smile, she headed for the bathroom. Her heart did a funny little flip-flop as his gaze silently followed her.

Patsy donned her PJs then took her time brushing her teeth, splashing cold water on her hot face. Staring in the mirror, she noticed her cheeks were flushed with a rosy hue.

Taking a deep breath, she went back to the bedroom. Luke's eyes were closed, and she thought for a moment he might be sleeping, but when she approached the bed, he lifted the covers to welcome her. When she slipped in beside him, his good arm folded around her shoulders and pulled her close. She pressed up next to his warm body and eased her arm around him.

Luke nestled his face into the fold of her neck, and minutes later, his even breathing brushed her skin, and she knew he was asleep. She closed her eyes, somehow knowing she was, at that moment, exactly where she belonged.

* * * *

The boys weren't up yet but Patsy took a dozen eggs out of the refrigerator, hoping the boys liked them scrambled. Maybe, this afternoon, she could visit Grams and get some other breakfast ideas. Even Patsy was getting weary of scrambled eggs. She remembered liking cereal when she was a kid but that wasn't an option since she'd dumped all the milk.

She sat at the table to relax and drink her coffee while she waited for Luke to come in or the boys to wake up. It struck her that she was behaving like a farmer's wife. The strange thing about it was the thought was somewhat comforting. Last night, she'd fallen asleep in Luke's arms and had never slept so peacefully in her adult life.

She was still digesting her thoughts when Luke walked in, carrying a gallon jug half full of fresh milk.

"Where did you get that?" she asked surprised.

He laughed. "This is a farm. Farms have cows. Cows give milk."

"You have milk cows? Where?"

"Only one, in a corral behind the barn."

Patsy frowned. "But…don't you have to milk them…every day?"

"Nope," he replied, setting the milk in the refrigerator. "She has a calf. I take the calf away when I need milk."

"Huh, learned something new again."

Luke grinned. "I guess that means you're not having a sad day."

She felt her cheeks grow warm when he bent down and tickled her ear with his tongue. "Don't you need two hands to milk a cow?" she asked, laughing, squirming away from him.

"Not necessarily. It just takes longer with one hand. I have to go tend to the chickens. I'll be back in a few minutes." He eyed the eggs on the counter and visibly grimaced. "Looks like it'll be scrambled eggs for breakfast."

"Hey, now that we have milk, we can have cereal."

Luke's face brightened. "Good plan, especially with the boys here. Never let it be said that you aren't resourceful. Maybe, next time, we need milk I'll show you how to get it. A cow with a calf might kick, and it's really not safe for me. I could get kicked with these sore ribs—unless you're afraid, of course."

When he walked out the door laughing, she stared after him, speechless. Was he kidding? She was still contemplating cow milking when Scott came bounding down the steps carrying an object cradled in the crook of his arm.

Patsy's heart gave a jolt that put her on the verge of fainting.

Chapter Fifteen

"Where did you find that?" Patsy asked, not recognizing the sound of her own squeaking voice.

"In Betsy's room," Scott chirped happily as he held up the faded yellow rabbit for her to see. "Do you think she's coming back to get it? She never goes anywhere without Binky."

Binky. The old tattered rabbit. Luke's only motivation for believing Betsy and Lola were alive. She couldn't let him see it.

"Show me where?" she said, bounding to her feet and turning Scott back toward the stairs, keeping an eye on the door at the same time to make sure Luke wasn't coming in. "Quick, show me where you found it."

Scott whirled around and ran for the steps, eager to show her where he'd made his find. She followed him straight to the girls' room. He jumped on one of the twin bed and pointed between the wall and the bed where the unmade quilt was tucked.

"Here, see, right here, it was stuck right behind the bed."

Patsy took a deep breath, trying to stay calm. "Are you sure this is Binky?" she asked shakily.

"Uh huh. See his nose is gone because she chewed on it."

Sure enough, there were bare threads hanging where the nose should have been.

The erratic thudding in Patsy's chest made it difficult to think. One thing was certain. She couldn't let Luke see this, not right now.

"Can you keep a secret?" she asked Scott.

"Sure, I know lots of secrets. Daddy always tells me secrets."

"What kind of secrets?" she asked

Scott giggled. "I can't tell you or they won't be secrets. That's what Daddy says."

She wondered what secrets he had with his father, but right now, that wasn't important. Obviously, the boy could be trusted. "All right, here's what we're going to do. We're going to hide Binky and not tell anyone, not Mark, not Luke and not your daddy. You think you can do that?"

He nodded with the exuberance of a child. "Sure, except if I see Betsy, I have to tell her."

"Of course, because he belongs to Betsy, she'd want to know where he is. Where do you think we should hide him?"

Scott's face grew serious at being assigned such an important task. "In the closet. Maybe in a shoebox. Mommy always hides stuff in a shoebox."

"Okay, let's see if we can find one." Patsy prayed Luke wouldn't come in the house until they had Binky safely secreted away. They hunted through the closet but didn't find a shoebox. Instead, they settled on a box that held building blocks. Working quickly, they took all the blocks out, stuffed Binky in then piled the blocks on top of him.

Finished, she held out her hand to Scott for a high five. He slapped her hand, grinning. She made a zipping motion over her lips, and he copied the action, his bright blue eyes shining with mischievous glee.

Downstairs, she heard Luke come in the front door.

"Hello. Where is everybody?" he called.

She got to her feet, pulling Scott with her. "How about cereal for breakfast?" she said hoping to distract him from their secret.

His face brightened into a wide smile. "Come on, let's go wake up Markie. He's such a sleepy head."

She pulled the door to the girls' room shut behind her, hoping that a five-year-old knew what keeping a secret meant.

* * * *

After Darren had picked up his boys, Patsy told Luke she'd like to go into Ashville to see her grandmother and pick up some groceries. She didn't mention that she hoped to get more recipes, like how to make a pie, or that she wanted to call her brother.

As she suspected, he had no interest in going along. "There's some cash in the can above the stove," he said. "Take whatever you need. Maybe you could stop at the hardware store and pick up a couple pounds of ten-penny nails for me. I have to make some repairs on the corral behind the barn."

Sounded like a strange way to classify nails, but she didn't question it. Instead, she went to her room to get her purse and cell phone. Back in the kitchen, she took sixty dollars out of the can then paused to look at Luke, who sat at the table, coffee cup in hand, silently watching her.

She suddenly experienced an awkward moment. Did he expect her to kiss him goodbye? He looked so sexy with a lock of hair falling over his forehead and those arresting gray eyes watching her every move. She really did want to kiss him, but for someone who was never shy about anything, she held back, uncertain. Finally, she said goodbye, blew him a kiss then hurried out the door, grabbing the truck keys on her way.

As soon as she reached the end of the drive, she checked her cell phone. No signal. When she passed Darren's place, she saw the boys playing out in the yard. They waved to her, and she waved back, the small gesture gave her a warm feeling. She wondered how the Marsh family would feel about her when she left to go back to Minneapolis. Would they feel she'd deserted Luke like Kelsey had planned to do? That wasn't fair, she decided. After all, she wasn't married to him; she was his employee. At least, she hoped she was. They still hadn't talked about wages. That reminded her of another call she had to make in town. She had to pay her Visa bill.

Suddenly, she had another dilemma to think about. Would Luke expect her to work for free now that they were having sex? Correction—they weren't *having* sex; they'd *had* sex—once.

It may have happened only one time, but the recall had her body heating up and ready for more. They hardly knew each other; what had she been thinking? Unless she got another job, she had to stay there the rest of August and another two months after that.

The Ashville city limits sign appeared at the side of the road, and she the last thing she remembered was driving past Marsh's farm. Damn, where was her mind?

She drove up in front of the assisted living building, parked, and took out her cell phone. Conner had left three text messages.

Patsy call me
Patsy where are you CALL ME
Patsy R U OK? Need to talk to you!

Holy Guacamole. Were his pants on fire of what? She punched in his speed dial code, and he didn't answer. Where was he? It was one o'clock. He should be through with his class. Oh, well, she'd have to call him after she saw Grams. He was probably with his girlfriend.

Her visit with her grandmother went wonderfully. Patsy had forgotten how much fun she'd always had at her Grams' house. Patsy was supplied with an armful of cookbooks, a list of things to make, along with another list of items to buy to make them.

Apparently, word had gotten to Grams that Patsy was staying with Luke—no surprise there—and Wilma made a point of telling her what a nice young man she thought Luke was. She remembered him coming to the farm to help out when Hank was laid up with a back injury.

Pleased with her successful visit, Patsy kissed Grams goodbye, then once again, chastised herself for ignoring her grandmother all those years.

In the hall, Patsy ran into Grams' friend Shirley. Shirley asked how Peg was doing, which reminded Patsy she should stop by and see her neighbor and assure her the boys hadn't been any trouble at all.

Of course, she had to stop and ask Wanda which room Peg was in.

"Two fifty-four," Wanda said, nodding toward the stairs. "How's Luke?" she asked then without waiting for an answer, she added, "I should really stop out and see him."

"He's pretty busy," Patsy said before she could stop herself.

Wanda gave her a scowl and said, "Sorry about the chickens."

Patsy nodded an acknowledgement and headed for the stairs. *Cripes, was losing five chickens national news in this town.* Only if they belonged to Luke McAlister and were poisoned, she thought cynically. She didn't bother to ask how Wanda had known about them.

Peg was reclined, in bed and greeted Patsy with a tired smile. "Hi, Patsy, thank you so much for taking the boys in last night."

Patsy returned the smile. "No problem. Fortunately, Luke knows how to entertain kids."

"I'm sure he does. I hope he was okay with it."

"He was fine." It was stretching the truth a bit, but Peg didn't need to know how much it troubled Luke having them there.

They talked about the kids and Patsy's plan to bake a pie, then Peg said. "I'm worried about Luke. I wish he'd give up the idea of looking for those girls. I think it'd be better for him if he could accept the fact that they're gone and move on with his life."

"You don't believe they're alive then?" Patsy asked.

Tears filled Peg's eyes. "I wish I could... It's just that... Well, you know. It's hard. I miss them, and so do the boys. They were all so close in age—" Peg wiped her eyes. "Sorry, Darren says I should stay out of it. It's just that we care so much about Luke. I'm glad you're there for him," she added with a watery smile.

A heavy weight pressed on Patsy's chest as she left the room. Was Luke chasing a wild dream? She never had any doubts until Scott found that rabbit. It wasn't fair for her to keep that from Luke, but she was concerned about his reaction.

When she got back to the truck, the first thing she did was try Conner's number again. Still no answer. She told his voicemail she'd call back.

Her next stop was the hardware store where she asked for Luke's ten-penny nails. Unfortunately, along with the nails, she got a warning about living *out there* alone with Luke McAlister. She noted wryly that the clerk wasn't so down on Luke that he wanted to give up doing business with him. It served as a reminder as to why Luke didn't like coming into town. As the disgruntled clerk dropped seventy-five cents change in her hand, the back door opened and she heard a voice she recognized.

"Hey, Clint, my mower blade ready yet?"

Clint gave Patsy a wary look and called out, "Yeah, Glen, it's sitting right against the wall there."

Seconds later, Luke's brother appeared at the counter. "Oh, hi, Patsy, how's it going?"

"Fine," she replied, managing a smile.

"Damn shame about the chickens. I still can't understand why some idiot would do such a thing."

"What happened?" Clint asked.

Patsy stifled a groan.

"Some ignorant fool poisoned Luke's chickens."

Glen was pulling money out of his wallet so he likely didn't see the smirk on Clint's face. "Well," she said quickly. "I have to run to the grocer's. See you later, Glen."

She put the nails in the truck then walked the half block to Rudy's Dry Goods, hoping she wouldn't run into Gertie again. Maybe Patsy would ask about her husband if she did. *Have I always been this catty?*

Rudy greeted her with a wave from the cash register where he was just finishing up with a customer. Five minutes later, he sought her out and asked if she needed help finding anything. Since there was no one else in the store, they had a genial time while they filled her list. He also showed her how to pick out the best produce, including the right apples for pie, then gave her tips on a number of other purchases. A new customer who'd come in and overheard them talking recommended Patsy buy readymade crusts from the cooler for her pies instead of going through all the work of making them herself.

Apparently everyone in Ashville, population fourteen hundred and twenty–three, knew she was a novice cook. But all in all, unlike her first trip to Rudy's, this one was a fun and enlightening experience. Rudy even invited her to come in for Customer Appreciation Day on Friday. He made a point of including Luke in the invitation.

Yeah, like that's going to happen.

With Rudy's help, she loaded her things in the back seat of the truck then got in, drove to the edge of town, and tried Conner's number again. This time he answered after the first ring.

"Patsy, why the hell haven't you called?"

"I tried twice, and you didn't answer. Besides, I told you the phone doesn't work on the farm. If it was so urgent, why didn't you call on Luke's phone?"

"Because I didn't want him hearing our conversation."

Patsy's heart rate accelerated. "Why? What's happening?"

"I hope you're sitting down. I went through everything I could find on McAlister's case, and I think you should get your ass out of there immediately. Come here, you can live with me until—"

"Conner, what are you talking about. I'm not in any danger. He was released."

"Yeah. Well, he never went to trial, that doesn't mean he's innocent. The original evidence showed his wife died before he got home, but there's speculation that the evidence was tampered with, and it's not certain exactly when his wife and kids died. God, Patsy, he killed two kids. The man's an animal."

Patsy's stomach roiled, and she swallowed at the bile rising to her throat. "Listen, Conner. Some of the townspeople here will say anything to get him put in back jail. I've spent four days with him. He didn't kill anyone."

"How can you be so sure? Is it worth bargaining with your life? Not even the inheritance is worth that." Genuine concern edged his voice.

He'd probably go ballistic if she told him about the note she'd received. "First of all, I'm not in any danger. He took a fall, and he has two cracked ribs and a sprained shoulder. You know me—I can take care of myself, especially with a man who's injured."

"But—"

"There's more," she said, interrupting him. "He doesn't believe the kids are dead. There were no bodies found. I'm helping him look for them."

"Wake up, Patsy. They found blood from both kids in their bedroom."

"We believe it was planted there."

"We? You *are* on his side."

"Yes. I told you I believe him. There wasn't that much blood—"

"How much does it take to convince you? Maybe you aren't aware they also found Lola's blood in his pickup."

Patsy couldn't breathe. A suffocating sensation squeezed her throat. "There must be a mistake," she whispered.

"You didn't know that, did you?"

Conner's voice on the phone brought her back to reality. She hadn't realized she spoken the words out loud.

"I'll have to give him a chance to explain that. It seems to me he talked about taking one of the kids in for stitches shortly before they disappeared." Conner was quiet for so long she thought he'd hung up. "Conner, are you still there?"

"I'm here," he said in a subdued voice. "And the only reason I'm not driving out there and dragging you away tonight is because I do know you can take care of yourself. But I'm still coming on Saturday. I need to check this farmer dude out for myself. Don't even try to talk me out of it."

"All right I won't, but get to know him. Don't come charging in here like an enraged buffalo or I'll take you down myself."

She could hear him breathing, thinking, and decided to wait him out. When he finally spoke, his tone had lightened. "I'd like to take exception to that except that I know you could do it. Maybe I'll bring Debbie along so it will look like we're just visiting you. I can check him out on the sly."

Patsy's brain ached as she mentally ran through a gamut of emotions on the drive home. Between Connor and Peg, she was starting to have doubts. Was there really a mix up in the autopsy concerning the time Kelsey died? Was there a chance Luke had done it? She quickly abandoned that thought. It just wasn't possible.

And if the girls were alive, where could they be? The rabbit was the one thing that had convinced her they'd been taken away and hidden somewhere. Could they have been weighted down and sunk in the lake? Luke said they didn't drag it because it was frozen over. But what about the spring?

Her intense deep thinking had lights flashing behind her eyes. Then, she realized the flashing lights came from behind her. The sheriff's patrol car. Oh, Lord, what did he want? Had she been speeding? She didn't think so.

She pulled over to the side, realizing she was on a remote stretch of road. There wasn't even a farm in sight. Had he waited for this spot to make up a reason to stop her? Rolling her window down, she watched in the rear view mirror as Sheriff Harvey Wilson got out of his car and sauntered toward her. Knowing the man was a possible killer had her gripping the steering wheel to keep her hands from shaking, especially when she noted the gun hanging on his hip like some kind of a swashbuckling, quick-draw artist. All right, she decided. She would pretend he was someone she didn't know and behave accordingly.

He leaned his arm on the open window so he could look directly in at her. "Can I see your license, please?"

Moving to the side as far as she could, she reached for her purse, took her license out and handed it to him. A toothpick protruding from his mouth moved as he chewed on it.

"Did I do something wrong?" she asked.

He didn't answer while he studied the license, and she hoped he wasn't familiar with the Minneapolis area since her father's address was still on it. Would he recognize the high buck Minnetonka suburb?

"Yeah," he said shifting the toothpick to one side. "You didn't signal at that last turn." She had to catch herself to keep from laughing. She hadn't seen another car since she left Ashville, and he was worried about her signaling. She could just as well have laughed at him because she was pretty sure this was not going to be a routine stop.

He confirmed that when he backed up and said, "Step out of the car, please."

All right, she thought, what the hell? She opened the door and slid out then held her hand out, asking for her license back. Surprisingly, he handed it back to her, but as he did, he stretched behind her and closed the door to the truck. The next thing he did was look both directions, presumably to assure himself there were no cars coming.

He took small steps toward her, backing her up against the door of the pickup. If his body so much as touched her, she was prepared to bring her knee up hard into his groin. He stopped inches from her and put his hands on the top of the truck over her head.

"Are you carrying any weapons?" he asked.

"No," she answered. "None that aren't attached to my body."

"Very funny. What about drugs?"

"Would you like to search the truck?" she asked.

He spit his toothpick out to the side. "No, that won't be necessary. But I might have to search you."

Okay buddy, you just stepped over the line. Lay one finger on me and you'll live to regret it. Cop or not.

"I see a bulge in those tight jeans you're wearing. It looks to me like you might be packing a concealed weapon. You have a permit to carry?"

He must have read her mind because he stepped back and said, "Turn around and put your hands on the hood."

If he thought that would hinder her he, had his head up where the sun didn't shine. The only question she had was should she accommodate him?

"You do realize," she said, keeping her voice smooth and nonthreatening, "that you need a female officer to search me."

When he snickered, she moved to the hood of the truck, turned around, put her hands on the hood and waited. At this point, she wanted him to touch her. Stifling a bizarre urge to do her wiggle butt, she waited to see what he would do. He didn't move in on her like she'd expected, keeping his distance instead.

"Why are you so calm about this?" he asked, suspicion deepening his voice. "You want me to search you, don't you?"

"No, I do not," she said adamantly.

He moved to the open truck window, and out of the corner of her eye, she saw him study the interior. Then she realized he was looking for a camera. Satisfied, he turned back to her, but halted when a car came over the hill less than a mile away.

Swearing profusely, he quickly backed away. "Okay, we're done here. You can go. In the future, pay attention to your turn signals."

He wasted no time getting in his patrol car, making a quick U-turn, and heading back toward town. To say she was disappointed was an understatement.

Thirty seconds later, Darren slowed down and stopped. His boys were strapped in the back seat. "Having a little trouble with the sheriff, I see." he said, his gaze fixed on the receding car.

"You might say that. Thanks for coming along when you did."

He shook his head. "Somehow, we need to get him out of that position."

"I'll second that," she said, getting back in the truck. "By the way, I just saw Peg; she's doing great."

"That's where we're headed. Thanks again for watching the boys."

Their little hands waved from the back seat as he took off.

She started Luke's truck, muttering to herself. *Sheriff Wilson, your balls were just saved by the bell.*

Chapter Sixteen

Patsy walked in the door, her arms loaded with grocery bags. Setting them on the counter, she turned to get the rest then gave a startled cry when she saw Luke sitting quietly in the corner at the table. His eyes were dark and brooding. Even Reggie lay in a corner staring solemnly at her.

She paused to ask him what was wrong then understood when she spotted the tall brown bag in front of him. It was the kind of bag that liquor was packaged in. He had a coffee cup sitting beside it. Obviously, he'd been drinking.

"I—I have to get the rest of the groceries in." She rushed out of the house, her breath coming in short gasps. Her hand shook as it closed around the truck keys still in her pocket. She tried to sort her thoughts but they all jumbled together.

What had made him drink? Did he find the rabbit? Kelsey had been killed when he was drunk. Did he get violent when he had alcohol in him?

Conner's words came back to haunt her. *He's dangerous, Patsy. The autopsy results may have been tampered with. Did you know they found Lola's blood in his truck?*

She pulled the keys out of her pocket, glanced at them then looked back at the house. She'd told Conner she could take care of herself. But Luke was a strong man. Even injured, he might be able to knock her out with one slam of his powerful fist. Tears threatened her composure as she debated what to do.

Stay and face him or run; maybe go to Glen for help. He knew Luke better than she did—Glen would understand and know what to do.

Closing her eyes, she pressed her forehead on the cool window of the truck, trying to think. She didn't even know where Glen lived. About ten miles away Luke had said.

She screamed when a hand clamped around her wrist.

"Where were you going?" Luke asked his tone harsh.

Right at that moment, she could have overpowered him, but something held her back. This was Luke, not some creep like Harvey Wilson. She couldn't bring herself to attack him, not when he was already hurt. Maybe he just wanted to talk. She could always take him down later if he started to play rough with her.

"I—I was just getting the other bags in."

"Yeah, right. Well, they can wait."

She went along when he tugged her back into the house. He rounded the table and prodded her into the chair in the corner where he'd been sitting. Then he pulled up another chair, blocking any thoughts she might have had of escape.

"Did the sight of this bag make you want to run?" he sneered.

She wanted to yell, *yes*, but held her tongue. Something was off, then she realized what it was. She didn't smell any liquor on his breath, and he wasn't slurring his words. Maybe he'd taken some hallucinogenic, the same drug he'd accused somebody of putting in his drink the night Kelsey had died and the girls disappeared.

She should have been afraid, but she was more heart-sick then afraid. Unless he suddenly punched her in the face, she was confident she had the advantage. He had no idea she had a black belt in karate.

How could she have been so wrong about him?

"Why Patsy, why did you do it? Why did you come here?" Raw anguish coated his words and... Were his eyes moist? Probably from the drugs.

She didn't understand. What had she done? Try to help him find his girls?

"What did I do?" she managed to ask.

He pushed the bagged bottle over to her. "Here, have a drink. Maybe that'll help clear your mind."

"I don't want a drink," she snapped, pushing the bottle back to him. "It seems like you've had enough for both of us."

He sat back in his chair, one hand going to his ribs. "I'm not going to hurt you. Just explain why you came here and who you're working for. Then you can leave. Take the truck. I don't give a damn."

Good grief, he was back to the spy thing. "Luke, I swear to you. I don't know what you're talking about."

He took the bag and pulled the bottle out, threw the bag aside and slammed the bottle down in front of her. "What else did you contaminate beside the water in the chicken coop?"

Patsy stared at the nearly empty bottle dumbfounded. Strychnine! She shook her head, trying to clear the cobwebs that seemed to have materialized in her brain.

"Where did you get that?" was all she could think of to say.

"Right here under the sink, where you left it."

"Have you completely lost your mind?" she said forcefully. "What kind of drugs are you on?"

"Let me explain," he snarled. "After you left today, I was going to tidy up a bit, help you out. I started to take the trash out then I noticed a tall brown bag there beside the trash can. I've been under that sink dozens of times. It wasn't there until today."

"Are you sure?"

"Positive. I took everything out from under the sink two weeks ago looking for dishwasher soap."

It suddenly became clear to Patsy. She gave him a hard look, talking slowly. "Think about it, Luke. If I'd poisoned the chickens—or you—would I be ignorant enough put the bottle under the sink, right by the trash where you'd be sure to find it?"

It took all of eight seconds for her words to register. He pinched his eyes then dragged his hand down his face, muttering some vile curse words as he did so. Then, he looked at her with far more relief than apology. "The door wasn't locked. Anyone could have walked right in and planted it there."

"Not anyone," Patsy replied. "The same person who came in the yard, poisoned the chickens, maybe the milk, and who knows what else."

"The milk was clean," he said. "Flanders called this afternoon. The chicken water had enough strychnine to kill a hundred chickens, and there's no chance Harvey Wilson is Lola's father." He put his elbow on the table then dropped his head in his hand. "I must be losing my mind. How could I have thought you…" He lifted his head and looked at her. "I'm a fool, Patsy, Can you ever forgive me?"

She saw such anguish in his eyes her heart went out to him. She bent over and put her arms around him, letting him know without words that she forgave him.

When she pulled back, she reached up and pushed a lock of his wayward hair back in place, giving him a reassuring smile.

Luke grasped her hand and put it to his lips. When he released it, he managed a tremulous smile of his own then sobered quickly. "My God, you were afraid of me, weren't you? You thought I'd been drinking?"

"That thought did cross my mind."

"And you remembered Kelsey died when I was drunk. So you still have doubts about my innocence."

"I…I have to tell you—I learned some things while I was in town today."

"Oh, Lord, now, what are they saying?"

Patsy was at a point where she had to decide how much to say, without telling him the whole truth. One thing was for sure; she didn't want to tell him that her information came from her brother.

"There's speculation that the autopsy was falsified concerning the time of Kelsey's death."

Luke swore. "I haven't heard that one. People will say anything. That's one of the reasons I don't go to Ashville."

"I didn't hear it from anyone in Asheville. My...computer guy found it in a newspaper article."

Luke scoffed. "I was in jail, and it depressed me to read what was being printed, but it's not true, even Jim wouldn't go that far."

Patsy heart took a jolt. "Jim?"

"James Flanders, he did the autopsy."

"A doctor can do autopsies?"

"Yes. Actually, Flanders was an ME before he decided he'd rather practice medicine. He was already a licensed physician so the transition was easy. Besides, there's no one else in town qualified to do autopsies."

"So...because he's your friend, the press capitalized on it?"

"The glory of free press," Luke said sardonically. "What else did he tell you?"

Pasty hesitated then decided to just blurt it out. "Lola's blood was in you pickup."

"That's easy. About a week before everything went to hell, Lola gashed her leg open on a barbed wire fence. It bled pretty heavily. Flanders stitched her up. There's a record of that in the clinic."

"Yes, now, I remember you mentioned that when Flanders was here yesterday."

"This computer expert of yours is pretty thorough," Luke said. "I'd like to meet him sometime. Maybe he could teach me something about computers."

Saturday, she thought glumly. *You'll meet him Saturday.* "First, you have to get a computer," she told him.

He gave her a weak smile that suggested he was getting back to normal. "I have one. It was Kelsey's, and it's packed away in my office. We even had internet service," he expounded before she could bring it up. "Anything else you want to ask about?"

"Yeah, can you put the refrigerated stuff away while I get the rest of the bags in?"

He bent over and kissed her on the lips. "Your wish is my command."

"I'm going to remember that."

That evening, as they enjoyed her first attempt at apple pie. Luke all but licked his plate clean then waved his also licked-clean fork at her and said, "You know, I've been thinking."

Oh oh, Patsy thought. Luke quietly thinking... Whenever Conner announced he'd been thinking, it never boded well for her. Had Luke figured out her sugar daddy was really her father.

"About what?" she asked consciously.

"Somebody put that strychnine bottle where I could find it. Only the chickens were poisoned. Nothing in the house that we've been able to determine was touched. I'm thinking it was a deliberate attempt to put the blame on you, so I would get rid of you."

Patsy's eyes widened. "You mean they expected you to kill me?"

"No," he said, frowning, "They expected me to fire you."

"Oh, of course—fire me."

"Who would most like to see you leave?"

Patsy said the first name that came to mind. "Wanda."

Luke rolled his eyes. "Wanda knows that getting rid of you wouldn't do her any good."

"Why not?"

"Because I have no interest in her and she's known that since high school. Can I have another piece of pie? Damn, that was good."

Patsy flushed with pleasure. "You really like it?"

"Do I strike you as the kind of man who'd give false compliments?"

She dished up the pie and handed it to him. "If it got you another piece of pie, yes."

"Wrong." He chuckled. "If it wasn't good, I wouldn't want another piece." He picked up his fork and dug in, making oohing sounds along the way. "It's kind of like having sex. If I didn't enjoy it the first time, I wouldn't pester the woman for more." He winked at her.

"Oh, now I get it. You didn't like it the first time you had sex with Wanda."

He let out an exasperated huff of air. "When will I learn I can't win a verbal battle with you?" When she opened her mouth to speak, he held up his hand. "No, don't answer that. Let's get back to the strychnine. If it was Lola's father and he suspected we might be getting close to him, I'm fairly certain he wouldn't have stopped with poisoning the chickens. If it had been someone from town wanting to cause me trouble, why implicate you?"

Patsy was only half listening. She was more intrigued watching Luke gobble up her pie, and thinking about what kind she could bake tomorrow.

"What really brought you to North Dakota?" he asked suddenly.

That caught her attention. "My grandmother."

"And what else? You came here driving a Maserati, claiming to be broke and needing a job. You have David doing some mystery work for you, and some guy neither Darren nor I know drives by here in a car with Minnesota license plates the same day the chickens start dying. Was David following him?"

When she didn't answer immediately, she knew she was busted. Luke pushed his empty plate aside, laid his arms on the table in front of him, and waited.

"My problems have nothing to do with you," she said finally.

"Your problems became mine when my chickens were poisoned. Talk to me, Patsy. You've helped me out looking for my girls. I'd never have known about Jerome Parker if not for you. If it has anything to do with your sugar daddy, I'll stand behind you."

Patsy had to think. Her father had warned her about using his name to find a job. But she wasn't doing that, she already had a job. Still, she didn't want to take a chance getting called on a technicality.

"Before I tell you anything," she said. "You're going to have to tell me what my salary is working for you."

His brows drew together. "Why is that important?"

"Because I can't have you reevaluating it after I tell you about how I ended up here. All I'm asking is that it's a fair amount for what I'm doing. And don't include the sex."

He smiled at that, but she could tell he was still totally perplexed.

"All right," he said after a moment's thought. "Since you have room and board, plus a vehicle to drive, I'll give you two hundred a week. Before you made the pie, it would have been one seventy-five." he added grinning. "Does that work for you?"

"Yes. I'm glad I didn't put you on the spot yesterday."

"What can I say—I have a sweet tooth. Go ahead, tell me your story."

She took a deep breath. "It wasn't a sugar daddy that kicked me out; it was my father. I grew up privileged as you've probably figured out by now. The last time I worked, I was thirteen, which is also when my mother died." She swallowed, thinking about Conner and decided to leave his name out of her story.

"I lived in my father's house; he paid all my bills, including my credit cards. Regardless of how much I spent. Nine months ago, he got on a kick that maybe I should be using the college education he paid for to try to make something of myself. He offered me a position in his company and—spoiled brat that I was—I informed him I expected a hundred grand a year and only wanted to work three days a week."

She watched as Luke's dark brow shot up, but other than drawing in a sharp hiss of air, he remained silent, allowing her to continue.

"I didn't bother looking for any other work. I figured, if he couldn't meet my demands, the heck with him. I liked my life, financially anyway, just the way it was. A few months ago, he had some kind of epiphany—said he talked to my deceased mother. Anyway, he gave me twenty-five thousand dollars and pretty much dismissed me from his house. After telling me he loved me, of course, and saying it was for my own good. He told me if I couldn't survive a year without asking for more money, or borrowing against his name, or using his name in any way. I would be disinherited. I don't even dare have a credit card balance at the end of the year."

She shrugged, avoiding Luke's gaze, and went on. "I didn't take him seriously and continued my spending habits until a few weeks ago, when I realized I'd never make to the deadline. That's when I decided to visit my grandmother, hoping she'd support me until my time was up."

"You didn't know she was in an assisted living home?"

"I'm ashamed to admit I've ignored my grandmother for the last fifteen years. In spite of my neglect, during all that time she continued to send money for my birthday and Christmas until about three years ago. She always sent a hundred dollars that I didn't appreciate and never once in all those years acknowledged with a call or thank you note." She swiped a hand over her eyes to wipe away tears she didn't realize she was shedding. "Now that you know what an awful person I am, if you pay me what you owe me and ask me to leave, I will."

Luke was silent for what seemed an eternity. When he spoke, his voice was surprisingly gentle. "It sounds like your father did you an injustice by not expecting more out of you sooner."

Those were not the words Patsy expected to hear. She felt she needed to defend her father. "Mom was the one who handle those things. After she died, he just took the easy way out, which was to allow me to do whatever I wanted. The only thing he was ever adamant about was that I finish college. I guess he figured after I had an education, I'd naturally want to do something with it."

Sometime during her talk, Reggie had come up and laid his head in her lap. She reached down and rubbed behind his ears, wondering how just a few days ago she hadn't liked him.

"How did Wilma receive you when you went to see her last week?"

Patsy sniffed. "She put her arms around me and gave me a hug as though all those years in between never mattered. She put a huge guilt trip on me without saying one word."

"We've all done things in our past we aren't proud of."

"Yeah, well, I could write a full-length book on it."

"I think your father would be proud of you now."

She smiled appreciating his generosity.

"You seem to have left something out," he said.

She looked up at him, confused. "What?"

"Why is your father having you followed?"

"It's not my father. He has a lawyer, and I think it's him. He's worked for my father for over twenty years, and my father trusts him explicitly and never questions what he does. But I think he's crafty—shyster comes to mind. I'm guessing that when he redid my father's will, to exclude me, he wrote something in there that will benefit him. We… I always had a copy of the will before, but I never saw the new one."

Luke rubbed the stubble on his chin. "Let me get this straight. At the end of the year, your father will reinstate you in his will, so if this lawyer has somehow written the will to his own advantage, if you last out the year, your father would have to die before the will was reinstated."

"I'm afraid so, but as far as I know, he's not sick."

"Is it possible his lawyer could be a threat to him?"

Her heart thudded at hearing the same concern from Luke as Conner had expressed.

"I'm not sure," she said, "but my computer friend is checking that out."

"Who is this computer guy, an old boyfriend?" Luke asked, frowning.

"No, just…someone I know."

"Someone you can trust?"

"One hundred percent," she said emphatically.

Luke stood and pulled her into his arms. She went eagerly, happy he didn't despise her after she'd revealed her horrible life.

His kiss was long, deep and tender. It warmed her, comforted her, and made her want to curl up in his arms and never leave. When the kiss ended, he whispered in her ear. "Sweetheart, I'm so sorry I distrusted you. I'll never do it again."

"I guess we were both harboring some trust issues today," she murmured. "Forgive me, and I'll forgive you."

"Will you come to bed with me and put a stamp on that deal?" he asked huskily.

"I wouldn't have it any other way."

Chapter Seventeen

Patsy was cutting up onions to put in an omelet when the front door opened and the phone rang simultaneously. She grabbed a towel to wipe her hands, when Luke appeared in the kitchen in time to pick up the old fashioned wall phone.

He said hello and, seconds later, dropped the receiver quite noisily in its cradle.

"I hate hang-up calls," he declared, walking up behind her. He pressed his lower body against her buttocks and wrapped his arms around her waist, nibbling her neck. "On the other hand, I love the smell of onions."

Patsy lifted her shoulder to restrict access to his tickling lips. "You must be sick," she said. "Nobody likes the smell of raw onions." She sniffed, rubbing her eyes with the back of her hand. "And nobody likes cutting them either."

"They smell good on you," he said, laughing. He released her with a sigh and a pat on the behind then poured himself a cup of coffee and sat at the table. "I have something to show you after breakfast. Guaranteed to make you smile."

"I've already seen it," she said, dumping the onions in a hot skilled with the green peppers and mushrooms.

"I don't think so, this is small and fuzzy and there are more than two of them."

She concentrated on stirring the contents of the skillet and gave him a sly look. "More than two, and *small*. Yup, you're right, I haven't seen it. So what is it?"

"Not telling; it's a surprise. That smells really good. You get some more tips from Wilma?"

"Uh huh. She was great cook. She made these wonderful chewy chocolate chips cookies and yesterday she told me her secret."

"Hey, I remember those cookies. She never shared that secret with anybody. You'll have to make some just so I can be sure they're the same."

Patsy flipped the first omelet onto a plate, added two pieces of toast and set it in front of him. Finishing her own omelet, she took a seat across from him, glowing at his compliments. As before, she was amazed at how much she enjoyed cooking. She especially liked sharing her efforts with Luke.

She'd just finished eating when the phone rang again. Her eyes locked with Luke in question.

His jaw tensed. "You answer it this time. Whoever it is, doesn't wanna talk to me."

Hoping it wasn't Conner, she reached for the phone, catching it on the third ring.

"Hello?" she said tentatively.

"Hello, Patsy. It's David."

"Yeah, David." She glanced at Luke. He was watching her impassively. "What is it?" she asked.

"I saw the SUV…you know, the gray one…with the dent."

Her back straightened as she went on full alert. "Are you sure?"

"Yep, I called LeRoy to come down and take a look at it. He's sure because it had the same headlight hanging out."

"Where is it? Do you know who was driving it?"

"He brought it in to Marty's repair shop to get the dent taken out. You know the place where your Maserati is."

"Who? Who brought it in there?"

Luke, she noticed, was suddenly hanging on her every word, trying to keep up with the one-sided conversation.

"His name is Jeff Brady," David said. "He farms west of Ashville, about ten miles past Hoskins Lake."

"Did you talk to him?"

"Nope, thought I'd leave that to you. He said he was going to the Ashville Café for breakfast. Just left here two minutes ago. If you came in right now, you could catch him."

"How will I know him? What does he look like?"

"Well, he's about sixty, wearing a blue western shirt and a raggedy old cowboy hat."

"Okay, good work. We'll be right in. Can you keep an eye on him in case he takes off before we get there?"

"You bringing Luke?"

"Yes, he knows about Fontaine, so it's okay to talk to him."

"Oh, well, tell him I'm sorry for hanging up on him."

Patsy hung up and glanced at Luke. His gray eyes had narrowed to slits.

"Who's Fontaine?" he asked unceremoniously.

"I'll explain on the way. We have to hurry. Grab the keys and get in the truck. I have to grab my purse in case the horse's behind stops me again."

By the look on his face she realized she hadn't told him about her encounter with the sheriff. "Don't ask. Just get in the truck. I'll tell you about that later." She raced for her room, hoping he'd take her at her word and head for the truck.

Thankfully, Luke was sitting in the pickup waiting when she got out. With a sulky look, he handed her the key. She started the truck, backed out and left a hail of gravel behind her as she headed for the main road. She drove past Darren's place then made a right toward Ashville.

"Okay," she said. "We don't have much time. I'm going to give you—"

"Who's Fontaine?" he demanded.

"Ben Fontaine is the man who is following me. The ugly guy Darren saw going past on Sunday."

"The chicken poisoner!"

"Yes, if it was really him, yes, but—"

Luke let loose with a volley of swear words Patsy had never heard before. They seemed to be in another language.

"Listen to me, Luke, we don't have much time. This isn't about Fontaine. It's about the SUV David saw out by your place. A vehicle Darren didn't see. It had a dent in the front—"

"An SUV? When were you going to tell me about that?"

"I'm trying to tell you about it now."

"Give me one reason I should listen to, or believe, anything you say?"

They were less than five miles from Ashville, she didn't have much time if they wanted to catch Jeff Brady at the café. "Because last night you said you'd never distrust me again."

He wasted a whole mile answering her. "Whatever we're doing appears to be urgent. Go ahead talk. I'll shut up and listen."

"David and his friend LeRoy saw this SUV, a gray Blazer, Sunday. It came from the back road and parked behind them while they were waiting for Fontaine to turn around." Luke's brows shot up but he kept silent. "According to Darren, it never drove past his house. That means it must have gone to your farm then turned around and left again by the back way. It had a dented right fender, and the owner brought it in to Marty's repair ship to get it fixed this morning." Patsy's heart began to hammer. They'd reached the city limits sign.

"Did he find out who owns it?"

"Yes, and we're hurrying because he's in the Ashville Café having breakfast. His name is Jeff Brady."

Luke stared at her woodenly. "Jeff doesn't own a Blazer. He drives a pickup exactly like mine."

Patsy swallowed convulsively as she pulled up in front of the café. "You know him?"

"He was one of the farmers with us in Bismarck the night I met Kelsey."

David was parked beside the café on his bike. He drove out and came up to her side of the truck. She took a dragging breath and rolled her window down.

David gave Luke an apologetic glance before telling Patsy, "He's still in there, hasn't even gotten his food yet. I asked Myrna to stall it a little."

Patsy smiled at him. "Thanks, David. We'll take it from here."

He gave her a little salute and grinned. "Roger, over and out." Before leaving, he looked past her at Luke. "I'm sorry for hanging up on you. I should have just asked for Patsy, but I panicked a little when you answered the phone."

Luke gave Patsy a look that could have meant anything. "That's okay, David, I'm sure Patsy told you to keep a lid on it."

David grinned, "Yes sir, she did. Bye." He wheeled his bike away then quickly turned back. "By the way, Ben Fontaine checked out and left this morning." He gave his little salute and pedaled across the street.

"That kid should be working for the CIA," Luke said dolefully.

Before she could ask him what he wanted to do about Jeff Brady, her phone rang.

Luke watched her, obviously waiting for her to answer it. She dug it out of her pocket and looked at the caller ID. Conner. Why was he calling? He should be in class. She switched off the ringer and stuffed it back in her pocket.

Luke's eyes narrowed on her. "More secrets?"

"My computer guy. We have to decide what to do here. I can talk to him later."

Luke gave a skeptical frown but let it go.

"I gave you what I know," she said. "It's your call. You know the man. Do we talk to him or not."

He opened his door. "Let's see what he has to say."

"You haven't been wearing your brace," she said as she got out of the truck. "Is that good for your arm?"

"I'm a fast healer. Besides, it's hard to have great sex with one arm."

She grinned at him. "Sometimes, *hard* is a good thing."

About six tables held customers in the café. Only one had a lone diner. Jeff Brady looked exactly as described by

David; his dusty hat lay on the empty seat beside him. Of course, Luke walked right up to the man.

Jeff held out a hand. "Luke, great to see you. Sit down; I'll spring for breakfast." His eyes slid appreciatively over Patsy. He extended his hand to her. "You must be Patsy. Have a seat; order something."

Patsy shook his dark, grease-stained hand. "Thanks, Mr. Brady, we already ate."

"Sheet, I ain't been called Mister since we whooped the south in the Civil War. Call me Jeff. So you already ate." He chuckled. "I hope it weren't pancakes."

Patsy felt her face heat up, realizing you didn't even have to live in town to get the latest gossip.

"Sorry about your chickens," Brady continued. "Who the hell would do such a dang fool thing?"

Patsy resisted the urge to lay her head in her hands, close her eyes, and say, "*Beam me up, Scottie.*"

Luke gave a little chuckle. "Patsy's turned out to be a right good cook, Jeff. She might even be able to give Bella a few pointers."

Jeff gave a wild hoot of laughter. "By golly, you got me there. If my wife can't boil it, she don't know what to do with it. That's why I make up any excuse I can to come in here."

The waitress, Myrna, according to her name tag, brought his heaping plate of food and set it in front of him. Her pretty brown eyes lit up like sparklers when she saw Luke. "Luke, honey! Fancy see'n you here. What can I getcha?"

Luke avoided Patsy's gaze. "Just coffee, thanks. Patsy made me a huge omelet this morning."

Myrna raised her finely painted brows at Patsy. "No kidding? Wow."

Patsy smiled through gritted teeth. Luke chuckled and she kicked him under the table. Jeff started stuffing food in his mouth.

"So, Jeff, when did you get an SUV?" Luke asked.

"Yesterday," Jeff said, talking through a mouthful of hash browns. "Got a good deal up at Wishek Automotive, the front end has a big dent in it. Light don't even work. I brought it in to Marty's to get fixed. Wife's gonna pick me up in a little while."

"What about your truck?" Luke asked.

"Agh, the Blazer's for Bella. She thinks it ain't ladylike to drive a pickup." He winked at Patsy. "That's one fine set a wheels you got in there, missy. Shame about it getting busted up like that."

* * * *

Debra was waiting for Conner when he came out of class. She looked distraught and told Willy to run along home, that she'd see him later.

"What's wrong?" Conner asked, resisting the urge to kiss her. Ever since he'd had a taste of her sweet lips the night before, it was all he could think about.

She glanced behind her where some of the kids were lingering, talking. "Let's go in the classroom. I don't want to be overheard."

He ushered her back in to his desk, sat her in the side chair then pulled his rolling chair up in front of her and took her shaking hands in his. "What is it?" he asked quickly. "You look like you've seen the devil."

"I think we both have. About an hour ago, I got a call from Teja. She asked me to meet her at the restaurant. Then, she pulled me in the back room and told me what the guy who's been watching us said to her."

Conner squeezed her hands. "Can't be all that bad, can it? What did he say?"

Debra drew her hands back and put them to her chest as to control her racing heart. "He said he was a social worker and he'd been sent there to keep an eye on you."

"I can tell you right off, he's lying."

Tears filled her eyes. "He told Teja that you'd been accused of molesting little boys."

Conner heart took an instant jump start. Obviously Morty Chambers had sunken to a new level. Resisting the urge to swear, he leaned forward and pulled her hands back into his. "Listen to me, Debra. He's lying. The man is a private eye, working for a lawyer in Minneapolis. I just found this out last night, and I can explain about it later. Did Teja tell anyone else?" he asked quickly, knowing how this thing could be blow up in his face in a heartbeat.

Debra shook her head vigorously. "No, she was pretty sure social workers didn't operate that way."

"Damn right they don't."

She gave him a watery smile, and he pulled her into his arms. "I just knew you couldn't do anything like that," she said, sobbing into his shoulder.

"Thank you for that," he said, stroking her hair.

She pushed back to look at him. "Teja didn't believe it either. That's why she called me right away."

Conner grabbed her hand. "Come on, let's go talk to her. We have to make sure this is stopped before it starts. I'll explain to both of you who this man is and why he's trying to discredit me." And then, he'd place a call to Charles Bartlett. If Chambers was willing to go that far to stop Conner, what was he doing to Patsy?

"I can't wait to get my hands on him," Conner said, gritting his teeth.

"He's gone," Debra said, blowing her nose into a tissue she'd pulled from a box on top of his desk."

"Gone?"

She nodded. "He told Teja he was leaving. He'd done all he could do and asked her to warn the school board."

* * * *

Silence hung between them on the way out of town until Patsy decided it was time to break it by admitting she'd run them up a dry creek.

"Well, that was a total bust," she said. "I'll have to tell David they got the wrong vehicle."

Luke shrugged as though it were no big deal. "I suppose we could contact the dealership in Wishek and confirm that he bought the Blazer yesterday, but I can't see him being involved in any of this."

"Yeah, me either. He's actually a likable old fart."

Luke chuckled. "Never a dull moment when you're around him. He warned me to stay away from Kelsey Kempler. Said she was high maintenance."

"Huh, so what's up with you and Myrna? She seemed awfully friendly toward you."

He looked at her, his lips twitching. "Jealous?"

"Don't be ridiculous," she snorted, deciding it was time for a change of subject. "Are you going to show me the small, fuzzy things when we get home?"

The look he gave her this time was a leer. "Can't wait, huh?

"My heart is in marathon mode."

Luke laughed. "First thing you're going to do, though, is call David and tell him they got the wrong SUV, and they should keep an eye out for another one."

"You believe there is another one then?"

"Of course. I never doubted they saw it. Your amateur sleuth seems to be pretty competent. And it's not out of the question to have two gray SUVs with dented fenders around a community this large. Plus, other than pickups, it's the vehicle of choice in a state that has a lot of snow. I even have one."

"Where?"

"In the barn. I bought it for Kelsey so she'd have a dependable vehicle when she took her monthly treks with the girls to Bismarck." He made a rude sound. "If I'd known what she was doing up there, I'd have gotten her a Kia."

"Oh, that's brutal," Patsy said as she pulled in front of the house. Then, she had an afterthought. "Maybe we should check her car for the money."

He leaned over and kissed her. "That's one of the things I like about you; you never miss a beat."

They walked in the house together, arm in arm, until she separated from him to go call David. Right now, they had no other leads to pursue. She finished the call and came in the kitchen to find him eating a piece of apple pie out of his hands.

"Lunch," he mumbled. He finished the pie, washed his hands, and directed her out to the barn.

It was the first time she'd been in there. The large, cavernous building with its pungent animal smells brought back wonderful memories of her grandfather. It seemed like every summer there'd been a new batch of baby kittens in the haymow. To see them she'd had to climb steep ladder steps, and when she was little, her grandpa had always stood guard below to catch her if she fell.

She wondered excitedly if Luke had baby kittens. Luke switched on lights and pointed to the stairs. These weren't steep ladder-steps but a regular stairway. She went up with him following close behind.

"There," he said, pointing to an open space surrounded by two layers of bales.

Giving him a curious glance, she leaned over the top and looked inside. She saw a cozy five foot square space and in one corner—

"A chicken!" she declared. "Why is there a chicken in here?" Before he answered, she noticed the hen had her wings spread, and there was movement beneath her.

"It's a cluck," he said, reaching—with a small grimace of pain—beneath her wings and bringing out a ball of yellow fluff. Opening her hand, he gently placed a baby chick in it.

He laughed at Patsy's delightful squeals as she put the chick to her face and rubbed her nose in its feathery down.

"What are they doing up here?" she asked, continuing to nuzzle her prize. "How do they eat?"

He pointed to food and water pans she hadn't noticed inside the bale cubicle.

"I have to take the clucks away and let them sit alone or the other hens will keep laying eggs in her nest. It only takes three week for them to hatch and when they're a couple of weeks old they can go down with the rest.

"How many are there?" she asked, reaching for another one."

"She had ten eggs, eight have hatched so far."

She giggled when the chicks pecked at her fingers. "They more than replace the ones we lost," she said, not even caring when she realized she said the "*we*" word.

"Unfortunately, half of them will be roosters. The phone's ringing," Luke said suddenly. "I'll get it." He left quickly and disappeared down the stairs.

While she waited for Luke to come back, she replaced her chicks and took two more, determine to give them all a chance to be held. She and Conner had always named Grandpa's kittens, but she suspected Luke would never quit laughing if she suggested naming chicks. Interesting, though, she found two with black spots.

She held those two in the hands when she heard Luke coming back up the steps.

"Good news." He sat on the bales beside her. "You don't have to make supper tonight. Glen's picking up pizza and beer in town. He thought you deserved a break."

"There's a pizza place in town?"

"Sort of. One of the bars makes it."

"Wow! I love pizza. And I'm hungry. This chicken feed is starting to look good. What time will he be here?"

"At least three hours; he's still at home. He said he wanted to let you know early so you wouldn't start cooking."

She made a disappointed face, thinking hungrily about the pile of hash browns on Jeff Brady's plate. Might as well stay busy, she decided, get her mind off her stomach. "Then we have time to search the car," she said with more enthusiasm than she felt.

Luke did the trunk, and she took the inside. After forty-five dusty minutes, they both came up empty handed.

"I didn't expect to find anything," Luke said. "I searched in here when I was hunting for Betsy's rabbit. Of course, I merely glanced in the trunk. My priority was places where it could have accidently fallen out of sight."

"What if you found the rabbit now?" Patsy asked, broaching a sensitive subject as they left the barn together. "Would you still believe the girls were alive?"

He didn't answer until they'd reached the house. "Until I see proof otherwise, yes."

She looked up in his face and saw the tired lines around his eyes. "You look beat, Luke. Why don' you go up and rest until Glen gets here? I'll go get the eggs."

When he started to protest, she stood on her toes and kissed him. He responded immediately by putting his hands on her face and deepening the kiss. His lips were so ardent and full of promise, her knees started to buckle.

"I will," he whispered, releasing her, "*if* you'll come up and just lay with me when you're done."

"Only after a quick shower. I think there was an inch of dust in that car. When was the last time you drove it."

"The tabs expired in April. Somebody, I suppose Glen or Daren, put it in there while I was…locked up."

Patsy heard the sadness in his voice and when he turned and walked toward the house his tread seemed slow and laborious. Her heart went out to him. With a deep sigh she headed for the chicken coop.

As Patsy gathered the eggs she tried to imagine an outdoorsman like Luke spending two months in a small cell accused of a murder—three murders—he didn't commit. She wondered how he'd come out unscathed. He seemed to have had a lot of female admirers from the time he was a teenager. But…had any woman ever really loved him…until now?

Yes, she realized, she loved him. But could she be happy spending the rest of her life here on the farm? On the other hand, would she be happy going back to the life she had? She sucked in a deep breath, pondering the dilemma as she walked to the house cradling her pail of eggs. The count had gotten smaller. Grams, Patsy mused, often gathered eggs in her apron, and Conner would…

Conner! She hadn't returned his call. Quickly, she pulled her phone out of her pocket and hit his speed dial number. He answered right away.

"Patsy, I'm really glad you called. Listen to this…"

What he told her about the accusations made against him had her stomach churning.

"You think it's Chambers?" she asked.

"I know it is," he declared adamantly. "And he has to be stopped. I'm concerned that he might do something to Dad. If Chambers thinks we're going to make it to November first, the only way he can keep control of whatever he's scheming is for Dad not to reinstate his will. I only hope I can convince Dad I'm not blowing smoke. He thinks Chambers walks on water."

"You're right on there. What about your class?"

"No problem. It's only a three-hour drive, and I'm halfway there now. If Dad will listen to me, I can be back for class by morning. I'll be in touch, dangerous talking while driving."

"Good luck. I love you, Conner."

"Me too, you sis."

Patsy closed her phone and hurried into the house. Tonight, after Glen left, she decided, she'd tell Luke about Conner—and the rabbit. She was tired of secrets.

She put the eggs in the refrigerator, then raced to her room and stripped off her clothes. After a five-minute shower, she dried off, put on a new T-shirt and her last clean pair of jeans. To save time, since she knew Luke would be waiting, she didn't bother blow drying her hair, sopping the water out of it with a towel instead. Before leaving the room, she glanced in the mirror and realized this was the second day in a row she hadn't bothered with make-up. She spared ten seconds to rub some musk oil she'd bought on a trip to Greece on her wrists and behind her ears.

Luke had pulled the drapes in his room. In the dim light, she could see him sprawled on his back in bed. She tiptoed closer, wanting to surprise him, then realized, by his even breathing, he was sound asleep. For a moment, she just stood there quietly watching him. With his face relaxed, he bore no sign of the tension that usually clouded his features.

Very quietly, she eased onto the bed and laid down beside him in the curve of his good arm. It tightened around her, though he never woke up. She closed her eyes, hunger forgotten, and hoped it would be a while before Glen arrived.

* * * *

"Anybody home?"

Patsy was startled awake by the sound of Glen's voice calling from downstairs.

She leaped off the bed. "Luke, wake up. Glen's here with the pizza."

Luke's eyes were wide open, and by the humorous look on his face, he'd been awake for some time.

"Why didn't you wake me up?"

"I like watching you sleep," he said, in no obvious hurry to move.

"Glen's here."

Luke chuckled. "I know. Go ahead; go down. I'll be there in a minute."

"He's going to know we were—"

"What? *Sleeping* together? Just explain to him that's all we were doing."

She threw her pillow at him and left the room, belatedly remembering how her hair must look after sleeping with it wet. Vowing to have it cut at the next opportunity, she absently wondered if Ashville had a beauty shop as she went downstairs to find Glen. He was in the kitchen, sticking a six pack of beer in the refrigerator. The pizza was in a box on the table, and it smelled heavenly.

"Hey, girl," he greeted her, his eyes taking in her disheveled appearance. "I was beginning to think I'd have to eat this pizza by myself."

"No way," she said. "I'm as hungry as a bear. Luke will be down in a minute. It takes an act of congress to get him to rest, macho man that he is." She thought about how explain that they were, in fact, just sleeping then thought he wouldn't believe it anyway so the less said the better. "I need to comb my hair. I'll be back in a minute to set the table."

"No hurry. I brought paper plates. I'll take care of it."

She finally got her hair tamed somewhat, and when she came back, Luke was sitting at the table holding a bottle of Guinness beer. Glen motioned her to take a seat beside Luke indicating he would take care of everything.

"Can you handle a beer?" he asked as she sat in front of an empty plate.

"Sure," she said. Dark ale wasn't her favorite choice of drink, but as long as he was springing for the best of the best, why not.

"You want it in a glass?" he asked.

"Nope, bottle's just fine."

He opened a bottle set it in front of her and flipped the lid back on the pizza. "Go ahead, dig in. You know I just missed you guys in town this morning. Jeff said you were in having breakfast with him."

Patsy laughed, taking a sip of the rich, bitter beer. Luke had already finished half of his. "Is there anything you can do in this town without everyone knowing about it?"

Laughing, Glen took a seat and grabbed a piece of pizza. "Not much. Hope you like pepperoni."

She pulled a piece free and took a bite. "Love it," she said, smiling, already feeling the effects of the beer.

"He knows it's my favorite," Luke said, scooping a large slice in his plate.

The phone rang, and since she was closest to it, she reached behind her head to answer it. She swallowed a mouthful of pizza, washed it down with beer, and said hello.

"Patsy, it's David."

"Oh, hi, David. What's up?"

"Well," David said, starting slowly as though reluctant to continue. "LeRoy was positive that Blazer Jeff Brady bought was the vehicle we saw. So...we took a drive to Wishek this afternoon and went to the dealership. We asked a salesperson if that Blazer had been driven on Sunday. He checked it out and said it was taken for a test drive. Said the guy had it for over an hour before he brought it back."

Patsy glanced at Luke, who had stopped eating and was studying her face. He still looked tired, his eyelids drooping. She bobbed her brows at him, indicating it was good news.

"So, who was it?" she asked when David didn't continue.

"Well...it was Luke's brother, Glen."

Before she could stop herself, her eyes flew to Glen's face. He'd been watching her. A dark, malicious glare replaced his cheerful demeanor. She looked at Luke who seemed to have trouble keeping his eyes open. The beer. She dropped the phone and quickly jerked the half empty beer out of Luke's hand. Before Glen could stop her, she'd slammed both bottles in the sink, smashing them.

She whirled to confront Glen and found a gun pointed at her. He walked around the table and hung up the phone, while Luke's confused gaze went from Glen to her and back to Glen. Patsy already knew he was under the effects of some drug. She could feel it buzzing in her own head, but it was nowhere near incapacitating her.

"Why?" she asked Glen, her voice raspy with shock. "Why are you doing this?"

"I didn't want to kill anyone," he said. "Not even Kelsey. Especially not Kelsey. I loved her."

"You lusted after your brother's wife?" Patsy said incredulously.

With that Glen laughed. It was an evil sneering laugh that ran chills up her spine.

"You might as well know." He glanced at Luke who may or may not have been cognizant. And, speaking more to Luke then to her, said, "She was the love of my life, but she didn't want to settle for being a farmer's wife. She wanted more. She wanted this farm after I told her what my father had discovered."

"What did he find?" Patsy asked, trying to piece his story together.

"First, let me tell you about the plan my darling Kelsey concocted. She said she'd marry Luke then arrange an accident for him, and we'd have the farm together."

Patsy gave a quick glance at Luke to see if he comprehended. He was silent, not moving. His eyes, only half open, were fixed on Glen, his hands clenched into fists. Was he pretending to be out of it but keeping silent to buy time and let Glen talk? Waiting for the right moment to attack? She prayed he'd stay out of it. Luke was injured, and

Glen held a gun. He waved it back and forth between then as he talked.

"You knew her before she married Luke?" Patsy prompted.

Again with the laugh. "*Knew her?* Lola is my daughter. You have any idea how I felt knowing she was going to bed with my golden brother every night?"

Luke hadn't moved but something gleamed in his gray eyes.

"And she had to screw him," Glen sneered. "If she was going to get pregnant." He turned his malicious glare back on Luke. "But she didn't get pregnant because he's obviously shooting blanks. So then she tries to get him to adopt Lola, but the asshole wouldn't cooperate unless he could have Betsy, too. And she damn sure wasn't going to give up her security blanket from Parker."

He waved the gun back at Patsy. She inwardly flinched, and her heart pounded so loudly her ears rang, but something told her he wasn't planning to shoot either one of them. That would implicate him. She was sure he intended to set up a scene exactly mimicking Kelsey's death. Only this time both of them would die.

"It was your damn snooping that found Parker. I thought when you poisoned his beloved chickens; he'd bounce you out of here…"

She didn't bother mentioning she wasn't responsible for that because he already knew the truth. One thing still didn't make sense, though. "Why did you want her to get pregnant? Or adopt Lola. She was married to Luke; if something happened to him, she'd get the farm anyway."

"Oh, yeah, she'd have gotten the farm all right, but Luke's conniving father set it up so only his heirs could inherit the mineral rights."

"But there's no oil here."

"You think you're so smart, don't you? Not even old man McAllister knew what was really back in those hills. My father was the one who discovered it. But he couldn't do anything about it because only Golden Boy here would have benefited."

"What did you expect to gain by killing Kelsey?" she asked.

Glen snorted. "She was going to quit on me. Take the girls and run. I didn't mean to kill her. I was just going to shut her up, convince her to come and live with me. She scoffed at me and said she didn't want to live on *any* farm, much less one without money attached to it."

"What did you do with the girls?" Luke whispered, speaking for the first time.

"What do you think? You killed them. I buried them in my own backyard to cover for you."

"That's a damn lie," Luke spat out. "Especially since I don't believe they're dead."

"Really? You mean because of that old rabbit? Why don't you ask your girlfriend here about the rabbit?"

Luke's dark brows drew into a heavy frown. His head swiveled slowly toward Patsy.

Her face burned. And she wondered how Glen knew about the rabbit unless he'd planted it there. Even if he had, how could he know she'd found it? She sent a pleading gaze to Luke, silently begging him not to judge her until she could explain. Explain what, though? That she'd kept yet another pertinent secret from him?

Glen obviously took pleasure in the exchange. He laughed. "Maybe your little spy really did poison the chickens?" He backed toward the refrigerator, selected a bottle of Guinness, and removed the cap with an easy twist of his fingers. Patsy was certain it wasn't the first time the bottle had been opened. He slammed the beer down in front of Luke. "Have a drink, brother dearest!"

"Why?" Luke asked, not touching the beer. "Why do you hate me so much? You're the one who had a father growing up. A father who gave you everything you wanted. He bought you a new Schwinn bicycle when you were ten. I got a used one I had to fix up. Then I had to work my ass off to buy my first car. You got one for your seventeenth birthday without doing a lick to earn it. You got a skateboard, a stereo, video games—"

"Not quite everything," Glen interrupted "You got the farm; I got a paltry hundred thousand dollars."

"Because my father owned it. When he died it went to my mother, our mother."

"Yeah, and *my dad* worked it, paid the debt on it, so that you could inherit it free and clear."

"Where are the girls?" Patsy asked, hoping to distract Glen from Luke and the tainted beer. At this point, she didn't know if the one he'd given Luke held drugs or poison.

"Well, honey, they ain't in Kansas anymore." Stepping toward her, he pointed the gun at her head, less than a foot away. "Drink the beer, Luke, or I drop her where she stands." He shrugged nonchalantly. "Doesn't matter to me either way. In case you haven't recognized the gun, it's yours. You'll be back in jail for killing your latest lover in a heartbeat. Of course, just like when you killed Kelsey you'll be under the influence of drugs, but this time, you'll spend the rest of your life in the slammer. Now, drink!"

Patsy had good training. Her instructor had even pointed a modified gun at her head, challenging her to wrest it away from him. The gun held a graphic imitation of blood red dye. Each time she'd reach for the gun, he'd pull the trigger. She had to do it eight times before she managed to avoid getting splattered by the dye.

But this wasn't play time. She faced the ugly barrel of a real gun that she was sure held real bullets. Her hands shook uncontrollably, her heart was speeding at a mind boggling rate, and she could still feel the buzz of the drugs in her system. When Glen turned, smiling, to watch Luke put the beer to his lips, she moved.

Shoving his gun hand aside, she grasped his wrist at the same time. She did a head-under-the-arm maneuver and twisted until she had his arm pinned behind his back. In that position, she could break it with an easy snap if he so much as attempted to fight her. The gun dropped with a noisy clatter to the floor, and the words that came out of Glen's mouth would have made a hardened criminal cringe.

When Luke stumbled to his feet to pick up the gun, Glen made a final attempt to swing his foot out and throw

Patsy off balance. She was ready for him, and he came within half an inch of having his arm dislocated from his shoulder. Glen wailed like a wounded hyena.

The front door burst open, and Sheriff Wilson bust in, his gun drawn. The thought crossed Patsy's mind that he planned to arrest her and Luke, especially with Luke standing there with a gun in his hand. Then, David and LeRoy charged in behind the sheriff.

"Dammit," Wilson yelled. "I told you brats to stay outside."

They ignored him and stared at Patsy in awe. "Wow, we were watching through the window," David said, excitedly.

"Yeah," Leroy chimed in. "We thought he was going to shoot you."

Wilson shook his head disgustedly and snapped a pair of hand cuffs from his belt. "You can let him go," he said to Patsy. "I got it."

Patsy cautiously released her hold on Glen's arm and stepped back. Glen immediately sprang into action, grabbing the gun from Wilson's hand. Wilson reached for his gun, trying to wrestle it away from Glen. They both fell to the floor, and the gun discharged with a muffled blast.

David and LeRoy simultaneously jumped back two feet, both releasing screams that blended with the echo of the gun shot. Everything happened too fast for Patsy to react, and Luke stood frozen, obviously still numbed by the drugs. They all watched in stunned horror as blood gushed over the floor coming from between the prone men. When Glen's legs moved, Patsy quickly took the gun from Luke's fingers and pointed it at Glen, waiting to see which one stood.

The sheriff, his chest covered with blood, pushed back from Glen, and got to his knees. He was gasping for breath, and when Glen quit moving, Patsy drew in a gulp of air, not realizing she'd been holding her breath. Wilson slowly got to his feet and stared in shock down at Glen, his chest still seeping blood on the floor.

"I've never killed a man before," Wilson whispered gruffly.

LeRoy said, "Holy crap. The kids will never believe this."

Wilson shot a glance at the two boys. "The next time I give you two to an order to stay outside, you damn well better listen."

"Yes, sir," they said as one, both staring at the blood on his shirt.

"You guys, okay?" he asked Patsy and Luke.

They both nodded. Wilson bent down and put a finger to Glen's neck. "He's dead." He straightened back up and spoke at David. "Make yourself useful and call the ambulance." He then looked at Patsy. "I've never seen anything like what you did in here—from a man much less a woman. I understand now what you meant when you said you didn't have any weapons that weren't attached to your body."

Chapter Eighteen

By the time everybody left and the ambulance had taken Glen's body away, it was almost midnight. Patsy sat at the kitchen table, nursing a cup of coffee. She was mentally and physically exhausted, the events of the day having finally caught up with her. She'd called Dr. Flanders, and he'd readily agreed to come out and check Luke. It seemed Luke hadn't drunk enough of the beer to do him any harm, and by the time, he'd consumed a carafe of coffee he was already coming out of it. Thankfully, the boys had helped her clean up the blood before they left. David had beamed when she credited him for saving their lives by his phone call. That's when she learned he had called the sheriff when he sensed what was going on, and they'd both nearly broke the sound barrier getting there—Wilson with his lights flashing minus the siren and LeRoy on his tail in his supped-up Mustang.

Luke walked slowly into the kitchen and sat across from her. He looked even worse than she felt.

He released a sigh that seemed to come from the depths of his being. "I had no idea Glen hated me so much. I knew he was upset when he didn't get the family farm but…to carry out the scheme he and Kelsey had planned is beyond comprehension."

She had no answer for him. Finding out the little brother you loved could do such a thing had to be like taking a ride on an emotional roller coaster. She thought about Conner and the close relationship they'd always had, and she couldn't even began to imagine what her reaction would be if he betrayed her the way Glen had Luke.

Luke laid his head in his hands, willing the throbbing to go away. He remembered all too well the last time he'd woken up with a similar headache—except *that* one had been worse.

"I wish we could say it's all over," he murmured as much to himself as to Patsy. He dropped his hands and looked at her. "Did you really find the rabbit?"

"Scottie did. He came running down the stairs with it. I'm sorry, I know I should have told you but... I didn't want you to give up looking for them."

"Where was it?"

"Behind one of the beds between the mattress and the wall."

He shook his head. "That's just not possible. I swear I went through that room with a fine tooth comb. I stripped both beds even moved them away from the wall."

Patsy's head shot up. "That means he planted it there, probably when he put the strychnine under the sink. He wanted you to quit looking for them. That tells me they must be alive somewhere."

"But where? He's dead. We may never know what he did with them. Maybe they *are* buried on his farm; they didn't search that far away." A stab of pain shot through Luke's chest. He wouldn't believe it. He couldn't believe it. Glen loved those girls. Luke had to trust that he wouldn't have hurt them.

Patsy frowned. "What was it he said when I asked him where they were? Something about Kansas. Does he have relatives there or something?"

"Not that I know of. I was like in a trance. I just barely remember him mentioning that. What exactly did he say?"

Her brow furrowed in thought as she ran a hand through her glorious red hair. He couldn't believe he'd once called her a carrot-top floozy. She griped a chunk of it as though trying to squeeze the answer out of her head.

"Something about them not being in Kansas. Wait I know— he said, *they ain't in Kansas anymore.*"

"That sounds like something from a movie the kids have. Was it *Alice in Wonderland?* Or *Snow White?*"

Her eyes lit up. "No! It was The Wizard of Oz. What's her name? Dorothy said it to her dog. Toto, we aren't in Kansas anymore."

Frustrated, Luke threw his hand in the air. "So, what the hell does that mean?"

"I don't know," Patsy said. "Is there possibly a clue in that silly movie? Do you still have it?"

Luke shrugged. "I suppose. All their things are still up there. I say let's watch it tomorrow. I'm beat tonight. And I'm hungry. Is there any of that pizza left?"

"I think the boys put it in the refrigerator. Do you trust it?"

"Well, Glen was eating it."

Patsy gritted her teeth. "He was also drinking the beer, but he likely had all the bottles marked.

"The pizza looked all the same to me. Why don't we get it out? I love cold pizza."

* * * *

"I'm curious about something," Luke said the next morning at breakfast. "Where did you learn that little maneuver you did on Glen?"

Patsy laid French toast, her newest creation, on his plate, sat, and smiled. "I started taking karate lessons when I was ten or eleven. Mostly, as a kid, I used it to embarrass my older brother. He was the school runt and was constantly being bullied. Once, I'd learned a few moves, all I had to do was show off a little and the bullies left him alone."

"You're older brother? Ouch, must have been a blow to his ego. I wasn't aware you had a brother."

"I guess I should have mentioned him. Actually, I have. He's my computer expert." She went on to explain about Conner's teaching job and what was going on with their father and his lawyer. "Conner went to Minneapolis yesterday to try to talk to Dad."

"If Glen poisoned the chickens, and I'm not fully convinced he did, then your Fontaine guy must have put the note in the mailbox or vice-versa."

"If he didn't do it, how would he know about the bottle under the sink?"

Luke got up and refilled his coffee cup along with hers. "Well, I've been doing some thinking on that. How did he know we'd be gone that day? How did he know you found Betsy's rabbit? And there are a few other things he's been privy to."

"You think he could have the house bugged?"

"Wouldn't surprise me in the least. In fact, I'm thinking it was happening before you even got here. Unless Kelsey called him—and that doesn't seem likely—I think he knew about the argument we had that night. What do you say we take a drive over to his place?"

"Good idea, maybe we can find something that will lead us to the girls. Right now, all we have is the Oz movie, and I don't expect much to come of that. My guess is he was just trying to be clever when he quoted Dorothy."

She took a bite of her French toast, once again amazed at how good it was. "What do you think he was talking about with the mineral rights thing? What did his father find that you don't know about?"

Luke licked the syrup off his fork and waved it at her. "I've been mulling that around in my head, too. Do you still have that rock you picked up out there on the hill?"

"I guess. It's probably still in the pocket of my jeans in the hamper. Want me to get it?"

"Please. I'd like to take a look at it."

Patsy ran down the steps found the rock, came back up, and handed it to him. "I just picked it up because it was pretty."

A thoughtful frown creased Luke's brow as he turned the rock over in his fingers. "Doesn't look like anything special to me."

"I thought it kind of looked like the granite countertops we have in Dad's house."

"Huh, I've never heard of anyone finding granite around here." He handed it back to her. "Hang on to it; maybe we can have somebody look at it. There was something in those hills that had him all het up, and I don't think it was oil."

Luke suddenly leaned over and kissed her. He tasted sweet like maple syrup. "Thanks for breakfast,' he said. "It was very good—and thanks for the late night dessert upstairs. That was very, very good. Do you have any more secrets I should know about?"

"Yeah," she murmured. "I forgot the powdered sugar."

"Is that a promise of kinky sex later?"

Patsy thought about how near they'd both come to dying, and she had an instant urge to be closer to him. She got up, went around the table, sat in his lap and put her arms around his neck. She nibbled on his ear and whispered, "How much later?"

"Not much," he murmured. "Will you show me one of your *moves?*"

Luke stood and, still kissing her slowly, backed her toward the stairs. "One of these days, my love, I'm going to carry you to the bedroom," he said, talking past the lock he had on her lips.

Out of the corner of her eye, Patsy saw Reggie watching them, a poignant look in his big brown eyes. When they reached the steps, he gave a deep sigh, lay down, and closed his eyes.

It was almost noon by the time Luke and Patsy headed over to Glen's farm. Over Patsy's protests, Luke insisted on driving, saying he had to get back to exercising his testosteronial rights.

"There's no such word," she grumbled, crossing her arms over her chest and watching his every move, making sure he wasn't disobeying any doctor's orders.

"Doesn't matter. I know what it means."

"Did I tell you I have a black belt?"

He arched a brow at her. "Won't help you keep me from driving. I'll just drop the keys down my pants—like women in movies always hiding things in their cleavage."

Patsy gave him an unabashed grin. "Like that would stop me from getting them."

He leered at her. "I was hoping you'd say that. Should I pull over?"

She rolled her eyes at him. Bantering with Luke gave her a special kind of pleasure, and today, she had an ulterior motive—keep his mind away from Glen. Luke didn't show it, but she knew he was troubled and hurt by his brother's death and betrayal. It was an awful thing to love somebody then find out it was all one-sided. Had Glen always been envious of Luke—even when they were kids growing up? How was it possible when Glen's father gave him everything he wanted—everything except the farm.

She thought about her and Conner. They had always been close, had always shared a common bond, but what if one of them had been clearly favored? How would that have altered their feelings toward one another?

The sight of Glen's house jolted Patsy from her thoughts. Weeds grew around the older two-story building that reminded her of her grandparent's farmhouse, except this one was greatly in need of paint and repair. The whole farmyard was run down and poorly kept. Glen was always clean and nicely dressed; this did not fit the image she had of him.

Luke stopped the pickup in front of the house and looked around. "I guess now I know why Glen let this place go to hell. He had no pride in it. Darren told me Glen had spent more time at my place than he did here while I was in jail. I imagine he was hoping I wouldn't be coming back. Of course, he had that covered, too. He probably expected me to be killed when that ladder collapsed on me."

Shuddering, Patsy asked if he had a key.

"Nobody locks their doors around here." He got out of the truck and walked up the porch steps, warning her about a broken plank as she followed him.

Inside, the house wasn't that bad. Things were fairly tidy, no worse than any other bachelor pad, which explained his neat personal habits.

She followed Luke as he walked through the house. Both kept an eye out for any clue as to where the girls might be. In a small bedroom upstairs, Patsy spotted a pair of lace-top girl's socks. She picked them up looking at Luke hopefully.

He shook his head. "They periodically spent time over here with their *Uncagen*, as Betsy called him. Both girls adored him," he added sadly.

"Uncagen?" Patsy repeated. "Doesn't that sound like the name Powers used when he asked Betsy where they went when they left his apartment?"

He stared at her like he'd been sucker punched. "Hot damn, you're right." Walking up to her, he planted a lusty kiss on her lips. "You really would make a good spy. I don't know why I didn't catch that."

"Too much testosterone," she said, kissing him back. "It gets in the way of men's brainwaves."

He swatted her on the butt. "Keep looking, Miss Black Belt."

"Oooh, are you into whips and chains, too?" she said, wriggling away from him.

They found nothing else of interest until they came to one bedroom that seemed to be locked.

"Now, what the hell?" Luke said, ramming his good shoulder against the door. "Is it stuck?"

"Don't hurt yourself," she warned. "Let's go back in his room and see if there's a key." She turned and led the way to the master bedroom without waiting for a comment. It took her all of two minutes to go through everything on top of Glen's dresser and come up with a key. She held it up, giving him a crafty grin.

He snatched it out of her hand. "You have a gifted mind, Miss Bartlett. Just one of the things I love about you—I think."

It was her turn to give him a butt swat as he preceded her out the door. "What are the other things?" she prompted.

He turned to give her a bodily survey. "You mean besides your…" he grinned, "hair?"

She gave him a shove. "Try the key, smart ass. Let's hope it works."

"Ow, that was my bad shoulder."

"Liar."

The key turned. He swung the door open, and they crowded in at the same time. What they found looked like a sophisticated security setup, with several television monitors and computers, all running. One camera showed movement—Reggie eating from his food bowl, another pictured a bedroom, Luke's bedroom, where they'd.... When the reality hit her, she felt a weakness in her knees threatening to drop her on the floor, where her mouth was hanging.

Luke swore, loudly and viciously. His face had gone pale as he walked around staring from one monitor to the other. One wall full of shelves held stacks of dated discs.

"If the son-of-a-bitch wasn't dead, I'd have to kill him."

"How can they still have disc space?" Patsy heard herself saying. "They must be running nonstop."

"Motion activated," Luke said. "Glen worked for a security company in Bismarck before he bought the farm."

"How long has he been doing this?" Patsy asked, moving in a daze, hardly daring to breath.

Luke shook his head. "I have no idea. He was there a lot while I was in jail but he also had plenty of opportunity to set it up while Kelsey and I were on our honeymoon for three days. He stayed there with the girls. So they could be in their own room."

"Maybe in a twisted way he wanted to know if the woman he loved enjoyed sex with his brother," Patsy said, surveying the room.

"Sick bastard," Luke growled.

Patsy moved past him scanning the wall of discs.

"Do you suppose he monitored himself while he killed her?"

Luke's gaze shot toward her. "Let's check the dates. Find March seventeenth."

He stood behind her searching the top shelf while she ran her fingers ran along the cases on the bottom

"It appears each discs covers about a week," she said. "Here's one that ends March fifteenth. The next one starts May twenty-first, nothing in between."

Luke swore again. "That's the day I got out of jail. He probably stopped the system for those two months I was gone, but even if he did, the one for March seventeenth is missing."

"Of course he wouldn't keep something that would absolve you and implicate himself. But he appears to be the kind of sick person who might like to watch it over and over again." Patsy went to the desk and started flinging drawers open, looking for anything the size of a disc or larger. Nothing.

Luke, she noticed, was tediously going through the discs obviously looking for one that might be out of place. She glanced around the room, spotted a metal file cabinet and quickly rifled through that with no results. Next came a small bookcase full of mostly hardcover books. She threw all the books out, looking behind them. When she came up empty-handed, she quickly flipped though each book, thinking one might be carved out like she'd seen in a movie.

When that proved futile, she sat on the floor and scanned the walls and ceiling. Her grandparents' house had an attic you accessed through one of the bedrooms, but Patsy was sure Glen would have kept the incriminating disc in the only room with a lock on the door.

She noticed Luke was angrily tossing discs into a large wastebasket. By the number of discs present before March fifteenth she realized Glen must, in fact, have set up his cameras when Luke and Kelsey were on their honeymoon.

Sighing dejectedly, she starting cleaning up her mess, setting the books back in the selves That's when she notice the shelves didn't go all the way to the floor. There was an empty cavity under the bottom shelf. She stood and threw the heavy bookcase forward only to find nothing but dust beneath it.

Luke had paused in what he was doing to stare at her knee deep in scattered books, the bookcase lying face down on top of them. He must have thought she'd taken leave of her senses.

Thinking she might have watched too many mystery movies, she reached down and ran her hand up under the area she couldn't see. Her fingers touched on something that was definitely not part of the bookcase. It was the size of a disk duct-taped to the top of the under cavity. As she pried it loose, she told herself not to get her hopes up. It could merely be assembly instructions.

She managed to get a sliver under one fingernail, but she finally pulled it free.

Bingo. It was a disc with a March sixteenth date scrawled across it with big red letters.

Luke was on the floor beside her in an instant. "Oh, my God, he actually kept it."

The look on Luke's face made Patsy realize what the disc meant to him. It would clear up all the things about that night he couldn't remember and possibly provide a clue as to whether Betsy and Lola were taken out alive or…

When they got back home, Luke immediately searched for the cameras. They were so easy to spot he chastised himself for not realizing they were there. He'd disabled all the monitors and recorders before they'd left Glen's place but he still didn't want the cameras in his house.

Patsy had gone to the kitchen to make coffee.

They had hardly spoken on the way home. Now, she asked if he wanted anything to eat. What she didn't add was *before you watch the disc.* Could he even bear to see it, he wondered. Of course that notion was moot; he had to watch it, if for no other reason, for Betsy and Lola.

He put the disc into the DVD player and sat on the sofa to wait for Patsy. His stomach was in knots, and he gave her a grateful look when she passed him a mug of coffee heavily laced with milk then sat beside him.

Taking a deep breath, he pressed the play button. There'd been two cameras, one in the kitchen with a wide lens covering both the kitchen and the walkway leading to the front door. The other camera in the bedroom showed a clear view of his bed and the door. As he'd suspected, it was movement activated. Nothing happened until Kelsey walked into the kitchen and started to make breakfast. A date showed on the top of the video. It was the morning of March sixteenth.

It was like watching a horror movie until Lola and Betsy came bouncing into the kitchen. While Luke liked seeing the girls, seeing them there with Kelsey made his stomach churn. Moments later, he walked in, gave each of the girls a kiss on the forehead and greeted them good morning. It was like viewing a replay of his life. He pressed *skip* and continued to do so, watching only brief segments each time, just long enough to get a sense of what was happening and what time of day it was. When the date changed to the seventeenth, he kept skipping until it was eight o'clock in the evening, and he was having the argument with Kelsey.

By now, he understood how the cameras worked. When there was movement at both cameras, the screen split and you could watch both scenes at the same time. When the lights went out in the room or the motion ended, the camera ran about ten seconds then stopped. If he'd felt the least bit charitable, which he did not, he'd have admired Glen's ingenuity.

Patsy sat beside him, sipping coffee, wisely remaining silent. If she had any comments about what he was doing, she didn't voice them.

He ceased skipping and let it play when Kelsey started packing her suitcase and he stormed out of the house. It broke his heart when the girls came into the room crying after he left. She comforted them then told them to go to their room and pack their favorite things because they were going to go on a little vacation. When Betsy asked, "Is Daddy coming too?" a lump blocked Luke's throat. Blinking rapidly, he drew deep breaths of air until he began to feel lightheaded. Patsy's hand slipped to his thigh offering comfort with a light squeeze. He couldn't look at her, his vision was blurred, and his eyes were transfixed on the screen.

Kelsey told her, "Daddy will come later", and Betsy should take Lola and help her pack. After the girls left, Kelsey spent about twenty minutes choosing her clothes. He was surprised to see how calm she was. No ranting or slamming things in anger. She simply took her time folding her clothes and placing them in the suitcase as though she truly was going on a vacation.

She snapped her suitcase shut, took her time packing a duffle bag with shoes and accessories, then left them both on the bed and walked out of the room. Ten seconds later, the screen went blank. It picked up moments later in the kitchen where she went in the pantry and came out with what looked like a five pound bag of sugar. She headed straight to the bedroom with it where she stuffed it in the duffle bag.

"The money," Patsy whispered. "She knew you didn't cook, she kept her money in a sugar bag."

Luke moved his hand over hers, squeezed and held it without moving his concentration from the screen.

Kelsey took a large suitcase from the closet and left the bedroom. When she returned, an hour had passed.

"She must have gone in to help the girls pack," Luke said.

The screen split, and there was a blurred movement in the shadows by the front door. Glen suddenly appeared in the bedroom.

"What the hell are you doing?" he asked eyeing the suitcase on the bed.

"Can't you see," Kelsey snapped, angry now. "I'm leaving. I'm done with this charade. I'm tired of smelling cow shit and chicken crap. I'm sick of pretending I enjoy sex with your brother. I'm just plan tired of it all."

"Where are you going?" Glen asked.

"Back to Bismarck, to Minneapolis, anywhere but here."

"You don't have to go. I love you, Kels. Tell Luke you want a divorce and come and live with me."

She scoffed. "Your place is a dump. Why the hell would I want to live there? I haven't seen one dime out of you since I moved in here. If it weren't for Jerome, I'd be destitute. I'm sick of Luke, and I'm even sicker of you. Luke expects me to be his frumpy little farm wife, and all you want me for is sex. And by the way, Luke is a hell of a lot better at that then you are."

Glen pounced on her like an enraged bull.

He picked her up, and body slammed her on the bed. When she screamed, he straddled her and wrapped his hands around her throat. They remained there, squeezing until Kelsey McAlister stopped kicking, stopped moving altogether.

Patsy couldn't breathe, couldn't believe she was actually witnessing a murder. This wasn't television. This was real—a real murder. This was a woman Patsy didn't know. It was beyond her to fathom the agony Luke was experiencing watching his wife die right before his eyes. His fingers tightened over her hand like a vise. If she'd been able to move, she might have reached over, grabbed the remote out of his hand, and turned the gruesome scene off.

Then it was over. Glen pushed himself off the bed, stepping back, staring down as in disbelief at what he'd done. Then, acting swiftly, he positioned Kelsey's body, facing her to the far wall, and threw covers over her to make it appear as though she was sleeping.

Just as he finished, a phone rang. He looked around franticly until apparently realizing the sound came from his pocket. He dug it out, opened it, and pressed it to his ear, saying a muted hello. He listened a moment then said, "Yeah, okay, I'll be right there." The time was ten thirty-five.

As he stuck the phone back in his pocket, a small figure appeared in the shadows behind him, partially hidden from the camera's eye by his body.

"Why are you hurting, Mommy?" a small sobbing voice said.

"Oh, God," Luke cried out, leaning toward the screen as if there might be something he could do. "It's Lola."

Glen whirled around, picked the little girl up, and hugged her against his chest. He pressed her face into his shoulder, running a hand over her head "It's okay, honey. Mommy's not hurt; she's just sleeping." He'd turned so the girl's back was to her mother and in doing so he faced the camera. Tears streamed down his cheeks.

Oddly, Patsy felt a wave of sympathy for a man who'd just murdered the woman he loved and was trying to shield his daughter from the scene. Then, she remembered he'd tried to frame his own brother, and if the evidence hadn't proved Luke was innocent, he'd have gone to prison probably for life, and Glen would have sat back and let it happen.

"Come on, sweetie," he said, his voice floating back as he carried her out of the room, "I'll put you to bed. You can sleep, and tomorrow everything will be fine." He switched the light off as he left the room, causing the picture to go instantly black.

A few second later, it lit up to show Glen running out of the house.

"He didn't take them," Luke said. "I don't understand. He didn't take them."

"Of course not. He was on the way to town to pick you up. He couldn't have bought them with him."

The remote fell to the floor, and Luke bought his elbows to his knees and rested his head in his hands. When his shoulders began to shake, Patsy had never felt so helpless in her life. She simply put her hand on his arm, letting him know she was there if he needed her.

A light drew her attention back to the screen. "It's coming back on," she said quickly.

Luke raised his head, and together, they watched as Lola switched the light on and tiptoed back in the room. She crawled on the bed and lay down beside her mother. The silent but visual aftermath lasted ten seconds.

Luke scrubbed his sleeve across his eyes. Patsy wondered at the thoughts running through his head.

The screen flashed again. The front door had opened, and a man's figure stepped into the shadowed foyer. His back was to the camera as he walked to the stairs and climbed them as though he bore the weight of the world on his shoulders. Suddenly, the screen split, and Luke walked into the bedroom.

Patsy felt Luke tense beside her.

He approached the bed and, for a long moment, stared down at Lola as she slept. Then he bent down, picked her up, and carried her body out the door. Moments later, he came back and fell on the bed without bothering to remove his clothes.

This time when the screen darkened, he looked at Patsy. His face seemed to have aged ten years. "This might sound crazy," he said, "but I dreamed about doing that."

"Maybe it wasn't a dream at all; maybe you remembered it."

He shook his head. "Possible, I suppose." He ran a hand through his hair. "So the girls were there when I got home. I don't understand—"

"It's back on," Patsy said, clutching at his arm. "Thirty-five minutes have passed since you came home."

"That's exactly how long it takes to drive to Ashville and back.

This time they watched another figure come in the front door and hurry to the stairs. About six minutes passed when he came hurrying back out carrying a crying child. He disappeared out the door and was back shortly empty handed. The next time, it only took him five minutes to appear with the second sobbing girl, larger than the first one. He returned for a third trip to carry suitcases. After that, the screen remained blank.

"He must have gone home and removed the disc to hide the evidence just in case he became suspect," Patsy said.

"You do realize why they were crying," Luke said woodenly.

She nodded slowly. "He must have cut them to make them bleed on the sheets."

Luke swore profusely, "And I slept right through it."

"He wouldn't have bothered with their suitcases if he planned to kill them," she assured Luke."

"They're alive," he declared adamantly. "But where are they? Because of the blood there were never any posters with their pictures hung up and not a word in the media about them missing. Everyone believed it was just a matter of time until their bodies were found. For all I know, they could be secreted away right here in the neighborhood."

"We'll find them," she vowed, putting her arms around him.

Chapter Nineteen

The next day the phone didn't stop ringing. It seemed like the word of Luke's proven innocence had spread throughout Asheville faster than a prairie wildfire. Especially when Sheriff Wilson swore it was so. LeRoy and David couldn't stop talking about their part in the event and even touted the sheriff's bravery for wrestling with Glen. Of course, they never failed to mention the blood.

That incident, however, took second fiddle to Patsy's heroics which both boys and the sheriff had witnessed though the window.

What amazed Patsy the most was Gertie showing up at their door with a sweet potato casserole. Patsy thanked her and put it in the refrigerated with the lemon pie, the wild-rice hot dish, and the salads.

By noon, the well-wishers had stopped coming and calling, giving Patsy and Luke a chance to breathe. Since Peg was still laid up, Patsy sent Luke over to their place with some of the food. He was also to question them about the suitcases and show the rock she'd found to Darren.

Patsy had another job to do.

Fully convinced the girls would be coming home soon, she tied a bandana around her mop of hair and tackled their bedroom. Cleaning, dusting, putting on the new pink fairy sheets she'd found in the linen closet and making the room over all welcoming for them.

While she was dusting and tidying up a bookshelf, she came across *The Wizard of Oz* disc. Turning it over in her hand, she examined the case, the pictures, the wording, even looked inside at the disc itself, but found nothing that could be construed as a clue.

Setting the disc aside to watch later with Luke, she doggedly continued her work. She had just about finished with the room when the phone rang yet another time. Expecting it to be another well-wisher, she hurried across the hall to answer it in Luke's bedroom. It could, after all, be news of the girls.

It was Conner.

"Patsy, do I have news for you." She wondered if his news was better than hers but he sounded so excited she let him talk first. "I went to see Dad yesterday. It took some doing, but after I told him about the guys following us and what they'd done, I finally got his attention. He called Mr. Morton Chambers into his office and demanded to see a copy of his will. Are you still with me?"

"Yes, of course, so what happened then?"

"When we weren't taking his threat to disinherit us seriously, Dad asked Morty to rewrite the will and set up a scholarship fund for under privileged kids. He was putting everything that would have gone to us in that fund."

Patsy's heart took a leap of shock. She supposed it shouldn't have surprised her, and yet, it did. "Oh, my gosh. He really would have done it."

"He not only would have. He did. Morty hopped right on that opportunity. He drafted a new will and Dad actually signed it. But I ran a check on this the scholarship foundation and discovered Morty may as well have called it the Morton Chambers Retirement Fund. If Dad had conveniently died before our year was up, Morty was set to get control of everything."

Patsy's suddenly felt nausea rising up in her stomach. "You actually think he'd have done something to Dad?"

Conner gave a short laugh. "What do you think?"

"So…what did Dad do?"

"Fired him on the spot. He already has a new lawyer who's working on a new will. Then he offered me a job in the company."

"You're going back to the cities to work for Dad?"

"Nope, I turned it down. I like what I'm doing. So…that brings me to another thing. I was going to suggest that he take a chunk of that money and do his scholarship fund. How do you feel about that?"

Patsy thought on it a moment. She didn't know if she wanted to spend the rest of her life on a farm, but…the thought of leaving Luke had her stomach lurching again. Enough money could get them started someplace else. Luke wouldn't even have to work if he didn't want to. But did she dare even ask him to leave the place he loved?

"Good idea," she said finally. "I certainly don't need his whole fortune to live. I may even become a cook."

Conner gave a hoot of laughter. "You always were good at telling jokes." He didn't wait for her reply. "I have another surprise for you—I'm in love."

"Congratulations, big brother. Are you still planning to visit this weekend?"

"If all goes as planned…and I may not be coming alone. So what's going on in your life?"

Patsy took a deep breath and filled him in.

That was where Luke found her, sitting on his bed, still on the phone talking to Conner. Luke sat and stuck his tongue in her ear. She giggled and tried to wriggle away from him but he had a firm hand on her hip.

"Sounds like you just got real busy," Conner said into her other ear. "I think you left something out of your report. I'll talk to you later. Debra's waiting for me by now anyway to take her son to his karate lesson. Bye."

Patsy wanted to ask more about that, but Conner had already hung up, chuckling as though he sensed what was going on.

"Important call?" Luke asked moving to her neck.

"Hmmm, just my brother. He had good news."

"Tell me later," Luke murmured, pushing her back on the bed when she set the phone aside. "I have something to show you.

"Later" turned out to be an hour.

Patsy nestled in Luke's arms, basking in the afterglow of their love making, and relayed her brother's good news. Luke, in turn, told her what he learned from Darren. There were no suitcases for the girls at the house, which Luke had already known, and unfortunately, after checking Kelsey's bags for anything of importance, they'd given most of the contents—with Glen's permission—to Good Will in Bismarck. There was a bag of jewelry they'd left on his dresser which he'd found. Luke hadn't mentioned the sugar bag because he didn't want to distress them. After all, it had been over four months.

Patsy groaned, wondering who the lucky recipient was. "What about the rock?" she asked after a moment.

"He kept it, said he had a brother-in-law who knew about rocks."

"I can't imagine anything will come of it," Pasty said. "The rock was pretty but..." she shrugged. "I only picked it up because Conner collects rocks .He has lots of agates and even a few arrowheads he found on Grandpa Hank's farm."

"I guess we'll just wait and see," Luke said nibbling on her ear.

She giggled at the tickling sensation. "Are you hungry? Or what?" she asked.

Luke laughed. "I'm hungry for both food and *what*. Let's go raid the refrigerator. Just don't feed me any of that sweet potato casserole Gertie brought. I hate sweet potatoes."

They had a grand supper gleaned from the goodies in the refrigerator, then snuggled up together to watch the Wizard of Oz. Luke was skeptical but Patsy was convinced they'd find some kind of a clue in the story.

Even if no one else, with the possible exception of Darren and Peg, believed Lola and Betsy were alive, tomorrow they were going to post photos of the girls from here to Bismarck and beyond if necessary. And they'd run the same photos in every newspaper in every town and city starting within a fifty-mile radius. Explaining that they'd been missing for so many months might be difficult but it was worth a try.

As the movie started, Luke had his arm around Patsy's shoulders, his fingers absently rubbing her upper arm. The movie had barely stated when his fingers stopped moving. She turned to look at him, frowning.

"What is it?" she whispered, not wanting to disturb his thought process.

"It's... I'm not sure... Something... Auntie Em!" he said suddenly. "Glen's father had a younger sister. He name was Emilie. She was kind of slow, but not so much that she couldn't live alone as long as someone looked in on her periodically. I've never even met her but about a year ago, the girls told me they went with Uncagen to visit *Auntie Em*. They giggled because it rhymed."

Patsy sat up to stare at him, her eyes wide. "It's certainly worth looking into. Where does she live?"

He shook his head. "I don't know, but I don't think it's very far. They were only with him for about three hours that day while Kelsey and I drove down to Aberdeen to look for a new dress she wanted for a wedding."

"*The Hub City of the Dakotas*," Patsy said, quoting Grandpa Hank. "So would her name be Emilie Johnson or did she marry?"

"I doubt that she married."

"Johnson is a common name but Emilie isn't as much so, not in the age group she'd be in." The movie forgotten, Patsy charged to her feet and raced to the phone book in the kitchen drawer. She flipped through the pages and found no Emilie Johnson, not even an E. Johnson.

"Who would know," she cried dejectedly to Luke who'd followed her into the kitchen.

"Glen," he said. "Glen would know. He'd have an address book in that high tech office, probably handy somewhere."

"There was a rolodex on the desk," Patsy said excitedly.

Luke was already heading for his keys. "Let's go."

They both ran to the truck, Luke beating her to get behind the wheel. This was no time to argue about doctor's orders, she decided. When he took the back road through the water, she was glad he *was* driving. It took them fifteen minutes to get to Glen's house.

They both got out of the truck and dashed to the front door, and from there, rushed upstairs to the room they'd left unlocked. The rolodex was setting on the desk right where she'd remembered it Her heart pounder as she stared over Luke's shoulder while he flipped though it stopping the J's.

"Got it!" he shouted as he yanked the card from the file.

Patsy grasped his wrist, pulling it toward her so she could read the card. "There's an addressed and a phone number," she said, rapidly scanning the information. "Zeeland? How far is that?"

"About twenty-five, maybe thirty, miles."

As one, they wasted no time heading for the truck. While Luke drove, Patsy had a lot of time to think about how disappointed they'd both be if this turned out to be a wild goose chase. She sat forward on the seat, willing the vehicle to go faster.

"Buckle your seatbelt," Luke said.

"What?" she asked, aware that he'd spoken to her.

"I said, buckle your seat belt; it makes me nervous when someone claws at the dash."

She gave him a withering look, pushed her butt back, and buckled up. "How far is it yet?"

"About ten miles. Why don't you enter the address in the GPS so we don't have to waste time looking for it? It'll give you something to do."

She took the hand held GPS from the dash and programmed the address in. Her fingers where shaking so badly she had to repeat the process. When the map finally appeared on the screen, it read seven miles to destination. They entered the Zeeland city limits with three miles left to drive. The town was barely a pit stop, even smaller than Ashville. After passing through the town, they made a right then a left, driving until they'd left the town behind and the homes were spread far apart.

They arrived in front of a small house set back from the road and hidden by trees. A short sidewalk walk bordered by tiny purple flowers led up to the front door.

Patsy looked over at Luke, suddenly feeling panicky. The feeling turned to elation the minute she stepped out of the truck. Children's voices carried from the back yard. Luke and Patsy took off at a trot, rounding the house only to be brought up short by a solid tall brown fence. Luke found a gate, opened it, and stepped inside.

Two pale blue pairs of eyes stared at them from under a tree where they were playing on a swinging rope hanging from a branch.

"Daddy!"

It was Betsy. She came running toward them, and Luke went to his knees and reached out to her catch her.

"Daddy, Daddy, you came," she squealed, flinging herself into his arms. Behind her, running slower on shorter legs, came Lola. Luke spread his arms to encircle her as well. His shoulders shook as he buried his face in their long blond hair.

Patsy felt her own tears sliding down her face.

"What's goin' on out here?" A voice called from the back door. "That you, Glen?"

A woman, somewhere in her mid-seventies, hobbled from the back door into the yard. She wore slippers with holes in them and a threadbare old housedress half hidden under a grimy apron. Patsy would have thought she'd be alarmed to find two strangers in the back yard; instead; her gaze darted about, taking in the scene, looking almost relieved.

"No," Patsy told her quickly. "It's not Glen. This is his brother Luke. He came to pick up the girls."

"Well, praise the Lord for that. Glen ain't been here since yesterday, and I was wondering what I was going to feed 'em. They surely do eat a lot. They're a handful, they are. I keep tellin' Glen to take 'em home, tellin' him I'm too old to be taking care of little kids..."

"Can we get their things?" Patsy asked, interrupting her ranting. The girls had not released their hold on Luke, and he didn't seem too anxious to part from them either.

"Help yourself," she said, waving an arm toward the house.

"Who's going to help me pack?" she asked no one in particular.

Betsy finally released Luke and looked at her. "Who are you?" she asked. "Where's Mommy?"

Luke struggled to his feet taking Lola with him. Patsy knew it must have cost him dearly to hold her. "This is my friend, Patsy. She's here to help me take you home."

"Patsy?" Betsy said. "That's a funny name."

Patsy held out her hand to Betsy. That's when she noticed the girl's stained dress, uncombed hair, and scuffed shoes. Why hadn't Glen seen to their care?

"Come help me pack your things," Patsy said. "Then you can go home with your daddy."

"Come on, Yoya," she called to her sister. "We get to go home with Daddy now." She looked up at Patsy, frowning. "Is Binky at Daddy's house? He was here but he went missing."

Patsy smiled through her tears. "Yes, honey, he's there waiting for you."

Lola wriggled free of Luke. When he set her down, he pressed his elbows to his sides, breathing heavily. Patsy raised her eyebrows to him in question and he mouthed the words "I'm okay," giving her a smile that outshined a Christmas star.

Chapter Twenty

"You certainly made Jerome Parker a happy man when you called him," Patsy whispered as she stood beside Luke, watching the girls sleep.

"Yeah, I promised him we'd bring the girls up to see him first chance we got."

Patsy blinked back her tears. "They're so sweet. How could you not love them?"

"God only knows what they've gone through," Luke said, his voice low and husky. "The amazing thing is how well they took it when I told them their mother had gone to heaven."

Patsy nodded. "It sounded like Glen might have prepared them. Whatever he was and did, I think he genuinely loved them both."

"Yeah, I know." Luke said hoarsely. "It's heartbreaking. I loved Glen from the day he was born, and I never realized how envious he was of me. I still have a hard time accepting it."

Patsy smiled. "At least the girls are home safe and sound. I can't wait to get to know them. You'll have to help me out since I don't know a whole lot about kids."

He put his arm around her, kissing her temple. "The important thing is you knew how to bring them home. I can't thank you enough for that. I don't know if I could have done it without you."

She put her arms around him and squeezed. "We both did it. We make a good team."

He smiled down at her. "I guess we do. In spite of everything, they seem healthy and amazingly cheerful. I guess kids know how to adapt."

"It sounded to me like they lived on cold cereal and eggs most of the time."

"Yeah," he said, drawing Patsy out of the room. "Look at the bright side. They won't complain about anything you make."

She drew back her fist, pretending to sock him in his wounded ribs. "Did I mention that tomorrow I'm making you a sweet potato soufflé?"

"Guess I better eat it if you do." Laughing, he enclosed her in the circle of his arms. "Did I mention that I love you?"

Pasty gently put her arms around his waist and smiled up at him. "I don't believe you have, but as long as you brought it up, I think I love you, too, Luke McAlister."

He brushed his lips across hers. "You think?"

"I've never been in love. How do I know?"

"I know, because I'd follow you anywhere if you didn't want to live here. I've never felt that way about anyone before."

"I feel the same way," she said. "You'd never believe the kind of life I lived before I came out here. I could do anything I wanted to do, go anywhere I wanted to go. I never even considered what things cost. Now, I realize I had everything but happiness." She looked up at him, smiling. "Maybe that's what love is all about. Finding happiness and knowing you'd do anything to hold on to it."

"You might have something there," Luke said. "But do you really think you could be happy living out here?"

Patsy sighed. "I never thought I'd say this, but I'd miss this farm if I left—especially the chickens."

"What about me?"

She gave a throaty laugh. "Take me to bed and remind what I'd miss about you. Maybe then I can decide if I'm really in love."

* * * *

Saturday afternoon, Patsy was out in the yard with the girls, throwing a fetch-ball for Reggie, when, true to his word, Conner's Escalade came up the drive. To Patsy's delight, he'd brought Debra and her twelve-year-old son, Willy. But the biggest surprise came when Charles Bartlett stepped out of the car. He held out his arms, and Patsy flew into them—something she hadn't done since she was a little girl.

Betsy immediately took Willy to the haymow to show him the baby chicks, and Patsy went into a panic about what she was going to feed all these people.

She called Peg who was home, feeling restless from being tied down after her surgery.

"We'll be right over," Peg said. "We'll raid your freezer and the pantry. Besides Darren has some interesting news for Luke, and the boys have been driving us nuts to see Betsy and Lola, not to mention the chicks."

Forty-five minutes later, Peg and Debra followed Patsy into the kitchen. While Patsy started making pies, Debra worked on the salad mixings Peg had brought with her, and Peg discovered the meat balls.

"We can make spaghetti," she announced "Everybody loves spaghetti."

"There's ton of noodles in the pantry." Patsy declared. "But we don't have any sauce."

Peg laughed. "Then I'll just have to teach you how to make your own. Much better anyway."

Patsy went to the pantry, got the pasta for Peg, and a bag sugar to refill the canister so she could finish the pies, marveling at how much she enjoyed the camaraderie of having friends in *her* kitchen. She hadn't had so much fun in a long time. Of course, knowing Luke was outside getting acquainted with her brother and father may have had something to do with that.

She opened the canister to dump the sugar in it and along with the grainy white sugar came small green bundles of hundred-dollar bills. She jumped back, shrieking.

Both Peg and Debra stared at her in alarm.

"What is it?" Peg asked, coming to look over her shoulder.

"Money," Patsy choked out. "It's Kelsey's money." She excitedly explained to Peg how they thought it was given away with Kelsey's bags.

"I found that," Peg said, staring at the green bills, with wide eyes. "I thought it really was full of sugar. I even tasted it. I couldn't figure out why in the world she'd packed it, but I just put it back in the pantry and forgot about it."

"What's going on?" Luke asked, walking in the kitchen.

Patsy held up the bundles of money, laughing. "Look what I found, Kelsey's money. It was in a sugar bag."

Luke shook his head incredulously. "Well, that'll make a nice college fund for the girls. But, hey, I can top that. Darren just told me that the rock you picked up was actually granite, so he did some checking and found out that the hill was tested just before Glen's father died. He said it's worth a fortune. Obviously, Glenn knew all about it. I don't even know if I want to tear up those hills to mine it."

Patsy laughed. "With the three million dollars my father is giving me, I don't think we need it. By the way, my Maserati will be done some time next week. I think it will look real sharp parked beside your John Deere tractor."

That evening, Lola climbed on Luke's lap. She looked at him very seriously and said, "Daddy, can we have pancakes tomorrow morning?"

About the Author

Born and raised on a North Dakota farm, Jannifer Hoffman started writing at the age of twelve, creating novels in her head while walking home from a one-room schoolhouse. A lifetime avid reader, she began writing in 1974 after reading The Flame and the Flower and Sweet Savage Love. After completing two historical novels Ceremony of Deception and Silver Shadows, Jannifer decided to try her hand at contemporary romance.

She readily admits it took thirty years of hard work, writing classes and writers' groups to finally realize what "serious writing" meant.

Her limited free time is spent sewing for a boutique and enjoying time with her family, including three children, five grandchildren, and a special man who has been her partner for some some twenty-six years. Jannifer lives on a lake in northern Minnesota during the summer and migrates to Yuma, Arizona for the winter. Besides writing her biggest passion is seeing the world from a cruise ship.

Jannifer loves to talk to her readers and can be found at www.janniferhoffman.com.

Also Available from
Resplendence Publishing

Rough Edges by Jannifer Hoffman

When Julia Morgan M.D. miscarries twin girls, she divorces her husband, believing he is to blame. He forces her out of her position at the hospital and threatens her credibility as a doctor if she attempts to practice medicine. Without mentioning her medical degree, Julia accepts a position as nanny on a Colorado ranch 900 miles away.

Dirk Travis is in trouble. His wife has gone missing, and his housekeeper is threatening to quit. He is in desperate need of a reliable person to look after his four-year-old twins. Even though Julia appears to be the answer to his prayers, he can't help but think she's a bit too perfect.

Both insist their relationship will be business only. While those plans start to go awry, other things begin to happen. People are getting killed and Dirk is the prime suspect, but that doesn't stop the heat index from rising between Dirk and Julia, even as she appears to be the next target.

Tonight by Patricia Pellicane

South Tiana Road Series, Book One

After months of hard work, Carlie Russo took a night off to attend her best friend's birthday party. While there she met a man who caused her to forget her usual common sense. Influenced by his magnetism, combined with the sensual entertainment provided, she grew intoxicated with desire. The outcome of a night sexier, and more wildly erotic than either could ever have imagined left both yearning for more.

Their intention was to meet again, only there are times when circumstances ruin the best laid plans.

Blood of His Fathers by Michelle Chambers

Sinners and Saints Series, Book One

Alexander McCormack has secretly orchestrated Jessica's life for the past fifteen years. Decisions she's deemed to have made are an illusion. Even her marriage proves to be nothing more than elaborate manipulation.

Jess is no longer content with a life that brings her little joy and no passion. With divorce comes unexpected danger for her and her young son, and her only recourse for safety lies in the unlikely savior of Alexander's son, Jason McCormack.

A hidden backdrop of age-long deceit, hatred and murder slowly manifests as Jessica finds herself drawn physically and emotionally closer to the man her every instinct—and cold hard fact—tells her she should avoid at all costs.

Long Relief by Abigail Barnette

Hard Ball Series, Book One

Successful entrepreneur Maggie Harper has lived and breathed baseball since birth. But when her father, once a legendary player, later a team owner, leaves her the Grand Rapids Bengals in his will, she's in over her head. Orchestrating a successful season is foreign territory, complicated by a sizzling one-night stand with a player who definitely wants something more.

After pitching a disastrous game that cost the Bengals the championship pennant, veteran pitcher Chris Thomas knows his days as a player are numbered. There are more important things to be worried about than the sexy new team owner, but Maggie's hot-and-cold act is driving him to distraction. A woman has never come between him and the game before, but now he has to make a choice between his love of playing ball and his love of Maggie.

When their entanglement is discovered, the stakes are even higher. Caught between doing what's right for the team and what's right for them, Maggie and Chris have to decide what's more important, a championship season, or a chance at love.

Lie to Me by JL Wilson

Grace Jamison has always been unlucky in love but this is ridiculous. What was supposed to be a blind date has turned into an FBI sting operation, complete with handsome Special Agent Ben Braden, a train ride and chase through the Badlands, and a final confrontation at a safe house—which turned out to be not so safe. If she can survive that, she can probably survive having her heart broken by Ben...unless she can convince him to take a chance on love.

Home for a Soldier by Tatiana March

Grace Clements is unemployed, lonely and broke. When she agrees to marry Rory Sullivan before he ships out to Iraq, she expects nothing but a Las Vegas wedding, a key to his New York apartment, and a divorce two years later. Instead, she gets a three-day honeymoon and a heart full of dreams of what could be... if he loved her.

Ten years ago, Rory Sullivan lost someone he loved. He gave up a life of wealth and privilege and joined the army. Hiding behind a wall of isolation, he avoids all emotional ties - until injury sends him home to recuperate. Home to

Grace, whose quiet dignity and gentle concern break through his defenses. As Rory fights his feelings, his gruff resistance drives Grace away.

But even when he believes she has betrayed him, he can no longer forget her. Can he make peace with his past in order to win back his wife?

Checkmate by Kris Norris

For years he's hidden in the shadows...watching...hunting. His attempts have never been successful, until now. And his game is just beginning.

Kendall Walker and her brother, Trace, share a passion for adventure racing. But when Trace is kidnapped by a psychotic figure from their past, Kendall finds herself immersed in an adventure race beyond anything she's ever known. And if she doesn't reach each checkpoint in time, Trace will die. She'll do anything to get her brother back, even surrendering to a man intent on becoming her lover. Luckily for her, Dawson has other plans.

Special Agent Dawson Cade doesn't know how his life went from complacent to complicated in what feels like a heartbeat. He has absolutely no leads on the bastard terrorizing Kendall, and he can't stop himself from wanting to take her into his bed. He knows he needs to keep distant, but when circumstances force him to succumb to the desires of a man intent on possessing Kendall, Dawson must face the truth. He's going to be Kendall's next lover, even if she doesn't know it yet.

And as the race begins, he can only hope he's able to save Trace, and keep Kendall from sacrificing herself, in a game where even victory has a price.

Find Resplendence titles at these retailers

Resplendence Publishing
www.ResplendencePublishing.com

Amazon
www.Amazon.com

Barnes and Noble
www.BarnesandNoble.com

Target
www.Target.com

Fictionwise
www.Fictionwise.com

All Romance E-Books
www.AllRomanceEBooks.com

Made in the USA
Charleston, SC
14 February 2013

HUNTER'S CURSE

ERYN & LARCEN: DELTA UNDERGROUND OPERATIVES

KAT HEALY

THE AUTHORS OF DUO

Sarah Noffke
Jamie Davis
Kimbra Swain
N. A. Grotepas
Kat Healy
Fatima Fayez
Scott Walker
Jenn Mitchell
S. W. Clarke
Mel Todd
Charley Case
Ben Zackheim